ZOE MAY lives in south-east London and works as a copywriter. Zoe has dreamt of being a novelist since she was a teenager. She moved to London in her early twenties and worked in journalism and copywriting before writing her debut novel, *Perfect Match*. Having experienced the London dating scene first hand, Zoe could not resist writing a novel about dating, since it seems to supply endless amounts of weird and wonderful material! As well as writing, Zoe enjoys going to the theatre, walking her dog, painting and, of course, reading.

Zoe loves to hear from readers, you can contact her on Twitter at: @zoe_writes

As Luck Would Have It

ZOE MAY

ONE PLACE. MANY STORIES

HQ
An imprint of HarperCollins*Publishers* Ltd
1 London Bridge Street
London SE1 9GF

This edition 2019

First published in Great Britain by
HQ, an imprint of HarperCollins*Publishers* Ltd 2019

Copyright © Zoe May 2019

Zoe May asserts the moral right to be
identified as the author of this work.
A catalogue record for this book is
available from the British Library.

ISBN: 978-0-00-833094-1

MIX
Paper from
responsible sources
FSC™ C007454

This book is produced from independently certified FSC™ paper
to ensure responsible forest management.

For more information visit: www.harpercollins.co.uk/green

Printed and bound in Great Britain by
CPI Group (UK) Ltd, Croydon CR0 4YY

Chapter 1

This is not how my life was meant to be.

How is it that at 32 years old, I've somehow wound up in my childhood bedroom? I'm sitting at the same desk where I revised for my GCSEs and I've been ticking off a to-do list compiled in a pink sparkly notebook I discovered gathering dust in the back of a drawer. My bedroom is like a museum exhibit entitled 'the habitat of a 13-year-old girl'. It's frozen in time. There's a Take That poster on the wall, for goodness' sake! And not one from their reunion tours, a *genuine* Take That poster from back when the band was young. When I was young. God, I feel like such a relic.

I cross out the last item on my to-do list – 'Send Katy press cuttings' – with a long satisfying swipe of my purple glitter pen. Did I mention that I'm using a glitter pen? It's one of those ones with a random tuft of fur at the end. That's just how I roll. Katy is a celebrity make-up artist and she's one of my clients, because believe it or not, I run a fashion and beauty PR agency. And no, I haven't always run a PR agency from the comfort of my child-hood bedroom. I'm not a total freak. I used to have an office in Camden in this seriously cool co-working space filled with tech geniuses, cutting-edge fashion designers, artisan coffee sellers and general hipster entrepreneurs. And then there was me. Not quite hipster, but not quite geek. A businesswoman. Unlike a few of the people there who rolled in at midday and 'brainstormed' over team-building games of ping pong, I was really committed. But then shit hit the fan. And now I'm back at home, living in a terraced house with my mum in the quaint Surrey village where I grew up, and instead of a cool Camden office with shabby chic exposed brick walls and co-workers lounging around on expensive bean bags, I'm surrounded by wallpaper printed with tiny hedgehogs wearing aprons (not even joking) and the closest thing I have to colleagues is a row of Beanie Babies lined up on the windowsill, their colours having faded from decades in the sun.

When I say shit hit the fan, what I really mean is my ex, Leroy, cheated on me with a girl from the gym where we met. In fact, Leroy wasn't just my ex, he was my ex-fiancé. Even saying his name makes me cringe. *Leroy*. What was I thinking going for a guy called Leroy? Did I really think I could marry him? Imagine standing at the altar saying, 'I take thee, *Leroy*, to be my lawfully wedded husband'. Bleurgh. His name was obviously a red flag. Everything about him was a red flag actually, from the tattoo of Dr Dre on his shoulder to the way he made these horrendous grunting noises when he did bench presses like he was experiencing some kind of demonic possession. And then there was his ridiculous job as a furniture upcycler, which essentially involved buying old chests of drawers for a tenner from car boot sales, painting them blue and then selling them on for a five quid profit to someone who probably needed to go to Specsavers. Okay, maybe I'm being a bit harsh. Sometimes Leroy made a ten-pound profit. Sometimes even fifteen. Basically, he wasn't exactly going places. And yet somehow (I blame pheromones) that didn't matter to me. I decided that his furniture upcycling was trendy and cool and creative. I told my friends that he 'wasn't really an office person' which, looking back on it, was just a nice way of saying he was pretty much unemployable. I'd stress how Leroy 'liked to work with his hands' as though he were an artisanal god.

Ha. Artisanal he was not. A god he was definitely not. But he did like to work with his hands. He loved that. He certainly loved working his hands on Lydia – the annoyingly chipper personal trainer he started seeing while we were still together.

I know I sound bitter but I'm not. I mean, not that much. Okay, a bit – but can you blame me? I thought Leroy was the one. I was willing to overlook a Dr Dre tattoo for crying out loud! It didn't matter because we were together. We were in love. We were going places. Leroy moved into my flat and somehow –*through many frenzied sexual encounters and a lack of respect for reproductive biology* – I ended up pregnant. P-R-E-G-N-A-N-T. When I saw those two red lines, I knew this was a problem that had to be solved. When you've spent your entire adult life avoiding pregnancy, that's just how you see it, right? At least you do when you're me and the only experience you've ever had of looking after something living is the time you bought a Venus flytrap and managed to kill it within two weeks. I ran through my options:

- Morning-after pill (probably too late)
- Abortion (eek)
- Buy another test in the hope that this one was faulty (fingers crossed)

I ran to the shop and bought another test, but the damn thing wasn't faulty. I was pretty sure it was too late for the morning-after pill so that left me with one option: an abortion. *Abortion.* Even the word made me shudder, but I braced myself to talk to Leroy about it. We'd get through it together.

But then that annoying furniture upcycler went and upcycled my mind, didn't he? He turned me from an IKEA desk – good for work, reliable, decent and functional – to a rainbow-coloured child's table, that with a few clicks and manoeuvres could turn into a cot. In Leroy's eyes, I could become multi-purpose, a businesswoman and a mum. He made me feel like anything was possible. As long as we were together – a team – we could make it work. The timing wasn't ideal, but we'd find a way.

To begin with, it was all going swimmingly. Leroy was so excited about our baby coming that he started buying the most adorable things – miniature Converse trainers, a tiny tracksuit, a rattle. He even came to antenatal classes with me without grumbling, and I started to feel like this pregnancy might be a gift. The catalyst needed to give my life and mine and Leroy's relationship a bit more substance. Until then, I'd just been a businesswoman and a party girl, and I thought that with the arrival of a baby, my life might start to mean something more. And then Leroy proposed and even though it wasn't the most epic proposal ever (a cheapish ring presented midway through eating a calzone at Pizza Express), I still felt like everything was starting to work out. That all the pieces of my life were coming together like a completed jigsaw. But then suddenly, pretty much overnight, Leroy's whole attitude changed, and he became completely hands off. Literally. He stopped wanting to come anywhere near me in the bedroom. He said he felt weird about 'disturbing the baby'. I mean, he was well-endowed but not disturbing-the-baby-by-piercing-my-womb big. I could tell it was about more than that.

Leroy quit coming to the antenatal classes. He stopped buying things for our baby. He stopped hanging out at my flat like he'd been doing the whole time we'd been together and went back to his tiny studio, claiming he 'had a ton of work', but there's only so much time you can spend upcycling furniture. When that excuse got old and I asked him to come home, he said he 'was feeling under the weather'. I didn't know what was going on, but I desperately missed him, so one evening, I dragged my pregnant arse over to his place, with a carrier bag filled with Lemsip, Jaffa Cakes (his favourites) and even a box of gourmet cupcakes, only to find Leroy wasn't under the weather at all. He was under Lydia. Leroy had forgotten that he'd left a spare key at my place and when he didn't answer the front door, I assumed he might be too ill in bed. I burst into his flat and headed to his bedroom, only to find him having such wild passionate sex that he clearly hadn't even registered my knock at the door. It took so long for him to notice my presence in the room that I began to feel like I was witnessing some kind of live sex show, and gawping in horror throughout the whole thing. Finally, Leroy spotted me and sprung apart from Lydia – but our relationship was over. I yanked the cheap ugly engagement ring he'd given me off my finger and flung it in his face. That was when it first dawned on me: I was going to be a single mum.

'Natalieeeee!' My mum's voice bellows up the stairs now, interrupting my thoughts, which is probably a good thing since they weren't exactly going to the best places.

'Yes?' I call back. The fact that my mum and I are still communicating like this – down a staircase in a similar way to how she used to call me down for dinner – is a little cringeworthy. Okay, it's *really* cringe-worthy, but my mum's been a life-saver recently. She let me move in with her when I realised I couldn't cope with looking after my baby alone while trying to keep my business going. And living rent-free at home has allowed me to save up for a deposit so that my daughter and I can have our own little home at some point.

'Come down here!' she shrieks.

'Okay!' I call back, placing my glitter pen on the desk, before heading downstairs.

My mum's got my daughter Hera downstairs and it's been a few hours since I saw her, which is a long time for me. Even if Leroy turned out to be a complete waste of space, I have to give him credit for helping me make the World's Most Perfect Baby. My little Hera is adorable, and I'm not just saying that because I'm her mum. She really is a gorgeous baby. She has the biggest brownest eyes, the longest lashes, a cute button nose and the prettiest little rosebud lips. She's so uniquely beautiful that I wanted to give her a unique name. I chose Hera because it's the name of the queen of the Greek gods – a powerful, strong, leading woman, just like I want my baby to grow up to be.

I head into the kitchen and immediately spot Hera sitting in her highchair, playing with her favourite toy – a teddy that somewhere along the line was dubbed 'Mr Bear'.

'Hello angel!' I coo, giving her a kiss on the head.

Hera immediately drops Mr Bear and reaches out for a hug. My heart melts. It never gets old. I pick her up and hold her close to my chest, rubbing her back and bouncing her up and down while she plays with my hair. It's only then that I notice that my mum is leaning against the kitchen counter fully made up and wearing a party frock she bought last week from TK Maxx. It's pink, embroidered with gold fuchsias, and she was incredibly happy to get it for 70 per cent off. She's munching on a cracker with brie, carefully cupping one of her hands under it so the crumbs don't fall on her dress.

'How come you're wearing that?' I ask, gesturing at her dress and noticing her face of full make-up. She's gone all out with blue eyeshadow, lashings of mascara, blusher and bright red lipstick.

'It's Mick's fundraiser!' my mum says through a mouthful of cracker. 'Remember?'

'What?' I head over to the counter and take a cracker from the open packet on the side.

'Mick's fundraiser. At the village hall?' My mum eyes me expectantly, as though waiting for the penny to drop but I have no idea what she's talking about.

'Remember? We're going!' My expression is blank. 'Oh Natalie! Don't tell me you've forgotten? Baby brain isn't meant to hang round for a year after you give birth!' She tuts, reaching for another cracker.

I roll my eyes indulgently. 'Seriously Mum, I have no idea what you're talking about. What fundraiser?'

'Down the village hall. Mick's annual fundraiser for Cancer Research. It's been happening every year since you were 12. Held on the anniversary of his wife's passing. Maggie, remember? The fifth of May. Ring a bell?'

'Oh *that*,' I reply, finally realising what she's on about.

Mick has been our neighbour my whole life. He lives just a few doors down in a narrow terraced house just like ours. Our village is incredibly close-knit. Chiddingfold is a small place. There are only a few thousand residents and most of us know each other or know someone who knows someone we know. Sadly, Mick's wife Maggie died from breast cancer around twenty years ago and Mick has been organising a charity fundraiser every year since in her memory. The whole community gets together in the village hall. There's a buffet, drinks, an auction of donated items, a disco, and one year there was even a talent show for the kids. It's a great event and it's certainly been going on for a long time, but it's hardly the highlight of my social calendar. It's not exactly been at the forefront of my mind.

'You used to love that fundraiser!' my mum reminds me as I chew my cracker and feed a little bit to Hera.

She's right. I used to love the fundraiser. I used to love the cake stand selling the prettiest cupcakes ever, the most choco-latey brownies and the fluffiest, most delicious Victoria sponge. The village hall would always be decked out with streamers and bunting and there'd be a massive bowl of non-alcoholic fruit punch for the kids and real punch for the adults. I used to love the disco, which was overseen by a Rick, a guy who worked at the Spar but doubled up as 'DJ Bubble' for the fundraiser. His rousing catchphrase was 'DJ Bubble, you're in trouble!' which we all loved when we were kids even though, looking back, it was totally awful. He'd play what I used to think were the best sets ever but were probably just the top tracks from *Now That's What I Call Music 6*. One year there was even a smoke machine. Oh, and there was a raffle that everyone used to get so excited about. I used to love the raffle, even though the best thing I ever won was a John Lewis spatula.

'Yeah, I did love that fundraiser, Mum, but the last time I went I was a kid! How am I meant to remember the dates of events I haven't been to for nearly two decades?' I ask exasperatedly before shovelling another cracker into my mouth.

'It was on the calendar,' my mum comments, nodding towards the calendar on the wall, where in red marker pen in today's box are the scrawled words 'Mick's fundraiser'.

'Right, so I'm supposed to just check the calendar every day to see if there are events I'm meant to be going to?'

'Umm, yes love, that is what calendars are for!' My mum laughs. I love my mum but she's impossible sometimes.

'You could have told me, Mum. You know, reminded me or something. Verbally?' I suggest.

She simply shrugs. 'Oh well, I forgot.' She looks at her watch. It's a gold and silver bracelet-style one she always wears for special occasions. 'We'd better head off. It starts in half an hour.'

'Mum, I can't go! What about Hera?' I remind her, stroking Hera's head.

'She's coming with us, love! Mick's included loads of prizes in the raffle this year for baby stuff. There's a baby rocker up for grabs. Even a baby forklift truck. Hera might win!'

'Hera has a rocker!' I point out. 'And she doesn't need a forklift truck!'

My mum just shrugs. 'It'll still be a fun outing!'

'I don't know, Mum, Hera will get tired. You know what she's like after late nights,' I remind her. Hera can get pretty loud and cranky the following day if she doesn't get a good night's sleep.

'We'll put her in her buggy, she can relax, and then we'll duck out early. We don't have to stay for the disco! Oh come on, Natalie, Hera can handle a little outing. And it would do you good as well,' she says, giving me a pointed look as I grab another cracker.

Ever since I moved back home, my mum's been on at me to get out more, and it's not that I'm anti-social, but I honestly don't see how I can. I have a business to run and when I'm not

8

working, I'm taking care of Hera. My mum offers to babysit but she already looks after Hera while I'm working, and I feel bad asking her to do any more. She only recently retired from her job as a nursery school teacher and I don't think spending more time with small children was quite what she expected from retirement. And anyway, she has a life too. A few years ago, she started seeing the landlord of the pub down the road – a good-natured divorcé called Tim and they're totally smitten with each other. My dad upped sticks when I was little and moved to the French alps to start a new life as a ski instructor and I know it's taken my mum a very long time to trust a man again. I should probably have been a bit damaged too, but I was so young that I don't really have many memories of my dad and you don't miss someone you've never known. Plus, my mum's always been exceptional, so I never really felt I was lacking. She deserves happiness and she adores Tim. The last thing I want is for them to miss out on quality time together just because I decided to pop out a baby.

Besides, it's not like my social life is completely non-existent. My best friends Lauren, Danielle and Amber come down to visit when they can and we go out for lunch followed by shopping or a walk in the park. I was a bit worried that my friends might get bored hanging out with a baby, but they adore Hera. Amber – a lifestyle blogger I met at a press launch years ago – is six months pregnant so she's obsessed with everything baby-related. My uni mate Danielle and my best friend from school, Lauren, have very opposing views on children. Danielle longs to have three children and she and her boyfriend Jack have just started trying for a baby. She keeps asking me a ton of questions, like 'which sex position is best for insemination' and will she 'get pregnant faster with regular exercise' (like I used to). Unlike Danielle, Lauren, who's still single and playing the field, prefers cats to children and swears she'll never 'breed' as she puts it. Of all my friends, Lauren is the one I'm closest to, even if our lives are totally different these days. Lauren's a freelance social media marketer and her days are packed with spin classes, Starbucks laptop sessions and nights out at glamourous industry events. My mumsy lifestyle is definitely not for her, but even Lauren loves Hera. Hera's impossible not to love, really. She's just so cute. She's got the sweetest little smile imaginable and even her cry isn't that bad. I've heard some babies at the local creche whose cries should be played in place of fire alarms. They're *that* piercing.

I know I sound really boring, but I don't always do baby-friendly things with my friends. Every couple of weeks, I'll leave Hera with my mum and head to London. I find a nice café somewhere and have lunch with my assistant Becky, where we discuss our latest campaigns. Becky's awesome. We used to work together in the Camden office and I was worried she might lose interest in the business once I left London and stopped being as hands-on, but she's stayed loyal. After Becky and I catch up, I'll meet my friends for dinner and drinks, like we used to before I was a mum.

Okay, so my social life isn't much. It's certainly a lot less exciting than it used to be, but the weird thing is, I've stopped minding. I've got used to winding down at home with Netflix in the evenings and a bowl of popcorn. It's cosy, almost like a home cinema. And anyway, even if I did have the time or inclination to go out, where would I go? There's not much to do in Chiddingfold. There's a village green which may have seemed like a fun place to hang out when I was a teenager, but it's hardly appealing now, unless I'm taking Hera for a walk. There are a couple of cute, cosy pubs that are lovely for Sunday lunch, but they're not exactly happening. And then there's Chiddingfold Cinema, which is actually just a projector screen and a few chairs lined up in rows in the village hall. It's kind of adorable, but they show one film a month and it's usually a 'new release' that came out at least two or three years ago. Oh, and a state-of-the-art gym opened recently a few miles down the road, but the last thing I want to do is head there and find Chiddingfold's answer to Leroy.

'Come on, love. It'll be a great night,' my mum insists.

'I don't know …' I squirm. The fundraiser did used to be a laugh and I do want to show my support for Mick, but I only just finished working and I was looking forward to snuggling up on the sofa and watching the next episode of the latest sitcom I'm addicted to.

'Brian will be there,' my mum adds with a wink.

'Oh God!' I groan. Brian is a bicycle repair man who's tried it on with every woman with a pulse in the village, yet that hasn't stopped my mum trying to set me up with him ever since I moved back home. He's got weird googly eyes and an insanely annoying habit of saying 'do you know what I mean?' at the end of every sentence. You'll run into him in town and comment on the weather and he'll respond, 'Yeah, it's really cold. Do you know what I mean?' or he'll be talking about the latest bike he's been fixing and comment, 'It's got a really good gear suspension, do you know what I mean?' My brain just switches off every time I talk to him. I've told my mum a million times I don't fancy him, but she acts like I'm overlooking Prince Charming. I shudder to think of what it would be like to be with Brian. Can you imagine – 'I love you, do you know what I mean?'

'Mum, I'm not going to date Brian!' I remind her.

'He's a lovely lad,' my mum huffs defensively.

'Mum, seriously …'

'Alright, alright.' My mum throws her hands up in mock surrender. 'I'll stop trying to set you up with Brian, but I still think you should come. Mick knows you're back. He'd love to see you there. Just a few hours, for Maggie.' She eyes me imploringly.

How can I say no to the memory of Mick's dead wife?

'Okay, fine,' I relent. 'I wish you'd told me earlier though. What am I going to wear?'

I give Hera the last piece of cracker, before brushing the crumbs from my hands.

'I'm sure you'll find something!'

'Hope so! Keep an eye on Hera while I look?'

11

My mum nods as she nibbles on another cracker and cheese.

I race upstairs. She's right, I will find something. I have a *ton* of clothes. They wouldn't fit in my old wardrobe, so I had to buy two rails to put them on. I try to pass my clothes addiction off as an occupational hazard of working in fashion and beauty PR. When I lived in London, I used to go to meetings, product launches and networking events all the time and I'd be expected to look the part. I needed to show our clients that I had my finger on the pulse and knew about the latest trends, which meant buying into the coolest looks every season. But it's not like it was a chore, I do genuinely love fashion and I love getting stuff that isn't on trend too, whether that's a nice charity shop dress, a comfy pair of boyfriend jeans or a slouchy oversized T-shirt.

I rifle through my clothes racks a few times until I find a short-sleeved purple jumpsuit I bought six months ago and never got around to wearing. It's tailored and smart, but its purple shade and gold drawstring waist give it a playful edge. It's perfect. I pull off the leggings and T-shirt combo I've been living in recently, swap my sports bra for a regular one and slip into the jumpsuit. I check my reflection in my bedroom mirror. The jumpsuit looks good on, but it's too dressy to wear without make-up. I don't have time to do a full face of make-up, so I smooth a bit of BB cream onto my skin, add a touch of blusher, some tinted lip balm and a slick of mascara. That'll do. I pull my hair out of its messy bun and run a comb through it. I take in its slightly frizzy appearance and wonder whether I have time to use my straighteners.

'Natalie! Hurry up!' my mum bellows up the stairs.

'Okay! Okay!' I call back, abandoning all thoughts of straightening my hair. I grab a hairclip from the dish on my dressing table and attempt to pin my hair to the side, but it looks weird, so I just let it down again. It looks a bit scruffy, but it will do. It's only a fundraiser at the village hall, after all.

I grab my wallet and phone, shove them into a handbag and head downstairs.

'I'm ready!' I say as I walk back into the kitchen.

My mum's put away the crackers and cheese and is now playing with Hera, who is back in her highchair. She looks over her shoulder.

'Oh, lovely outfit you've got on,' she says, clocking my jumpsuit.

'Thanks Mum,' I reply, walking over to her and Hera.

'How's my gorgeous girl doing?' I ask.

'I'm good,' my mum replies, with a grin, as she waves Mr Bear around for Hera.

I roll my eyes. 'I meant Hera, Mum!'

'I know!' She laughs as Hera reaches out and grabs Mr Bear, before clutching him close to her chest. She starts blinking sleepily and her head drops forward a little.

'Oh no, she's tired!' I say. 'Maybe she needs to go to bed.'

'We'll put her in her carrier, and she can have a little nap on the way. Relax love. An hour at the village hall isn't going to kill her.'

Hera's eyes droop closed, and I begin to have serious doubts over whether going to this fundraiser is a good idea. 'Look at her!'

'Well, let her have a nap in her carrier then. That baby sleeps like a log. She'll be fine. We'll only be out for a bit anyway,' my mum says impatiently. 'I just want to see if I win anything in the raffle. Mick's worked really hard on this year's draw. The top prize is a romantic getaway to Marrakech!'

'A romantic getaway to Marrakech!? Seriously?' I balk. 'I could swear the last time I went to Mick's fundraiser the top prize was a picnic hamper.'

'Well, it's come a long way since then! Mick's been pulling some strings.'

I raise an eyebrow. Mick, pulling strings? He's a retired office administrator whose social life revolves around the local bridge club, how many strings can he pull?

'A trip to Marrakech could be just the thing for you!' my mum says with a twinkle in her eye.

'Didn't you say it was a romantic getaway? Who am I going to take?'

It's a bit tragic to admit, but I haven't so much as held hands with another man since things ended with Leroy. I've been so preoccupied with trying to be a good mum and keeping my business running smoothly that I haven't had any time to go on dates. It's not like I meet anyone now that I'm a homebody. The only men I encounter in my daily life these days are the postman and takeaway delivery men (and unfortunately neither are sexy).

'You could go with Lauren. I'll take Hera for a few days. And anyway, you could always make it romantic,' she suggests with a wink.

I frown. 'Huh? Mum, are you suggesting that I seduce my best friend?!'

'No!' I'm suggesting that you might meet a nice man while you're there. Have a little holiday romance!'

'Oh God,' I grumble. 'Are you serious, Mum?'

'What?' She shrugs exaggeratedly with a cheeky wink. 'It wouldn't hurt!'

I stare back at her, deadpan. 'Somehow, I doubt a dodgy holiday romance in Marrakech would be a great move right now and secondly, I find your concern for my sex life a little disturbing!'

'I'm not concerned. I'm just saying, a little holiday romance might be fun. It might do you some good,' my mum says, waving Mr Bear for Hera. Hera ignores her, nodding off instead.

'Some *sun* might do me good,' I point out, when all of a sudden, an image pops into my head of me and Lauren lying on sun loungers sipping cocktails by a big sparkling pool. Going on holiday hasn't occurred to me once since I had Hera, but it is a surprisingly appealing image.

'Sun! Is that what they call it these days?' my mum sniggers.

'Oh my God, Mum!' I groan. 'This conversation is over!' I tut, picking a sleeping Hera gently up from her highchair and placing her in the carrier, where she continues to snooze.

My mum laughs. 'Well whatever, let's just hope one of us wins!'

Chapter 2

By the time we get to the village hall, my mum and I have already fallen out over whether the washing up has been done and whose turn it was to do it. The car has stalled three times and Hera has woken up. My mum parks wonkily in a space outside the village hall and as soon as the car comes to a stop, I jump out and open the back door to check Hera.

She reaches for me from her baby seat, wailing loudly.

'Baby! It's okay sweetheart,' I coo, attempting to calm her, while rocking her gently on my shoulder. My mum turns the engine off and gets out of the car.

Hera lets out a few more loud cries.

'Sweetie, it's okay, it's okay!' I rub and pat her back as I pace back and forth by the side of the car. My mum looks on with concern.

'Shall I just go home? Maybe this is too much for her?' I suggest.

'Give her a minute …' I can tell my mum's really desperate to have a night out at the village hall, so I keep patting Hera and making soft cooing noises in her ear.

She lets out a few more loud cries and then, strangely, she quietens down.

'Oh, thank God for that!' I breathe a sigh of relief when

15

suddenly, Hera's body swells and an eruption of green-tinged vomit spurts out of her mouth.

'Eww!' I yelp as the vomit lands on my jumpsuit and drips from my shoulder down over my right breast.

'Oh no!' My mum opens the car door and reaches into the glove compartment for a pack of baby wipes while I rub Hera's back, comforting her, while trying not to breathe in the pungent smell of fresh sick.

'It's okay, sweetheart,' I coo as my mum dabs at Hera's face, wiping the sick away. She chucks the vomit-soaked wipe into a nearby bin and then gets a fresh one and tries to mop up the warm sick that's dribbling down my jumpsuit.

'What do you think is wrong with her, Mum? Do you think she's okay?' I ask, fretting. My mum may wind me up a bit sometimes, but it's been a godsend having someone nearby who's been there and done that when it comes to motherhood.

'Yeah, she's fine. She probably just ate too much at lunch. I thought she was gulping down that apple crumble dessert a bit fast,' my mum comments.

'What? You gave her apple?' I gawp.

'Yes,' my mum answers hesitantly. 'Was I ... not meant to?'

'It doesn't agree with her, Mum, that's why she's vomiting,' I grumble. 'Poor Hera-pops ...' I rub her back some more.

'Oh dear, let me have her.' My mum reaches for Hera.

I hand her over and take a wet wipe. My mum comforts Hera, while I dab at the sick on my boob. I love my baby, but she's managed to produce the most disgusting slime-like vomit. The more I dab at it, the more it seems to be getting everywhere and before I know it, my entire left boob is soaked and gunky.

'Oh God,' I groan.

My mum looks up from Hera and eyes my jumpsuit in shock.

'It's everywhere,' she comments.

'Pam!' my mum's friend, Sandy, calls out, waving over her shoulder as she heads into the hall.

'Hi Sandy!' my mum calls back in a strained voice. 'Oh no, they're going to get all the raffle tickets, we need to go in,' she adds under her breath.

'But Mum, look at me!'

My mum plasters a smile onto her face as she takes in my frazzled, vomit-spattered appearance. 'You don't look *that* bad,' she insists.

'You just said it was everywhere. I look awful,' I sigh.

It's true, I do. I go over to the car window and take in my reflection. I'm a complete mess. My nice jumpsuit is covered in gunk and my whole boob area is dark and splodgy from all the dabbing I've been doing with the baby wipes. All the stress has made my hair go even frizzier than it was before and the BB cream that I'd convinced myself gave me a subtle glow when I applied it at home isn't even remotely covering the pale washed-out look of my face. I'm a far cry from the single glamourous girl-boss I used to be, and I don't exactly look like Mum of the Year either. I should just head home already. This is what happens when you tell yourself real life is better than Netflix.

'Oh! I have an idea!' my mum pipes up, interrupting my self-pitying thoughts. Hera has calmed down a bit now and is resting her head against my mum's shoulder.

'What?' I turn to look at her, questioningly.

'I have a top in the back. You can put it on over your jump-suit. The sick will dry in no time and you'll look right as rain,' she says, heading over to the car boot. She hands Hera to me.

'Really?' I ask hopefully.

'Yeah, really. You might not smell right as rain, but you'll look it!' She gives Hera to me and then reaches into her handbag for the car keys and opens the boot.

'Let me just find it.' She leans forward and rummages in the assortment of random stuff she keeps there. I peer over her shoulder, taking in the empty, deflated-looking duffel bag, a long-forgotten crusty towel from a swimming trip and a Jilly Cooper novel.

'Oh, here it is!' my mum says suddenly, pulling a sweatshirt out of a plastic charity shop carrier bag buried behind a plant pot with a Homebase sticker on it that she appears to have forgotten to unload. She holds up the jumper, shaking it out of its crumpled state.

'What is that?' I gawp, taking in the monstrosity she's holding. It's a gigantic grey sweatshirt with a massive print of a tabby cat across the front and the words: 'Cat Cuddles Sanctuary'.

'Mum! Why did you buy that?! You don't even own a cat?!' I balk.

'I know.' My mum shrugs. 'So?'

'Then why do you have a Cat Cuddles Sanctuary jumper?!' I ask through gritted teeth.

'I bought it from Oxfam to wear for gardening. Anyway, you've never listened to Led Zeppelin and if I recall correctly, you own a Led Zeppelin T-shirt,' my mum points out, still holding up the monstrous jumper for all the world to see.

'What?! I do listen to Led Zeppelin!' I huff.

'Name a Led Zeppelin song,' my mum fires back, still holding up the jumper. The beady eyes of the tabby cat are strangely distracting, and my mind has gone completely blank.

'Erm, "Purple Rain"?' I say eventually.

'That's by Prince, darling.'

'How about "Stairway to Heaven"? Or "Whole Lotta Love"?' a man's voice says. He starts singing "Stairway to Heaven" in a low lilting tone.

I turn around to look to see none other than Will Brimble. Will. Brimble. The most popular guy from my old school who I haven't seen since I left to go to London for sixth-form. Will was part of the reason I left my old school. I applied for an arts scholarship at a boarding school in London for sixth form. I didn't expect to get in, but when they offered me a place, I decided to see it as a fresh start after experiencing heart break for the first time. Will was my first love and I used to absolutely adore him, but he was also the first guy to teach me what complete and utter morons men can be.

'Oh my God,' I mutter under my breath, wishing the ground would swallow me up. Will Brimble is the last person I want to run into, especially now, as I'm standing here clutching my baby while covered in sick.

Will sings another lyric and my mum closes her eyes. 'I forgot how much I like that song,' she says, swaying a little to Will's singing, as though she's at Woodstock festival. Will smiles smugly before continuing his rendition.

'Can you stop singing, please?' I snap.

'So you're not a Led Zeppelin fan then?' Will asks wryly. He's clearly just as much of a smug know-it-all now as he was at school. My mum smirks.

'I am a Led Zeppelin fan!' I huff. 'How long have you been eavesdropping, Will?'

'Not long. I just parked my car and then saw you two having some kind of commotion,' he says, glancing over at a white Audi TT, perfectly parked four or five spaces away, before turning to my mum.

'How are you doing, Pam?' he asks.

My mum bats her lashes as she and Will chat away. She's always thought a lot of Will. Everyone has. He was the kind of boy who was both popular with his peers, and parents and teachers too, because despite his love of skateboarding and partying, he was also really smart and did well at school. He'd have a joke with teachers, but he knew when to knuckle down. He even encouraged his friends to get their heads down ahead of exams – a form of peer pressure teachers and parents were incredibly grateful for. But aside from liking him for just generally being an all-rounder, my mum has a soft spot for Will because she was really fond of his dad, Gary – a retired police officer who was also extremely popular in the village. He bought a black cab and set up a taxi service to keep himself busy; he was known in Chiddingfold as the man to call if you needed to get somewhere. He was always reliable and friendly, a trustworthy bloke you felt comfortable around. But sadly, he died of a stroke around seven or eight years ago. Everyone was distraught. Our hearts went out to Will and his mum, Sharon. I even sent Will a card and emailed him at the time, offering my condolences, but he never got back to me. I guess he was just too overwhelmed. Will loved his dad.

While Will and my mum chat away, I look towards his car. It's pretty impressive and it looks a little out of place among the old Nissans and Fords of the villagers, but I wouldn't expect any less from Will. Despite the upset of losing his dad, he's done alright for himself. He's a bit of a celebrity on the media scene. He took his gift of the gab, smarts and ability to get on with anyone, and decided to pursue a career in journalism after school. He studied at City University and managed to get a reporter role at a paper in north London when he graduated. Then he moved to another reporter job at a national, which led to a promotion to assistant news editor, another promotion to news editor and then, basically after a few years, he'd achieved the staggering feat of becoming Group Editor for a national newspaper group with three papers by the tender age of 28. I know this because it's been impossible to escape Will's meteoric rise to the top. His promotions were always covered in the media news websites I subscribe to for work and Will never turns down the opportunity to commentate on TV if there's a chance. He's regularly appeared on Sky and the BBC. He's remained just as much of a show-off in adulthood as he was at school. But although his rise to the top of the journalistic career ladder has been very impressive, Will's success story has suffered a bit of a blow lately. The company he was working for had been losing money for years and despite their efforts to boost their revenue, nothing's worked. They tried staff lay-offs and restructures, they even added pleas to readers at the bottom of each article on their website with details of how to donate. But after years of trying, they realised the business just couldn't survive and sold their titles to a rival media group. The takeover meant that Will and all of the staff were out of a job. It was a huge story. I read about it at the time and wondered how Will had coped, but I didn't realise he'd ended up back in Chiddingfold.

Our eyes meet for a moment. His are just as striking as I remember them – a jade-green shade flecked through with amber. Exotic eyes that mesmerised my infatuated teenage self. Eyes that inspired forlorn poetry and horrendously self-indulgent angsty diary entries. Suddenly, Will's gaze drifts down and I'm worried he's going to notice a splodge of sick I've only jut spotted on the sleeve of my jumpsuit but instead, his eyes land on Hera.

'And who's this?' he asks.

'Oh, this is my daughter, Hera,' I explain, turning a little so Will can get a better view of Hera's gorgeous face.

'Aww, what a pretty girl!' Will says. I smile and thank him, but I just know the next question he's going to ask is going to be something to do with Hera's father and standing here, covered in sick, the last thing I need is to answer questions about Leroy, who hasn't once tried to get in touch since I had Hera and, as far as I know, is still living in his studio flat painting bookcases and having wild sex with Lydia.

I give Hera to my mum to hold and take the cat jumper, leaving her to show off Hera to Will and deflect the 'where's the daddy' style questions. I pull the jumper over my head. It smells musty and stale, from having been in the charity shop, but also from having been stuffed in the boot of my mum's car for God knows how long. Combined with the smell of sick, I'm really not my best self tonight. I just hope I don't run into anyone else from school.

I sweep my hair out from under my collar and take in my bizarre reflection in the car window, before turning to Will and my mum. They've moved on from cooing over Hera to talking about my mum's dress. Will is telling her how 'sensational' she looks and she's lapping it up.

'Oh, thank you,' she says, batting her eyelashes like a flirtatious schoolgirl.

'Oh yes, it's very flattering. A great cut, very figure-hugging,' Will remarks. My mum smiles delightedly.

A great cut?! Figure-hugging?

'Do you mind?' I sneer, wondering if there's any low to which Will won't stoop. Clearly even 60-year-old women aren't off his radar. He hasn't changed a bit since school, and don't even get me started on the nitty gritty of what he was like back then.

'What? I was just saying how fabulous your mother looks,' Will comments defensively, before taking in my jumper, his eyes widening in alarm. 'Hmmm … interesting choice. I heard that you work in fashion. Is that top some kind of ironic statement?'

'What do you mean, ironic?'

'Well, surely you don't mean to look like a crazy cat lady?' Will remarks.

My mum giggles.

'Piss off Will,' I snap. 'And mum, this is your jumper. So why are *you* laughing!?'

I turn my back on both of them. I put Hera in her carrier and give her a dummy, which she sucks on contentedly.

'I need a glass of punch!' I declare, before picking up Hera's carrier and marching towards the village hall.

Chapter 3

Martha, a friend of my mum's, is manning the drinks table. Unlike Will, she has the good manners not to comment on my attire. Okay, so maybe her eyes linger for a beat on the huge tabby cat and the Cat Cuddles logo but she doesn't feel the need to say anything. She quickly diverts her gaze back to the bowl of ruby red punch. With painstaking care, she dips a ladle into the bowl and decants the liquid into a plastic cup, before adding two ice cubes, half a strawberry and a slice of lime, and finally handing it to me. I take it from her, thanking her gratefully, before plucking the cherry out of the way and necking it. I wipe my mouth on the back of my hand, before handing her back the empty cup.

'Can I have seconds? Thanks Martha.'

Martha takes the cup, looking a little taken aback, before dutifully refilling it. A boozy mum in weird cat clothes with a baby sitting in a carrier at her feet probably isn't the best look, but I'm beyond caring. Martha doesn't bother with the fruit garnish this time and simply hands me the glass. I thank her and sip hungrily at it, before wandering over to the buffet. The buffet table, with its striped plastic cups and matching paper plates laden with party food is exactly as I remember it from back when the fundraiser first began so many years ago. Even the hall is the same, with the exact same rainbow bunting and streamers.

A few of the older men who I vaguely recognise regard me as I approach. They're local busybodies that have been active in neighbourhood affairs for years. I think a few of them sit on the board of Chiddingfold Parish Council. They're always finding something to complain about, from the frequency of the bin collection to the meandering bus routes. One guy, a retired naval officer called Clive who always wears a flat cap even when indoors and has been poking his nose into other people's business for years, watches me closely as I reach for a bread roll. I pretend to be fascinated by the roll, taking a bite before inspecting the fluffy dough as though it's the most interesting and engaging thing ever; I really don't want Clive to speak to me. Once he starts, he doesn't stop. I last saw him at a Christmas party at the local pub nearly two decades ago and the memory's still disturbingly fresh. He was wearing the same grey flat cap and bent my 12-year-old ears off about unreasonable parking regulations near my school and blah blah blah. I can feel Clive zoning in on me, so I spear a few olives from a bowl with a toothpick and try to busy myself with the buffet, when I suddenly hear a different male voice over my shoulder.

'Sorry Natalie, you don't look like a cat lady,' Will says, reaching for a cheese and grape stick from a plate on the buffet. He pops the chunks of cheese and grape speared onto the stick into his mouth in one bite.

I ignore him and turn back to the buffet to spear another olive. Will's hand follows mine to the bowl. His fingers are long and surprisingly well-groomed, his nails and cuticles are incredibly neat and tidy, and his hands look soft and moisturised. Not like the hands of the rough-around-the-edges Will I remember.

'Okay, maybe you do look a bit like a cat lady, but that's not necessarily a bad thing, is it?' Will ventures.

'What?' I snap, before popping an olive into my mouth and shooting him a look.

'Well, cat ladies … If you think about it, they're just animal lovers, aren't they? And what's wrong with looking like an animal lover? Cats are lovely animals.'

I turn to look at Will, giving him a deadpan stare as he makes his case for why it's okay to go around saying how someone you haven't seen for over a decade looks like a 'cat lady'. Even though he's just as annoying as ever, as much as I hate to admit it, he's still handsome. His young self and his current self are like the difference between a picture with a filter and the original. He's got a few lines now, his face isn't quite as smooth and blemish-free as it used to be and his hairline is beginning to recede, but he's still good-looking. His eyes are as striking as ever and they have a depth to them now that they never had before, even if he's still chatting total rubbish like he used to back at school. As well as his ability to chat to anyone about anything, he has the same dimples he had all those years ago and the same trademark playful smile.

He smiles at me, waiting for a response, but as usual, Will baffles me. His habit of talking complete crap is strangely beguiling, because even though you know what he's saying is rubbish, you find yourself engaging with it nonetheless. I consider his statement.

'Well, while there's nothing intrinsically wrong with being a cat lady, it's not exactly style goals, is it?' I comment.

Will smirks. 'I suppose not. I forgot you were a fashionista these days,' he remarks.

'*Fashionista?!*' I echo, smirking. 'Who even says that?' I reach for another olive. Will copies me, diving his stick back into the bowl. I have to yank my hand out of the way to avoid being impaled.

'Do you mind? My hand is not buffet food!' I huff, reaching back towards the bowl and spearing an olive. Before quickly pulling my hand away.

'Sorry, just a bit hungry,' Will says as he takes an olive and pops it in his mouth. 'Mmmm, delicious.' I ignore him but he keeps talking. 'Anyway, you are a fashionista. I've seen you online, talking about your outfit or the day – hashtag O-O-T-D. And you say things like "style goals."'

'Well, fashion is kind of my job, Will,' I point out, rolling my eyes indulgently, even though I do feel a little embarrassed about how regularly I used to hashtag my outfits of the day. It wasn't exactly *all* relevant to work.

'Even your baby is a fashionista,' Will remarks, peering closer at Hera, who's wearing the cutest red patterned dress that I got on sale at Gap Kids the other day. I managed to find a headband in exactly the same red shade from Accessorize to coordinate with it. Red is kind of her colour. Although she also looks great in pink, and yellow, and blue. And green, for that matter. She basically just suits everything. She certainly looks a hell of a lot more stylish than me right now. Upstaged by a one year old!

'Doesn't she look cute, though?' I say.

'Yeah, she does.' Will peers at Hera with a soppy, charmed look. 'She's very cute.'

I smile proudly at her. She's starting to fall asleep now, but I can tell she's trying to stay alert so she doesn't miss anything. She's dropping off, blinking a few times, trying not to fall asleep and then dropping off again.

'She's sleepy. She's my little angel,' I say with a sincerity that surprises me. But it's true. Hera is my angel. Even though it wasn't easy having her while being heartbroken over Leroy cheating and then learning how to be a single mum while trying to let go of all the bitterness I felt towards him, I got there in the end. Hera saved me with her lovely cuddles, her cute little smile and her unbridled enthusiasm over the little things, from eating her favourite food (chocolate yoghurt) to playing with Mr Bear.

'Aww!' Will reaches for Hera's cheek and gives it an awkward little stroke. It's abundantly clear that he doesn't interact with children very often.

26

'Will, you just left a streak of olive juice over Hera's face,' I grumble, spotting a greasy smear where his hand has been.

'Oh sorry,' Will replies, looking a little embarrassed.

He grabs a napkin from a nearby stack and quickly reaches down to wipe off the streak. Hera blinks up at him, wide-eyed, as he wipes the olive grease away. It's actually quite cute how flustered he seems to be over having got Hera the slightest bit dirty. Little does he know that some of her favourite hobbies include smearing mud from the garden over her face, giving a new twist to the idea of a mudpack. And if that doesn't hit the spot, she also likes to grab bottles of shower gel, washing up liquid, bubble bath – whatever's in reach, really – and just drizzle them over her head.

Will discards the napkin. 'Sorry about that,' he repeats.

'Don't worry about it.' Hera's already forgotten all about it and she's now properly dozing off.

'So anyway, how do you know about my OOTDs?' I ask, casting my eye over the vol-au-vents in the buffet.

'Oh, I know all about your agency. You used to send us press releases all the time. If I recall correctly, the last one was for a vajazzle.'

I avoid his gaze and crunch through a few crisps. They're sweet chilli and they're delicious. I try not to look too awkward at the mention of the vajazzle campaign I worked on. Representing a company that specialised in adorning women's vaginas with glitter wasn't my finest hour, but they paid well and sometimes money has to come before taste in business.

'My mum mentioned you were back. I think she heard about it from someone in town. I was wondering if I'd run into you,' Will comments.

'Oh right …' I murmur a little uneasily.

I can't help wondering what Will's heard. He must know something about the whole Leroy thing or otherwise he wouldn't have tactfully not mentioned it. I've certainly heard about his divorce.

He surprised everyone by settling down in his mid-twenties, marrying an heiress called Elsa Millington-Brown. It came as a bit of a shock to the village, especially since Will seemed to have been playing the field when he was first making a name for himself on the media scene. I'd see articles from time to time on the *Daily Mail* site with him falling out of nightclubs looking cosy with other minor celebrities. He was pictured quite a few times with a candidate from *The Apprentice*. Then those articles dried up and all of a sudden, word got around that he'd found love and settled down. Except apparently, the couple split a few years ago – I have no idea why. And I had no idea Will was back in Chiddingfold either. I wish I'd had a heads up that he was in town. My mum is usually a pretty reliable source of village gossip, but she's probably been too busy with Hera to stay on top of her game. If I'd known Will was back, I might have actually made an effort with my appearance – not because I still fancy him after all these years, but just for my own sense of pride.

'So, do you still paint?' Will asks.

I used to paint at school. I used to spend all my time in the art room, and it was my artistic ability that helped me get a scholarship for sixth-form but I haven't painted for years. Even before I had Hera. I just kind of lost interest in it.

'No, not really,' I admit.

'But you were so into it,' Will says, sounding almost disappointed.

I shrug.

'You were Natalie, the arty girl.' Will has a wry smile on his face.

'Ha!' I laugh. 'And you were a skater boy, but people change. I doubt you still hang around at the skate park with your arse hanging out of your jeans, while pretending to be into punk even though everyone knew you preferred pop,' I tease him. 'I bet you're not still doing that now – or are you?' I raise an eyebrow.

'No, I'm afraid not. Although I can get my arse out if you want me to?' Will asks with a wink.

'Oh for God's sake, I really set myself up for that one.' I sigh, laughing in spite of myself.

Will watches me as I reach for another handful of crisps and I can feel my cheeks growing hot as a blush creeps into them. I'm trying to focus on the crisps, but all I can currently think about is Will's arse. And the fact that he's watching me having these thoughts is like being an insect examined under a microscope. I feel like I'm squirming in a hot beam of light.

You see, I used to really fancy Will. Like *really* fancy him. I had a crush on him from the very first time I saw him, when he joined the school aged 11 after he and his family moved to Chiddingfold from London His dad had quit his job as a police officer at the Met Police and wanted a quieter, calmer life. Of course, I didn't know that detail at the time, but over time, I gathered titbits of information on the grapevine and added them to my mental catalogue of facts about Will Brimble, building up quite a detailed picture of him even though it took us three years to finally speak.

Will's right, I was the arty girl at school. It was my thing back in those days and I really wanted to be a painter, but everything changed when I went to my new school for sixth-form. I'd enrolled to study artsy subjects – Fine Art, Media Studies and Drama, but we were expected to take four A levels so I opted for Business Studies as I'd heard it was quite easy. Little did I know how much I'd take to it. My tutor spotted an entrepreneurial streak in me and by the time I left college, business had become my thing.

The arty girl Will knew is long gone. Back in those days, I used to spend as much time as possible in the art room. It felt like home with its paint-spattered tables, jars of brushes and pencils and trays of paints. I loved it. But not many other people shared my enthusiasm. I persuaded my art teacher – Mr Reed – to start an after-school art club on Wednesday afternoons, thinking the club was going to be a hit, but I ended up being the only person who went, and Mr Reed said he was going to cancel the club if

29

I continued to be the only attendee. Somehow, Will heard about my plight and the next week, he came along with a few of his friends. He was terrible at art. All of his drawings looked like they were drawn by a toddler and I could tell art wasn't his forte, but I'll never forget the wink he gave me when he asked Mr Reed at the end of the session, 'So I guess you're not still cancelling the club then?'

He came every week after that and we gradually got to know one another. My infatuation reached epic heights, but I did my best to hide it. Even though Will had saved my art club, I still wasn't convinced he fancied me. You see, the fact that Will had tried to save my club wasn't entirely out of character. Will had a reputation for doing things like that. He had this knack for just seeing when someone was in need and helping them out. He made the school a better place. There was one time when this really quiet, earnest girl called Alice started fundraising for a village in Tunisia and no one would donate. Everyone just wanted her to stop hassling them, but then Will started fundraising with her and within days, she'd met her fundraising target. She seemed more confident after that, sort of happier in herself. Then there was the time Will started a petition to ban sports teachers from getting team captains to pick who was going to be on their teams one-by-one out of the class, meaning that one person would always be chosen last. Will petitioned to have the practice banned because he felt it was unnecessarily cruel even though he was the kind of guy who'd be selected as the team captain, or if not, would instantly be chosen first. Nevertheless, he still took issue with the mean approach, which would always leave one kid feeling glum and dejected. Will's petition garnered hundreds of signatures from pupils and parents alike and from then on, the practice was history. Things like that just fuelled my adoration for him. He was good-looking and had a heart of gold, what more could I want?

Will didn't just come to Art Club once or twice, he came every week and he and I got really close. It was easier to be my real self around him when I was in the art room, which felt like a second home, than it would probably have been otherwise. I'd no doubt have been completely giddy and over-excited under normal circumstances. But I didn't have Will to myself. Soon Art Club was the most popular club in school, and I realised I wasn't the only girl who adored Wil. A ton of other girls suddenly discovered a passion for painting the moment they realised where Will was spending his Wednesday afternoons. But Will always sat with me and I began to suspect that I wasn't just fantasising and that perhaps – perhaps – he might actually fancy me.

But then things got messy, really messy …

'Hi guys! Ready to get some raffle tickets?' Rita, Mick's sister who helps him organise the fundraiser every year, bounds up to me and Will, brandishing a pad of raffle tickets, before she notices Hera who's now fast asleep and starts gushing over how cute she is.

While Rita fawns over Hera, I suddenly remember the prize. I'd got so distracted by all the commotion with Hera being sick, the cat jumper, Will and the buffet that I completely forgot that the reason I agreed to come along to this thing in the first place (apart from being a good person and raising money for charity, of course) was for the chance of winning a holiday. My mum was right, I do need a holiday. If anything was ever going to reinforce that fact, it would be standing here with a wet boob in a Cat Cuddle's jumper emitting the faint odour of sick.

'So, erm, is there really a holiday up for grabs, Rita?' I ask breezily.

'There is indeed!' Rita replies, turning her attention away from Hera. 'Mick really pulled out all the stops this year. His niece, Hannah, got a job at a travel agency and she managed to sort it. Best prize we've ever had. An all-inclusive romantic four night stay in a luxury five-star hotel in Marrakech! It has a swimming pool, a spa, the works. Sounds like heaven, doesn't it?' Rita's eyes have lit up.

31

'It sounds amazing!' I enthuse. 'Five-star? Really?'

'Oh yeah, five-star. It's top notch. The best,' Rita insists, before glancing down at her pad of raffle tickets. She could be exaggerating to get me and Will to splurge on the raffle, but somehow, I get the feeling that this prize might really be a diamond in the rough. A five-star holiday amid a plethora of hampers, kitchen utensils and Debenham's gift cards.

I rummage in my handbag for my wallet. 'Okay, I'll have five tickets please, Rita. No, ten!'

'Feeling lucky, are we?' Rita jokes. 'It's two quid a ticket, so that'll be twenty pounds, please.'

Twenty pounds? This event really has moved on since I was 12, when raffle tickets cost 50p. I pull my wallet out of my bag. It's a quirky one I found at an independent boutique in London with a Fendi-style monster print all over it. Will raises an eyebrow at the bold print as I pull out a twenty-pound note.

'Interesting …' he comments as I hand Rita the money. He's clearly having difficulty getting his head around the new me. The businesswoman me who pays attention to trends rather than the head-in-the-clouds arty girl I used to be.

Ignoring him, I hand the money to Rita, who places it in a money belt around her hips, before tearing off a few strips and handing me the tickets.

'Thanks Rita!' I reply. 'Fingers crossed!'

'Good luck, love,' Rita says, with a warm smile.

Rita turns around, looking for her next target, before clocking Clive. She waves over at him and turns to head his way when Will suddenly taps her on the shoulder.

'Rita, wait. I want some.'

'I already sold you one earlier,' Rita points out.

'Yeah, but I only got one. I didn't realise people were buying multiple tickets,' Will comments, sounding a little petulant.

'It is for charity,' I mutter under my breath.

Will laughs. 'Oh sure, Natalie, charity is what's on your mind right now!' he jokes, and it's as though he can see into my brain and is witnessing the picture in my head of me lounging on a deck chair by a gorgeous pool, the sun making my straw hat cast shadows over my face, a novel open on my lap and a cocktail in my hand.

'How many tickets would you like, Will, love?' Rita asks, ignoring mine and Will's bickering.

'Twenty,' Will says.

'Twenty?!' Rita and I both echo in unison.

'Yeah, it's for charity,' Will reminds me, with a smirk. I roll my eyes as he reaches into his jeans pocket and pulls out a battered old wallet. He flips it open and hands Rita two twenty-pound notes.

She takes the money and gives him his tickets, which he folds into his wallet while smiling smugly.

'I'll have some more please,' I tell Rita, before she has a chance to walk away.

'What? How many more?' she asks, looking a little taken aback.

I peer into my wallet. I have a crumpled fiver, two one-pound coins, a fifty pence piece and a couple of twenty pence and ten pence pieces. I quickly add it up: £8!

'Four please,' I say, fishing all the money out and depositing it into Rita's hand. She takes it, counts it and slips the coins and notes into her money belt, before handing me four more tickets. I place them in my bag, feeling warm and fuzzy with excitement. At least I think it's the excitement and not just the punch I've had to drink.

She glances over her shoulder at Clive who is looking over. He waves and looks hungrily at Rita's pad of tickets, clearly keen to get involved.

'Good luck you two!' Rita says, before heading over to Clive.

'Thanks Rita,' I call after her.

I pat my handbag, feeling pleased with all my tickets.

'Why are you smiling?' Will asks, eyeing me. 'You only have fourteen tickets. I have twenty-one.'

'You're such a dick,' I tut. 'Anyway, I don't care if you have twenty-one tickets to my fourteen, I'm feeling lucky. I'm going to win. I can just feel it.' I cross my fingers, praying I'm right.

'Ha!' Will scoffs. 'Well, we'll see about that, won't we?'

Chapter 4

I devour another handful of crisps and wash them down with a third glass of punch, while listening to Rowena – the head librarian at the local library – extoll the mindfulness benefits of cross-stitch. Believe it or not, the party is in full swing now. A few people have taken to the dancefloor where they're currently grooving to Katy Perry. The bowl of punch is nearly empty. The auction has been held – the highlight of which was a dark-haired woman bidding £100 for someone else's used foot spa – and Mick gave a really moving speech about his wife Maggie and about the important work Cancer Research are doing. Will and I have mostly been avoiding each other the whole evening, but I keep glancing across the hall and catching him looking over at me, which is annoying but then I wouldn't know about it if I wasn't also looking over. God, I really do feel like I'm back at school.

At the moment, Will's standing across the hall with his mum, Sharon – a softly spoken petite woman with an incredibly pretty face. She has a sort of Audrey Hepburn charm with sparkly eyes and a wide gorgeous guileless smile. She has a neat grey bob that always seems to have a natural bounce to it, the kind of volume most women can only achieve through a blow dry. She's stayed single since Will's dad passed away and I don't think she's particularly interested in finding anyone else – they were absolutely smitten – but that hasn't stopped the hordes of admirers from flocking her way. From the looks of it, Sharon is currently being chatted up by Mr Price (a divorced history teacher from my old school known for his bad breath and terrible toupee), Matthew Black (a chronically single monotone-voiced bachelor who lives down the road and has a penchant for keeping pet rats) and some other guy I don't recognise who appears to be totally over-excited to be speaking to a woman. So much so that his entire face is beaded with sweat. Will is standing protectively close, shielding Sharon from this onslaught of undesirable admirers and she keeps giving him grateful looks that, actually, now that I come to think of it, are bordering on desperate 'get me out of this' stares.

'It's incredibly restorative,' Rowena insists, and I realise she's still talking about cross-stitching. 'It's like meditation. Your mind relaxes but your body becomes centred too as you stitch. It's almost better than traditional meditation because your mind and body are in harmony. You should try it sometime.' Rowena eyes me hopefully. 'Once you get into it you can use your creations as gifts or just decorations. I decorate my whole flat with them.' Rowena picks up her phone and shows me an array of cross-stich creations in frames on the walls of her book-lined flat. If there isn't a slightly dusty-looking bookcase against the wall, there's an array of cross-stich designs in shabby chic frames. There are traditional floral pieces, which are quite charming, if a little twee. There are a few slightly bizarre but surprisingly life-like portraits of her cat, who she tells me is called Mittens. There's even a feminist design of a uterus and ovaries with the slogan 'Grow a pair'. It's pretty cool.

'Oh wow!' I say, both shocked and impressed as I take in the fine needlework on the cervix.

'You should come over sometime and I'll show you how it's done,' Rowena suggests enthusiastically. As sweet as she is, cross-stich is hardly my thing.

I have a sudden vision of myself in a few years' time, still living at home with my mum, cross-stitching portraits of Mr Bear for Hera or cross-stitching a penis with an angry slogan about toxic masculinity or something, while drinking tea at Rowena's place night after night, having forgotten what it feels like to be touched by a man. I suppress a shudder.

'I'm quite busy with work and with Hera. It's hard for me to get out much.' I glance towards Hera's carrier. She's still fast asleep, sputtering slightly as she dreams. I feel a fresh wave of maternal love for her and not just because she's the loveliest baby ever, but also because she's a brilliant excuse to get out of doing stuff I don't want to do.

Rowena looks a little disappointed. 'Well, maybe I could come to yours. I could bring my kit.'

'Err …' I utter. I can't seem to come up with an excuse and just as I'm beginning to think there's no way I'm going to get out of this, Mick's voice suddenly booms from the stage.

'Ladies and gentlemen!'

Everyone goes quiet and looks towards the stage. Mick's wearing the same outfit he had on last time I was at this fundraiser back when I was 12 – an eye-catching red three-piece suit teamed with a white shirt and a black bow tie.

'It's the moment we've all been waiting for!' he says, grinning broadly. 'The raffle!'

A few cheers erupt across the hall.

'Oh my God!' I grin, gripping Rowena's arm in excitement.

I look over at Will to see him looking back at me, steely-eyed. He smiles smugly as he holds up his crossed fingers. I smirk and wave my crossed fingers back at him.

'This year, we have a host of brilliant prizes,' Mick enthuses, gesturing at a table piled high with goodies. 'From a bottle of Fortnum's vintage port, Amazon gift cards, a year's subscription to *Good Housekeeping* and many others, to the star prize – a five-star romantic getaway for two in Marrakech!'

We all cheer.

'Big thanks to my lovely niece Hannah for pulling out all the stops to get the travel agency she works for to gift us this marvellous prize,' Mick continues, explaining how Hannah couldn't make it to the event because of her 'busy London life.' Ha. Unlike me and Will who now spend our Friday nights in village halls. I look over at him and catch his eye, we exchange a wry smile.

'I'm delighted to reveal that we've raised a total of £4,428 tonight for Cancer Research, making tonight our most successful fundraiser ever! A big round of applause to everyone! To everyone who's bought a ticket in the raffle and gifted prizes; to everyone who donated items for the auction and all the generous bidders; and to everyone who's taken the time to help with everything from the buffet to the bunting – it means the world to me that you all get behind this event year in year out. I know if Maggie could see us all, she'd be so incredibly proud,' Mick says, his eyes glistening with tears. 'Give yourselves a round of applause!' he adds, smiling warmly.

We all start clapping enthusiastically. Everyone, including myself, has teared up a little. It's so touching just how sweet and loyal Mick is that after twenty years, he's still holding fundraisers for his true love. It really does bring a tear to your eye and I can't help feeling bad that I hadn't been particularly interested in coming along tonight. I glance over at Will and even he's looking misty-eyed as he claps enthusiastically, a tender smile on his face.

Rita suddenly gets up on stage and takes the mic from Mick. He seems a little taken aback.

'I'd just like to say that even though everyone has done a marvellous job to make this event happen I think we should all acknowledge Mick's efforts. Without him, this event would never be the success it is. Your dedication is an inspiration to us all, Mick. Maggie would be so touched and so, so proud,' Rita says, her voice cracking with emotion. She starts clapping and we all join in, with even more gusto this time.

She and Mick hug and he takes the mic. Rita heads back to her seat.

'Thanks everyone. I'm so very touched,' Mick says as the applause dies down. 'And without further ado, I'll now be announcing the prizes of the raffle.'

Mick picks up a tin from the table of prizes and gives it a shake. 'Right, who wants to help me pick winners?' Mick asks, looking encouragingly towards a few kids sitting with their parents at a nearby table.

A little boy in a *Transformers* T-shirt sticks his hand up. 'Me! Me! Me!' he cries out.

'Come up on stage, Edward!' Mick says. Edward's mum ushers him towards the stage and helps him up.

'Right, Edward, you can pick our winners,' Mick says, pulling off the lid of the tin. Edward smiles up at him delightedly.

'Okay, so our first prize we'll be announcing is a fifteen-pound Waterstones voucher and the winner is …' Mick presents the tin to Edward, who reaches for a ticket.

He pulls one out victoriously.

'Thanks Edward,' Mick says. 'What number is that?' Mick holds the microphone down to Edward.

'Number 231,' Edward announces shyly.

'Oh, that's me! That's me!' A red-haired lady I recognise as the receptionist from the local GP surgery calls out, waving her ticket in the air. She comes up on stage and Mick hands her the voucher. She seems delighted. I know it's only a raffle and I should just relax and have fun, but I can feel myself becoming totally gripped with excitement. I really want to win too!

Mick and Edward reveal the rest of the raffle winners. Will's mum Sharon wins a dinner for two at an Italian restaurant in town and I can't help feeling sorry for her as her admirers all seem to light up, clearly hoping to be her plus one. I suspect she'll probably end up taking Will. Rowena wins the bottle of port. By the time the final few prizes are revealed, Edward's beginning to look exhausted, like the novelty of choosing winners is starting to wear off. He goes back to sit with his mum. Edna, an elderly lady from the local church, comes up on stage to pluck the final winning tickets from the tin.

The table of prizes is growing increasingly empty and the tension in the room is mounting as we get closer and closer to the star prize reveal. I know it's only a charity raffle, but I can't help caring so much. A holiday to Marrakech is not something that people in my village take lightly. I know this prize and whoever wins will be the talk of the town for months. My mum was right. This is an important event on the village calendar. I can't believe I even considered missing it.

'Okay ladies and gentlemen, now the moment you've all been waiting for – we'll be announcing the winner of the star prize! A romantic getaway in gorgeous, exotic, exciting Marrakech,' Mick says. He switches a button on a projector on the table and suddenly, beautiful images of the most exquisite hotel fill the screen. It's stunning – a huge white palatial building with a tapering gold domed roof and tall majestic archways, lined with palm trees soaring to the sky. The images cut to the inside of the hotel and it's all dreamy-looking terracotta walls, sun-filled riads and wide marble hallways. The pictures cut to a photo of a plush sumptuous bed covered in fractured light flowing from ornate silver lamps and photographs of a giant tranquil aquamarine pool lined with sun loungers in the most stunning courtyard ever. Rita really wasn't exaggerating when she said this holiday was 'top notch'. The images of the hotel blend into images of Marrakech, with its bustling souks, full of spices, tagine dishes, rugs and elongated lamps that look like something you could use to summon a genie.

I drink in the images, my daydream of reclining on the sun lounger in a bikini and sunglasses growing sharper and sharper by the second. I really want to win this prize. It would be so great for me and Lauren. She seems to be loving the single girl-about-town life, but I know it gets exhausting and she could do with a break. We used to go on mini-breaks from time to time. She and I took the Eurostar to Bruges one weekend and we've been to Paris a few times, too. I've felt a bit bad since I had Hera and moved to Chiddingfold as we don't get to hang out anywhere near as much as we used to. This holiday would be perfect for us. We'd get to spend some quality girl time together.

'And the winner is ...' Mick holds the tin our to Edna, who reaches inside.

We all hold our breath. We're so silent you could hear a pin drop. Yet Edna is taking forever to choose a ticket, rummaging about in the tin. She probably feels like Dermot O'Leary right now, announcing the winner of the *X Factor*.

Eventually her hand emerges from the tin and she unfolds a piece of paper.

'Number 18!' she announces.

Excitement floods through me as I scan my raffle tickets. I'm pretty sure I had number 18 and then my eyes land on the winning ticket. Number 18!

'And number 102,' Edna adds just as I leap to my feet, waving my winning ticket and cry, 'It's me!'

My moment of joy is suddenly shrouded in confusion. Why is Edna calling out another winning ticket? *I* won!

'Ha! I have 102!' Will calls out, brandishing a ticket.

I look over at him. *What?* I glance around the room, trying to figure out what's going on, but everyone else is looking equally perplexed. We all look towards Mick, who seems baffled.

'It's just one winner Edna, not two!' he says eventually.

Edna blushes. 'Oh ... I thought it was a prize for two, so I just read out two names.'

'No love. A prize for two but the winner can take whoever they want.'

'Right,' Edna replies, looking completely out of her depth. I can't help feeling sorry for her. She's in her eighties and I don't think her mind is quite as sharp as it used to be.

'It's okay, Edna love,' Mick says, rubbing Edna's back.

Mick thanks her for her help and reassures her that she's done a good job. She smiles sweetly and goes back to her table to sit down.

'Right, well, er, this is a difficult situation ...' Mick looks towards me and Will. We're both holding our winning tickets.

'Well, my ticket was read out first so it would probably be easiest to just let me have the prize,' I suggest. 'Maybe next time, Will.'

Will smirks. 'Just because your ticket was read out first doesn't mean anything. My ticket was read out fair and square.'

'Yes, it does. Ever heard of first-come-first-served?' I remind him.

Will laughs. 'Raffles don't work like that, Natalie.'

I suddenly realise that everyone in the hall is watching us bicker.

'Why don't you just pull a ticket from those two?' Clive suggests, gesturing between me and Will. Not a bad idea actually, except I'll stand a 50 per cent chance of losing and I really don't want to lose.

I don't comment and neither does Will. I can tell Will's not particularly keen on the idea either.

'Good suggestion, Clive, thank you. But I've had an idea too,' Mick says. My ears prick up.

'How about you both go? Together.'

A laugh escapes my lips. 'Together?' I gawp.

I look over at Will, who's also laughing.

'That's a great idea, Mick,' my mum pipes up, a twinkle in her eye. She's sitting a few seats down from me at the table and I shoot her a look. I know she likes Will, but I mean, seriously? Suggesting I go on holiday with him. I haven't even seen him for sixteen years, I'm hardly going to just hop on a plane with him to Marrakech!

'You could ...' Rita suggests, looking hopefully between me and Will.

Suddenly everyone in the hall is murmuring in agreement.

'Maggie used to love our holidays,' Mick reminisces over the microphone. 'There was this quote she used to like – "The world is a book and those who don't travel only read one page". She loved that. I know she would have been keen for you both to have a read of the Morocco chapter.'

Oh my God, what is happening? How has this trip of a lifetime that I was dying to get my hands on five minutes ago suddenly turned into the world's most awkward holiday?! Now I can't even refuse to go without feeling like I'm somehow betraying Maggie's memory.

'Come on, love. It's what Maggie would have wanted,' my mum says. I blink at her in shock several times, unable to believe her nerve. She's not interested in what Maggie would have wanted, she's just trying to set me up with Will.

As I gawp at my mum, another voice pipes up.

'I have an idea …'

I look over to see Brian. Googly-eyed annoying Brian. I hadn't noticed him until now, but he's sitting at a table by the buffet eyeing me intently, almost hungrily. It's a little disturbing, actually.

'I'll come with you,' Brian offers. 'If Will doesn't want to. I'll take the ticket and come with you. Give you a bit of company, do you know what I mean?'

He stares at me with a look of impassioned intensity as he makes this offer. I'm not sure he realises he's not helping the situation at all. As if Will's going to just give up his ticket! I glance at Will who is now smirking mischievously.

'That's not a bad idea, Brian,' he says.

My eyes widen in shock. He's not seriously going to sacrifice his ticket to Marrakech purely to get a laugh out of making me go on a four-night romantic getaway with Brian? Actually, that's exactly the kind of thing Will would find hilarious.

'No, Brian! Thanks for the offer, but no,' I state firmly, my voice tight and a little erratic. Brian deflates a little, but I don't care. I know he'll bounce back and will probably have moved onto his next target by the time the raffle's over.

'Okay, well in that case, maybe we should just go together then?' Will throws his hands up in surrender. I glare at him. What is he doing? He smiles back, shrugging.

Suddenly everyone's eyes dart towards me, expectantly. I don't want to go on holiday with Will, but if I say that, I'm going to look like a total spoilsport.

'Come on, Natalie!' Mick says, with a hopeful grin.

'Yeah come on,' a few others echo.

Everyone's looking my way and even though only seconds have passed, it feels like a lifetime. I squirm, not knowing what to do. My mum's nodding encouragingly. So's Rowena. Even Clive looks keen on the idea. I glance towards Rita, who seems to be the only person in the room who's giving me a sympathetic look.

'I mean, you could always go together and just do your own thing?' Rita suggests in an upbeat, optimistic tone.

I suppose she's right. I could always go on the trip, enjoy the gorgeous hotel, hang out at the pool and explore Marrakech on my own. Just because the trip is billed as a romantic getaway for two doesn't mean Will and I *have* to be romantic. It may be a package holiday, but we can unpackage it. We don't have to do everything together. I glance over at Will.

'Don't worry Natalie, I won't cramp your style,' he says, smirking again.

'Okay, fine,' I sigh, giving in.

'Oh fabulous!' my mum cries out.

'Excellent!' Mick says. 'Maggie would be so proud.'

'Great.' I smile uneasily, sitting back down.

Chapter 5

'You're going on a romantic getaway with Will Brimble?' Lauren gawps over a coffee in Starbucks. It's the one around the corner from this really cool vintage shop in Soho we always used to go to. I was tied up in a meeting with Becky but Lauren nipped in before coming and she's now wearing a yellow polka-dot headband featuring a giant bow that she managed to pick up. It's from the Fifties, apparently. Only Lauren could pull a headband like that off. It goes surprisingly well with her black biker jacket and bright red lipstick, and despite insisting she has 'the hangover to end all hangovers', she looks vibrant.

'No, I'm not going *with* him! We're both going on the same holiday, but not together,' I point out.

Lauren looks blank. She takes a sip of her coffee, but discovering it's not sweet enough, tears open a third sachet of sweetener and decants it into the mug.

I try explaining again. 'So basically, the holiday is meant to be a romantic getaway but we're obviously not going to be romantic. So we won't be doing romantic things, like candlelit dinners and couple's massages or any of that stuff. We'll just do our own thing.'

'Oh, come on, how is that going to work?' Lauren scoffs, taking another sip of her now super sweet coffee, seeming satisfied this time. One of the perks of Lauren being a freelancer is that she can often squeeze in seeing me at a moment's notice so when I arranged an emergency trip to London to discuss the situation I've found myself in, she was more than happy to oblige. Regardless of the whole Will thing, it's good to see her. I've missed her plain-speaking and her love for overly sweet coffee and outlandish accessories.

'Won't you have to share a bed?' Lauren asks.

'Well, no, not necessarily,' I reply. 'Not at all. I think our hotel room has a sofa. Will can sleep there, I'll sleep in the bed. Maybe we'll take turns. But we're definitely not sharing a bed.'

'Right. It's just sleeping on a sofa doesn't sound particularly comfortable. You'll end up sharing a bed and you know it!' Lauren smiles naughtily, placing her mug back on the saucer.

'I won't. I really won't,' I insist.

Since Hera was born, I haven't shared my bed with anyone but her. I'm definitely not going to jump into bed with Will and certainly not in the sexy way that Lauren's suggesting. She may be my best friend, but she has a much more laidback approach to sex than I do. I've only slept with a couple of guys, including Leroy, whereas Lauren's had quite a few partners. I often lose track of the guys she's dating. There was a guy called Dennis or Darren or something who she seemed pretty into for a few months, but then she started talking about some 'cool, sensitive' physiotherapist and Reiki healer called Carl. I have no idea what happened to him. She's already seeing someone new, a lawyer who she insists has 'great hair and an even better sense of humour'. Apparently, he's the reason she's hungover today and has slicked lashings of concealer under her eyes.

'Lauren, you know how I feel about Will. There is no way I'm going to end up in bed with him,' I point out.

Lauren rolls her eyes. 'Seriously? You're not still whingeing about that time he called you "pancake boobs".'

'That wasn't Will,' I point out. 'That was his friend, Nathan.'

Before Will came to our school, this guy Nathan had been bullying people in our year. He dubbed me 'pancake boobs' back when I'd only just started developing. I was so self-conscious about my tiny breasts and I absolutely hated that nickname. But I wasn't Nathan's only victim. There was Susan Granger – a really sweet girl who I used to sit next to in English – who came into school one day with toothpaste on her mouth, earning the nickname 'jizz lips', which all of Nathan's mean friends seized upon for weeks. And there was this weedy maths nerd called Lewis, which Nathan shortened to 'Loo', which then morphed into 'Bogmeister'. Although 'Bogmeister' didn't really stick. Too many syllables probably. When Will came along, he put a stop to all of that pettiness. He was bigger, better-looking and cooler than Nathan, and he hated all forms of bullying. In comparison to Will's friendly, cool attitude, suddenly being nasty no longer seemed like such a good move and people like Nathan dropped all that pettiness.

'Will actually put a stop to pancake boobs,' I tell Lauren, reminding her of the story.

'Oh yeah, I forgot about that. Will's cool,' she says, casting her mind back to our school days, her eyes misting over with memories.

'He could be cool, but he could also be a real dick. Don't you remember the tent incident?' I ask, suddenly wishing we were in a pub and not a café. The memory is still raw, and I could do with something a bit stronger than tea. Although I do feel grateful that I had the foresight to buy a brownie.

Lauren pauses for a second. 'Ohhh …' The penny drops. 'The tent incident.'

'I can't believe you remembered Nathan calling me pancake boobs, but you forgot about the tent incident!' I balk.

'I didn't forget. It's just pancake boobs was funnier.' She smiles wickedly.

I pick up my spoon and slap her on the arm with it.

47

'Ouch!' She cowers away, giggling.

I take a bite of my brownie.

'So, the tent incident. If I recall correctly, Will made a move on you, you freaked out and then you guys never spoke again?' Lauren says, rubbing her arm even though I'm sure it doesn't hurt.

'Well, no, not really. I need to refresh your memory,' I tell her, before explaining exactly what happened.

What actually went down was that Will and I became really close at Art Club. We'd always sit next to each other and we realised we had quite a lot in common. It was the kind of stuff that matters when you're a teenager: we both loved The Strokes, we shared an addiction to *Neighbours*, we enjoyed English and hated maths, and we were in agreement that pineapple on pizza is amazing. One day Will asked for my number and we got into the habit of chatting in the evenings. I used to love taking my phone up to my bedroom, snuggling up in bed and listening to Will's voice. We'd chat about everything: the latest *Neighbours* episode, coursework, what we'd had for dinner, plans for the future, school gossip, all sorts. We could talk for hours and even though we played it cool at school, our growing closeness was hard to ignore. We both knew it had meaning and that something would happen between us eventually.

Then the time came. We'd been studying landscape painting in Art Club and Mr Reed, our art teacher, suggested a camping trip to a coastal national park not too far away where we could set up our easels and paint the scenery. I was excited about the trip for weeks and it didn't let me down. Our train arrived early in the morning and after putting up our tents and leaving our stuff at the campsite, we headed off to the coast and set up our easels. The scenery was beautiful – lush green grass, white chalk hills, deep blue sea and a bright azure sky streaked with wispy clouds. The weather was perfect too – bright and warm with a light breeze. It was ideal weather for painting, since everything was illuminated but the breeze dried the paint quickly from our canvases. It was heavenly. We were all moved by the peaceful atmosphere and there was none of the usual bickering, attention-seeking or crude jokes we usually made as teenagers. Instead, everyone was perfectly calm.

Eventually, the light faded, and we packed up and headed back to the campsite. Mr Reed and a couple of the other teachers set up a campfire and cooked jacket potatoes in tin foil with beans and cheese. We sat around the fire chatting away until it got cold and we headed back to our tents. I was meant to be sharing a tent with another girl from the club, Emily, but she fancied Will's friend, Raj, and we'd planned a swap on the train down. I'd share with Will and Emily would share with Raj. Once the campsite had gone quiet, Raj and I swapped places, sneaking across the campsite and slipping inside each other's tents. It didn't last long before the teachers realised what we were up to, but for a precious half hour, finally, Will and I were alone, after what felt like forever. I'd chatted to him under a duvet hundreds of times before, but never without a phone involved. It felt strange to be next to him. To be able to smell him and hear him breathing. To be able to touch him. Will gently ran his fingers up and down my arm, and I was silently begging for him to kiss me and also terrified of it. I'd only ever kissed one boy before (a regrettable sloppy incident with an annoying guy with bad breath during a game of Spin the Bottle) and I was worried the kiss with Will might be a disaster like that had been. I was also equally worried that Will wouldn't make a move at all and that it would finally dawn on me that he wasn't interested, and that after all this time pining over him, I'd been totally delusional.

But Will did make a move and our kiss was everything I'd ever wanted it to be: tender, gentle, heartfelt, passionate, adoring. Except then kissing became fondling, which I was okay with, even though it was the first time I'd ever been to second base. But then Will's hand started wandering further south and I freaked out a bit. I was sure Will had slept with girls before. A lot of guys in our year had and he was the coolest, best-looking guy, so I naturally assumed he would have done. I felt so embarrassed admitting I was a virgin and that I wasn't ready, but I had to get it out. I had to be honest, because if I didn't explain the reason I wasn't keen to go further, Will might have thought I just wasn't into him and nothing could have been further from the truth. Surprisingly, Will confessed to being a virgin too and promised he'd wait until I was ready. I couldn't believe it! Will Brimble was a virgin and wanted to lose his virginity to me! If I wasn't already head over heels for him, now I was truly, truly smitten.

The rest of the trip was bliss: painting, cuddling, kissing, snuggling around the campfire. It was perfect and I knew it wouldn't be long until I was ready to have sex with Will. I just wanted to go home and get my head around things. I wanted to research sex and read articles in Cosmo and chat to Lauren. I had so many questions, like should I shave my pubic hair? Do I need to shave all of it or just the bit at the front? Will he want a blow job and how do you even do them? I also needed to buy condoms. The last thing I wanted was to get knocked up on my first time. I needed a bit more time to psych myself about the whole thing, but my mind was made up: Will was the one.

'Oh yeah,' Lauren comments, taking a sip from the dregs of her now near-empty coffee. 'And then didn't he go off and sleep with Jo?'

'Yeah,' I reply, glumly. 'He did.' I take a massive bite of my brownie.

Years and years have gone by and yet and it still hurts. Things were great after Will and I got back from the camping trip, Will was still phoning every few days and as usual, we'd chat about everything and anything, but then one day, the calls just stopped. Will didn't show up at Art Club and all of a sudden, he was ignoring me at school. I asked around and I found out that he'd slept with this blonde sporty girl called Jo at a house party at the weekend. He had been meant to be waiting for me! I was devastated. My Will bubble burst in one cruel second. Not only had Will ruined everything but he'd chosen Jo over me. She was loud, bordering on brash, and obsessed with all things sports. She didn't like The Strokes, or art, or *Neighbours*, or reading. She wasn't like us and yet he'd gone for her when we were meant to be saving ourselves for each other. I still remember the sadness and disappointment like it was yesterday.

'Oh yeah, that was really harsh. Christ, I'd forgotten about that,' Lauren remarks, looking a bit more moved now.

'It was awful,' I admit, stuffing the brownie into my mouth.

'I can't believe he did that,' Lauren sighs. 'You guys never spoke again after that, did you?'

'Nope, never again,' I reply, thinking back to the months that dragged on from that point until the end of school. Will was the main reason I ended up moving to London for boarding school. I went to Westminster University afterwards and then set up my business in London too. In a way, that incident with Will changed the course of my life. I might never have moved to London in the first place if he hadn't made me want to get away from him so badly.

'God, what a nightmare,' Lauren muses.

'Yeah, a real nightmare,' I grumble.

'Let's get you more tea?' Lauren gets up to head to the counter to order more drinks.

She comes back with a bag of popcorn too. I love Lauren.

'I know you're not going to want to hear this,' she says, as she tears open the bag and places it on the table between us, 'but it was a long time ago. Will behaved in a really shitty way, I'm not denying that, but he was only a kid and a lot of time has passed. We were all different back then to how we are now. I'm sure Will's grown up a lot since then.'

'I know.' I reach for a handful of popcorn. 'He still seems kind of immature though,' I remark, thinking back to his competitiveness over the raffle the other night.

51

Lauren plucks a few pieces of popcorn from the bag. Unlike me, Lauren is an avid gym-goer and calorie counter. I have enough to worry about these days with Hera to pay much attention to my waistline and my once size ten figure has become more of a size fourteen. I used to care but right now, I'm just thinking that Lauren's restraint means more popcorn for me.

'He's done alright for himself, hasn't he? Didn't he marry some super rich girl? And he was Group Editor at a national newspaper. I mean, you have to admit, that's not bad,' Lauren comments, before popping a piece of popcorn into her mouth.

'No, it's not bad, but he's not editor anymore. He lost his job. And he's divorced.' Even as I say the words, I wince at how they sound.

'I don't know about Will's divorce, but losing his job wasn't through any fault of his own though,' Lauren points out. 'Over three hundred people lost their jobs when his paper went under. It's not like he was fired or anything.'

'Yeah, I know, but just because he was Group Editor at a national newspaper and stuff, it still doesn't make him a great person.' I'm clearly still smarting over the past.

'I guess.' Lauren shrugs. 'But I would keep an open mind if I were you. Don't hold stuff from more than fifteen years ago over the guy. That's a bit harsh.'

'S'pose.' I reach for another handful of popcorn.

Lauren plucks a few more pieces and eats them slowly, looking pensive.

'What are you thinking?' I ask.

'I was just …' Lauren chews another piece of popcorn. 'I was just thinking about that thing all the girls used to say about Will at school. Do you remember his nickname?' she asks.

'Knobhead? Asshole? Wankstain?' I suggest.

'No, nicknames that *everyone* gave him, not just you,' Lauren teases.

I rack my brains. Nicknames. I can remember the nicknames

Will saved other people from. I can't remember him having any of his own.

'No, I don't remember Will's nickname. Pray tell.'

'Everyone called him the cruise ship,' Lauren says, a mischievous twinkle in her eye.

'The what?! He didn't even go on cruises ... did he?'

'Oh, it had nothing to do with cruises,' Lauren says obliquely, with a dirty look in her eyes.

'What did it have to do with then?' I ask, narrowing my eyes at her as I grab some more popcorn.

'Okay.' Lauren shuffles on her seat. 'You know that phrase, it's not the size of the ship, it's the motion in the ocean?'

'Yeah, for guys who have small penises,' I say, a smile creeping onto my lips. 'Does he have a tiny penis?'

'No, there was this girl, Lydia. I don't think you knew her. She was on my hockey team and she'd been seeing this guy, Pete or Paul or something, I can't remember. But anyway, apparently, he wasn't particularly well-endowed and everyone kept telling her that it's not the size of the ship, it's the motion in the ocean.'

'Uh-huh,' I reply hesitantly, wondering where she's going with this. I never really knew any of Lauren's hockey mates. When I left to take up my scholarship for sixth-form, Lauren stayed at our old school. She developed an interest in hockey and joined the school's hockey team, competing at matches across the county.

'Well, eventually Lydia ended things with Pete and started seeing Will,' Lauren explains.

'Right ...'

'Well, one day she randomly came to practice looking really pleased with herself and she said it was because she'd spent the night with Will and that he was a "cruise ship".' Lauren smiles cheekily at the memory.

'Still totally confused, Lauren.'

'She called him the cruise ship because he was well-endowed

and he knew how to use it. A massive ship with a good motion in the ocean,' Lauren says with a snigger.

'Oh Jesus,' I groan, lowering my head into my hands.

'Maybe you'll get to see in Marrakech?' Lauren winks. 'You're both single! Maybe you'll get to hop aboard the cruise ship?'

'Shut up, Lauren!' I roll my eyes. 'Even if that was on my agenda, I don't actually know if Will's single. Just because he's divorced, it doesn't mean he's available. And even if he were, honestly, the last thing I need right now is to get involved with him. You know how I feel about men since Leroy.'

'Yeah, I know,' Lauren sighs, nodding to herself.

Lauren was my rock during my break-up with Leroy. I was an absolute mess. Seven months' pregnant and single. Heartbroken and hormonal. Lauren spent so many evenings listening to me bitch and rant about him. She sat with me as I cried, telling me it would all be okay. She pulled me through it. She even came to the hospital with me and held my hand until my mum arrived. She knows more than anyone how difficult that period of my life was and how anxious it's made me about getting involved with someone again. My singleness isn't just down to being a single mum living in my childhood home in Chiddingfold, it's also because I'm not sure my heart could take any more. If a man could cheat on me at seven months' pregnant, sometimes I wonder what chance I'll ever have of finding someone who'll be faithful.

'Okay, ignore what I said about the cruise ship,' Lauren comments. 'Just go on the holiday, soak up the sun, do some shopping in the souks, eat some amazing food and just *relax*. Will's an alright guy, despite what he did when he was 15. He'll be decent enough company, but just do your thing. Put yourself first and make sure you enjoy yourself. You really deserve a holiday, Nat.' Lauren fixes me with a sweet kind look, and reaches over and squeezes my hand.

'Thanks Lauren,' I reply, trying not to tear up. I do really need this holiday.

Chapter 6

It's two days until we leave and I'm beginning to feel really excited. I've bought a new swimsuit to wear at the pool, a wide-brimmed hat and a pair of cool oversized sunglasses. I've got a couple of fun holiday reads lined up and a bottle of sun cream and I can't wait to sit by the pool and just relax. It's going to be perfect, or at least as close to perfect as possible. The only drawback is Will, but I can't have everything. You can't have a sun-soaked holiday without *something* annoying you. It's a bit like mosquitos – you can be in the most beautiful tropical place, your pictures might be the most Instagrammable shots ever, and yet you still have to contend with those little bastards. Will is a bit like a mosquito: a minor drawback to an otherwise idyllic experience.

Hera's fast asleep in her cot and I'm painting my toenails a bright pink shade when my phone buzzes with a text. It's from an unknown number.

I've booked a taxi for 4 a.m. Shall I come and collect you?

I consider ignoring the text as it's clearly not meant for me, but I fire back a response just to give the person who sent it a heads up.

Wrong number, sorry.

My phone buzzes again.

Natalie? This is your number, right? It's Will.

Will? How did he get my number? I text back to ask him.

Ran into your mum in Sainsbury's. She gave it to me.

I sigh. Of course, she did. My mum loves Will and has talked of nothing else since we won the raffle. She's brought me fully up to speed on all the gossip. I think she made up for lost time at the fundraiser, chatting over glasses of punch to all the friends and acquaintances she's been too busy to see while helping out with Hera. Anyway, apparently, Will's moved into a flat only a few roads down from us and he's freelancing for national papers. My mum seems under the impression that Will's redundancy might have been a blessing in disguise and that he needed a break from London, although she doesn't seem to know why. Oh, and apparently, he's definitely single. Not that it's of any relevance to me, but my mum won't stop going on about how he's 'back on the market' as though he's a product to be snapped up and not someone who, like myself, is probably quite content on their own. She's become fixated with the idea that Will and I are going to reignite our spark on this trip. She even forwarded me a magazine article the other day entitled: 'Five Ways to Make Your Romantic Getaway Completely Unforgettable'. I immediately hit delete. She's more excited about the trip than I am and really, it comes as no surprise that she would have given my number to Will. She's *dying* for us to get together. In fact, she's probably already bought a hat.

Me: I see.

Will: So, the taxi. Makes sense for us to head to the airport together … I can be round at yours at about ten past four. Ok?

Taking a taxi at 4.10 a.m. with someone I've barely seen since school isn't the ideal wake-up call, but Will's right, it does make sense for us to head to the airport together.

Me: Ok, sounds good.

Will: Ok great. See you then. Hope you're as excited as I am

I stare at the text, unsmiling. What's with the winky face? It's bad enough having Lauren being suggestive about this holiday. I don't need Will to start being suggestive too. I type a response.

Me: Winky face? Please refrain from that in text or in person.

Will: Lol. See you bright and early on Thursday.

Me: See you then!

I place my phone down. So, this really is happening. I really am going on holiday with Will Brimble. I take a deep breath and add another brushstroke of nail polish to my toenail.

* * *

Two days later, my mum is answering the door at 4.05 a.m. in her best dressing gown – a silk floral Kimono-style number. She's even wearing lipstick – a rosy shade that could just about pass as natural but which I know is a result of the Clinique Chubby Stick she keeps in her handbag. She's a sucker for Will's charm, just like every other woman in the history of his entire life.

'Oh hello, Will,' she says in a husky voice as though she's just rolled out of bed. She bats her lashes which she's slicked with a light coat of mascara. I roll my eyes as I rummage amongst the pegs by the front door for my handbag.

'Pam, you're up early!' Will says, giving her one of his most charming, broad, pearly white smiles, despite looking pale and a bit bleary-eyed. He's wearing a hoodie, jeans and trainers, with a leather jacket thrown on top and a scarf hanging unevenly around his neck. He probably chucked it on half-asleep, as he left his flat. His slightly sloppy get-up makes me feel better about the leggings, slouchy jumper and long padded jacket I'm wearing, which bears more than a passing resemblance to a sleeping bag.

'I thought I'd see Natalie off! It's such a big exciting trip!' my mum gushes. 'My Natalie, my little girl going all the way to Africa,' she adds fretfully.

'I'm 32, Mum,' I remind her, rolling my eyes as I find my

handbag amongst the coats. I open it to double check my passport is still inside, even though I checked twice last night before I went to bed.

'Oh, don't worry, Pam, I'll take care of her!' Will insists, placing a hand protectively on my shoulder.

'You'll what?' I laugh, shuffling away.

'I'll take care of you,' Will repeats simply. 'You know, look out for you.'

'I can take care of myself, thanks very much!' I huff, spotting my passport in the slip pocket I placed it in last night.

My mum and Will exchange a look. 'Stop being such a sour-puss, Natalie.'

'I'm not! I just don't need Will to take care of me. I'd be perfectly capable of going on this trip alone.'

'Honestly! If I were in your shoes, I'd be incredibly grateful to have someone like Will taking care of me,' my mum jokes, giving Will a cheeky wink.

'I know you would, Mum!' I groan, cringing. I really wish she would stop making such cringey comments. It's so embarrassing.

Will laughs a little awkwardly.

'If only they'd pulled my name out of that hat!' my mum jokes, nudging Will.

He smiles widely although his eyes look a little afraid. 'Oh yes, we'd have had a brilliant time!'

I gawp at both of them. 'It's too early for this. Far too early!' I grumble. I turn around to grab my massive traveller's backpack, which I left ready to go in the hallway, and heave it onto my back.

'Let me help,' Will says, reaching over to give me a hand.

'I'm fine, thanks Will,' I insist in a slightly clipped tone before slipping past him to head to the taxi, which is waiting at the end of the garden path, its engine rumbling.

'Natalie's not a morning person,' I hear my mum tutting behind me.

It's pitch-black outside and my breath is misty in the cool

58

night air. The driver looks over as I approach and, spotting my bag, he gets out of the taxi and comes around to open the boot.

'Need a hand?' he asks as I struggle to lift the bag.

'Yeah, that would be great, thanks,' I reply, letting him help me position the heavy bag in the boot. I actually don't mind accepting help from men, I think it's good manners, but when an offer of help comes from Will, my instinct is to reject it like a stroppy teenager. I should really try to be a little nicer to him. He probably needs this holiday just as much as me what with his divorce and redundancy, I muse, as the cab driver tucks a trailing strap of my bag into the boot.

'Got anything else or is that it?' he asks.

'Just one more thing! One second,' I tell him with a grateful smile, before heading back to the house to get my suitcase. The backpack just contains my swimming pool stuff – my sunglasses, swimsuit, books, sarong, hat, sandals and a few cute kaftans. My suitcase is packed full of all the other things I might need, like hiking boots if I decide to go on a day excursion to the Atlas Mountains as well as jeans, trainers and tops for exploring Marrakech.

Will and my mum are chatting away about the weather in Marrakech as I approach.

'I hear it can get quite nippy there, even though it's in Africa! I hope you've packed some nice warm clothes,' my mum's saying.

'Don't worry, Pam. I'm prepared for all eventualities,' Will reassures her.

'I'm sure you are, Will.' My mum beams at him.

I ignore them as I slip past and retrieve my suitcase, pulling it down the hall.

'Don't worry, I'm not going to offer to help!' Will holds his hands up in mock surrender.

'It's okay,' I sigh. 'I could do with a hand, actually.'

Will frowns, giving me a slightly bemused look, before coming over to help. We load my suitcase into the boot. The driver slaps it closed.

'Ready?' Will asks.

'Erm … yeah, sorry, I just need to say bye to Hera,' I tell him, feeling a twinge of panic as I say the words out loud. Leaving my baby behind feels so unnatural that it makes me nervous.

'Go for it,' Will says, smiling sweetly.

I rush upstairs and tiptoe into Hera's room, making sure I'm extra quiet so I don't wake her. I've already said goodbye twice, but of course Will doesn't know that. Hera's fast asleep in her cot. She looks adorable. Her little chest is rising and falling under her blanket. Her long lashes rest on her chubby cheeks and she looks totally blissful and content.

'Bye sweetheart, I'll miss you angel,' I whisper, gripping the side of her cot.

I lean over and plant a delicate kiss on her forehead. 'I'll be back really soon, baby. Be good for Granny. I love you.'

A lump hardens in my throat. I take a deep shaky breath, willing myself not to cry. The holiday is four nights and five days, which is by far the longest time I'll have spent away from Hera and if I think too much about it, it seems an unbearably long time. It's better to just remind myself that she'll be with her granny who adores her and it's only a week. It could be a lot worse. *It'll be okay, it'll be okay*, I tell myself as I take one last look at Hera, and place Mr Bear right next to her, before slipping out of her room and gently closing the door behind me.

My mum's beginning to look a little chilly now, clutching her kimono around her waist as the cool night air sweeps down the hall. She and Will have moved on from discussing the weather to comparing opinions on different types of tagines. My mum isn't a big fan of lamb tagine, apparently.

'How's Hera?' my mum asks as I approach.

'Sleeping like a baby,' I joke.

Will laughs, while my mum just half-smiles, having heard my joke before.

'Right, are you ready?' Will asks in an upbeat voice that doesn't quite conceal the concern in his eyes. It's as though he can sense how on edge leaving Hera is making me.

'Yeah.' I nod, smiling despite the nervous feeling in my stomach. 'I'm ready.'

'Great,' Will says, his expression relaxing. 'Let's go.'

I turn to give my mum a hug, pulling her close.

'Have a brilliant time, love,' she says. 'Enjoy yourself, really.' She fixes me with a sincere look. 'And don't worry about Hera, she's going to be fine.'

'Okay. Thanks Mum.'

I give her another squeeze before turning to leave.

'Bye Pam,' Will says, pulling my mum in for a hug. I raise an eyebrow, watching them. They've barely seen each other for sixteen years and yet apparently, they're on hugging terms.

'Bye Will,' my mum says.

I grab my handbag and we head out to the car. We hop in, waving over our shoulder as we close the doors. My mum waves back as the taxi pulls away from the kerb. I watch her as we drive away, until she's nearly out of sight and I can just about make out her closing the door. I think of Hera again while I fasten my seatbelt and feel a little stab in my heart at the thought of her sleeping in her little cot, soon to be a whole continent away from me.

'So, a romantic getaway for two, eh? Excited?' Will asks, interrupting my ruminative thoughts.

'Oh please, you're as bad as my mum,' I groan, as I adjust my seatbelt and try to get comfortable.

'Ha ha. At least someone appreciates me,' Will says, smirking.

I eye him, taking in his face, which looks pale in the darkness. His eyes sparkle with humour even in the greyish light.

'I'm sure lots of women appreciate you, Will, I'm sure they're highly appreciative,' I say with a wry smile, before looking over my shoulder at my road, my baby, retreating into the distance.

'Lots of women? Care to introduce me because I'm not aware of them,' Will huffs.

'Really?' I mean, Will's hot. Despite my conflicted feelings about him, he's objectively very good-looking, and he's intelligent and charming, of course he'd get attention.

'Hardly,' Will scoffs.

'So aren't you seeing anyone?' I ask. I don't mean to sound like I'm interested, because I'm not! I'm really not, and yet, in spite of myself, the question makes me sound so keen.

Will laughs, smiling to himself. 'No, I'm not seeing anyone. Anyone at all. I've been single for ages, actually. I've been focusing on me,' Will says, slapping his chest where his heart is.

Focusing on me?! What does he mean? The Will I knew was not the introverted spiritual type.

'Focusing on you?' I echo.

'Yeah.' Will shrugs. 'Like self-care.'

'Self-care?' I try not to smile. When Lauren was dating the Reiki healer guy, she always used to joke that when he said he was taking some time for 'self-care' he meant masturbation.

'Yeah, self-care,' Will replies simply.

'You don't mean, like, you know, *self*-care?' I raise an eyebrow suggestively, feeling 16 all over again.

Will shoots me a deadpan stare, his lips twisting into a smirk. 'No, Natalie,' he tuts. 'Not that kind of self-care. I haven't spent the past year masturbating! Although, to be fair, I have had to engage in a bit of ...' Will scrunches his face up. 'Do you know what? I'm going to sleep,' he laughs, bundling his scarf up to form a makeshift pillow.

'Haha, good plan,' I agree, pulling my scarf off and doing the same.

I stuff it between my head and the car door.

'Night Natalie,' Will says, smiling affectionately.

'Night Will,' I reply, as I rest my head against my scarf

Chapter 7

I don't know if it's the coffee that Will and I have been mainlining since we arrived at the airport or what, but all of a sudden, I find myself feeling incredibly jittery at the boarding gate.

The British Airways stewardess takes my passport and frowns at it, looking troubled.

'Hang on a minute,' she says, smiling politely at me, before turning her attention to the computer behind the check-in desk.

My stomach sinks as she consults the screen and I have a sudden, horrible feeling that the holiday will be called off. It will be found to have been an administrative error or something. Perhaps Mick got confused?! The holiday did seem too good to be true. Maybe his niece Hannah didn't book it after all. I glance over at Will, giving him a searching look, but he seems equally perplexed. He shrugs, clearly not having a clue what's going on.

The stewardess – whose name badge informs me that she's called Rachel – leans closer to her computer screen and clicks her mouse a few times, until finally, after what feels like forever, she looks back up at me. This time, her frown is replaced by a wide, friendly smile.

'I'm pleased to tell you that you've been upgraded to first

class!' she says, as she hands my passport back to me, with my boarding pass.

'Oh wow! First class! That's amazing, thanks!' I enthuse, before looking over at Will, who's looking a little less thrilled.

'So I guess I'll just be in economy then,' he grumbles.

'Oh, no, you've both been upgraded due to your honeymoon package,' the stewardess informs us, with a bright smile.

Honeymoon package? I raise an eyebrow. What's she talking about? She must have made a mistake, but I'm hardly about to set her straight. I've only ever been upgraded once before, years ago, and it was totally brilliant. Worlds away from economy with delicious food, huge seats and free drinks.

'That's brilliant! How kind of you,' Will says, wrapping his arm around my shoulder and pulling me close to him. I smile weakly, even though I can feel my body stiffening. Will doesn't seem to notice though. He proceeds to rub my arm vigorously and gives me a kiss on the forehead. It's so cringeworthy that I can't help but wince.

'Have a wonderful trip,' Rachel says, glancing over Will's passport before handing him a boarding pass too.

'Thanks so much!' Will replies.

I thank Rachel again and then Will and I head down the passageway to board the plane. Even once we're far enough away from Rachel that she can no longer see us, Will still has his arm around me.

'Okay!' I trill, sweeping his hand off my shoulder. 'You can drop the honeymoon act now!'

'I was just trying to be authentic,' Will insists.

I roll my eyes indulgently. 'It's not like they're going to take our first-class tickets away from us because we're not tactile enough!'

'Okay, fine!' Will says, taking a step away from me. 'We can be a cold miserable couple instead. The kind that never touches each other.'

'Good! Remember, we're not actually a couple,' I remind him.

'I know!'

'This is going to happen everywhere isn't it?' I sigh, pulling my suitcase over a bump on the concourse.

Will gives me a questioning look.

'This whole couple thing. Do you think everyone's going to assume we're a couple?'

'Probably!' Will says with a cheeky grin as we approach the plane entrance. He's clearly quite enjoying pretending to me my husband.

The air hostess smiles broadly as we reach the entrance of the plane and takes our boarding passes.

'This way, please,' she says, guiding us to the left.

It feels odd to be taking a left in a plane, rather than going right towards economy. I look over at Will and we exchange an excited glance.

The air hostess, a pretty redhead wearing diamond stud earrings whose name badge reads 'Victoria', shows us to our seats. The seats in first class are detached with their own armrests and footrests, and they all have a window view. They look a hell of a lot more comfortable than the squashed seats of economy. I'd never pay for first class myself – as nice as it is, it does feel like quite an indulgent expense.

'This will be your seat, madam,' Victoria says, smiling warmly as she gestures towards my wide comfy-looking chair.

'Thank you!' I reply. That's another thing you don't get in economy – being shown to your seat.

'I'm afraid we couldn't seat you next to each other, but we have another seat just two down,' Victoria explains ruefully. I'd just assumed, since the airline seems to view us as a honeymooning couple, we'd be seated together.

'Oh, that's more than okay,' I reply effusively, before taking in my wide, comfortable-looking seat with a fold-out screen for watching the on-flight entertainment. Perfect! This is the life!

I stash my bag in the overhead compartment, then I look over my shoulder to see Will being shown to his seat.

'Wait!' A middle-aged businessman sitting in the seat next to me, pipes up. He seems to have noticed me looking over at Will.

'You can sit here,' he says, turning to Will. 'Why don't we swap? I don't mind!' He moves to get up.

Really?' Will asks hopefully.

'Of course,' the businessman replies. 'It makes no difference to me and if you two are together ...'

'Great, thanks!' Will enthuses.

'Great!' I echo weakly, before checking my manners and thanking the man for his kind gesture.

But seriously, it's like the universe is conspiring for Will and I to be as intimate as possible. Just when I thought I'd be able to have a few hours of peace, maybe get a little more sleep, Will is going to be sitting right next to me and not only sitting next to me, but he's going to be sitting next to me pretending to be my husband. Fabulous.

'Hey wifey,' Will says as he swaps places with the businessman.

'Hey hubs,' I reply sardonically as I sit down and press the recline button on my chair.

'They must think you're one of those progressive women who doesn't take her husband's name,' Will comments, looking at his name on his boarding pass.

'Well, to be fair, if I was married to you, I probably wouldn't have taken your name,' I point out.

'There's nothing wrong with Brimble.'

'Natalie Brimble.' I try the name out, saying it aloud, as though it's the first time I've ever done that. In fact, I feel like I've just gone back in time. I used to try the name 'Natalie Brimble' out loud all the time when I was in my bedroom as teenager, writing it in my diary surrounded by hearts.

'Natalie Brimble is a fine name,' Will insists.

'Ha, I prefer mine.'

'Suit yourself, Miss Jackson,' Will jokes as he sits down after stuffing his bag into the overhead compartment.

Natalie Jackson. I used to think my name was a bit ordinary, but over the years, it's grown on me. I named my PR agency after myself – Natalie Jackson PR – not because I'm self-obsessed or anything, but because I couldn't think of a better name and I thought it sounded quite professional. Plus, people tend to trust businesses more when the founder is willing to back it with their own name and reputation. Or at least that's the idea. Over the years, Natalie Jackson has become more than just my name, it's my brand too. Natalie Brimble sounds funny in comparison, even if I did used to love it.

I start scrolling through oi-flight entertainment to distract myself from pondering my marital name anymore. I really am beginning to feel 16 again. The plane is filling up with jet-setting holiday-goers and weary-looking businessmen taking to their seats. They don't seem in the least bit excited to be flying first class. They probably got used to it a long time ago and now it's routine for them. I watch as a few of them slide their bags into the overhead compartments. One guy looks tired and a bit stressed and immediately settles into his seat. He drapes a blanket over his body and puts on a sleeping mask, clearly determined to get some rest. Another guy retrieves a computer case from his luggage and pulls out a Mac. Will and I are like kids in the cinema, choosing what to watch, while these guys are either catching up on sleep or work.

Everyone eventually gets settled and Victoria informs us of the safety precautions, advising us to inflate the flimsy-looking life jackets in the event of an emergency landing. I eye the tiny life jacket that looks like it would barely keep you afloat in a paddling pool let alone save your life in the Mediterranean Sea. I feel a nervous tremor as I imagine the plane crashing and Hera growing up motherless. Oh God. What if she grows up telling her friends that Mummy died while gallivanting off on a romantic getaway with her long-lost childhood flame?! What kind of mother would do that? Arghh! Fortunately, the moment the safety precautions are over, Victoria instructs us to fasten our seatbelts for take-off and it all happens so quickly that my nerves are replaced by adrenaline.

With a lurch, the plane begins to rumble before picking up speed and gliding down the runway. Then it takes off, parting with the land, and my stomach does a little flip as we soar into the sky. I gaze in wonder as we sweep over the suburban houses far below. I gaze out of the window, watching the streets, cars and homes retreating from view.

My thoughts turn to our destination.

I look over at Will, who is now checking out the plane's film selection. 'What do you think Marrakech will be like? It'll be nice, won't it?' I ask.

'Oh yeah, it's fine.' Will shrugs. 'I mean, obviously after the Arab Spring, things got a bit dicey there for a while, but it was okay as long as you stuck with people you trusted and listened to the government's travel advice.'

'Right …' I reply, a little taken aback. 'So you've been before? After the Arab Spring?'

'Oh yeah,' Will says casually, as he flicks past a rom-com from the plane's movie selection. 'Several times.'

'You kept that quiet!'

'Well, I haven't been on a romantic getaway or anything like that,' Will says, looking over, a smile playing on his lips. 'I was just there for work. Reporting on the suicide bombing in the main square back in 2011. In and out. I never really got to explore or do any of the touristy things. I didn't really get to see the best side of Marrakech. I've never been there to just relax and unwind. It'll be nice to see that side of it, see what it's all about.'

'Of course,' I reply, still taking in this new information. 'I can't believe you've already been to Marrakech. Wow!'

'Yep!' Will replies, selecting an action film to watch.

I watch him, reassessing a little bit. I knew Will was a journalist, but somehow, I didn't think he did actual reporting. I thought he was too senior for that and I just assumed other people would be running around chasing the stories while Will spent his time in a cushy London office, making the odd TV appearance here and there. Now I realise that I was wrong. Will went all the way to Marrakech to report on a bombing. That takes balls.

'Where else have you been for work?' I ask him.

'Oh, I've been to loads of places,' Will says, selecting an action film to watch. 'Iraq, Syria, Yemen, North Korea, all for work. In fact, I haven't been on holiday since ...' He pauses, racking his brains. 'Ooh, ten years ago, when Nathan, Jonesy and I went to Ibiza for a blowout after uni ended.'

'Oh God,' I groan, thinking of Nathan and Jonesy, two totally annoying boozy, girl-chasing lads from our school days.

'What about your honeymoon?' I ask. 'Didn't you go away? Surely you went on holidays with your wife?'

'No, not really. We got married in Cornwall and we just stayed there for a few weeks after the wedding – that was our honeymoon. And we were both too busy for holidays, really,' Will says, coughing a little and pressing a button on his control that he's already pressed.

'I see,' I reply, dropping the subject. I get the feeling Will doesn't really want to talk about his failed marriage.

'When was your last holiday?' Will asks.

I think back to the last time I went away. It was a long weekend Leroy and I took to Bruges back when I was three or four months' pregnant. I should have known back then that things were never going to work out. I'd ended up booking the flights and hotel – which came to more than £600. Leroy had promised to pay half but as the holiday approached, he kept making excuses. The person who was meant to buy the table he'd been upcycling for the past month had changed their mind, he had to help his mum pay for her new bathroom refit and then there was a friend's stag do he had to go on. By the time our holiday rolled around, he'd paid a measly £40 towards the trip. He kept grovelling, apologising and promising he'd pay me back and I nearly let it go, but while we were packing for our trip and I was looking for a bottle of dry shampoo I'd left at his flat that I wanted to bring, I stumbled upon a bag stashed in his bathroom containing a Nike shoe box with a pair of fresh new Nike Air VaporMax Plus trainers inside. I gawped at it, looked into the bag and found a receipt dated two days earlier. The trainers cost a whopping £169.95 yet Leroy had only been able to contribute a paltry £40 towards the holiday! I was so furious, I could barely look at him.

We argued all the way to the airport. I had been so tempted to just call the whole thing off, but I didn't want to lose out on the holiday I'd already paid for so we went. I tried to let it go, but every time I had to pay for something because Leroy claimed he was broke, I just pictured those Nike trainers in my mind. I had this sinking feeling the entire trip that here I was, carrying the baby of a guy who couldn't even pay for his own dinner. When we got home, Leroy did end up managing to sell the table and he did pay me back eventually, for the hotel, flights and extra for all the other stuff I'd paid for, and I started wondering whether I'd overreacted ... but then he went and shagged his personal trainer and I realised that he was just a no good waste of space all along.

'Oh, just to Bruges with my ex,' I reply casually now, hoping Will doesn't ask about Leroy. He is the last person I want to talk about.

'I hear Bruges is beautiful,' Will replies. His uncharacteristically polite and restrained reply makes me wonder yet again what he's heard. It must have been bad for Will to be this well-mannered.

'It's so beautiful,' I tell him, steering clear of the subject of Leroy. Instead, I launch into a detailed description of the winding streets, epic medieval architecture and dreamy canals. I even start telling him all about some amazing waffles I had over there. Anything to not have to talk about Leroy.

Will nods. 'I've heard it's lovely. I'll have to go there sometime.'

Suddenly, Victoria swoops by with a drinks cart.

'How are you guys doing?' She smiles enthusiastically. 'What would you like to drink?'

'Oh, er ...'

'We have champagne, cocktails, spirits ... Here, have a drinks menu.' She hands me a drinks menu that could compete with a London bar. I glance over at Will, who is also handed a copy.

'You could have champagne, since it's your honeymoon,' Victoria suggests, glancing between me and Will, with a playful twinkle in her eye.

'Excellent idea! Let's get a bottle of Dom Perignon!' Will says, slapping his drinks menu shut, clearly feeling decisive.

Victoria's eyes light up. Even though we've been upgraded to first class, it's not like a bottle of Dom Perignon is complimentary. It seems ridiculously excessive to be splashing out on the finest champagne, especially since it's still so early in the morning. Hardly anyone else on the flight seems to be drinking.

'Will!' I hiss.

'Oh come on, it is our honeymoon after all!' Will reminds me, reaching over to give my hand a squeeze.

I resist the urge to glare at him.

'That's the spirit!' Victoria says, clapping her hands together. She seems tickled by the romance of our situation. She looks to be in her mid-twenties and probably thinks we're madly in love. I feel bad puncturing the fantasy.

'Oh, okay then,' I sigh.

Will grins triumphantly.

'Fabulous!' Victoria beams, before reaching into the drinks trolley for a silver bucket, which she begins filling with ice cubes.

'It's on me by the way,' Will adds quietly while Victoria's distracted. 'Got a really good redundancy pay-out,' he whispers.

'Oh, really? Are you sure?' I reply, feeling touched.

'Yeah, of course.' Will smiles, giving my hand another squeeze. He may be being lovely but he's really milking this whole hand-holding thing.

71

Victoria places the bottle in the bucket and hands it to us with two champagne flutes. I glance around but none of the other passengers seem remotely surprised by our early morning boozing. Perhaps this kind of thing happens all the time in first class.

'So, what was your wedding like?' Victoria asks as Will begins twisting the cork off the bottle.

'Oh, er, it was lovely,' I tell her, smiling enthusiastically. I glance at Will, who has a slightly unnerved expression. He clearly hadn't anticipated this blindingly obvious question.

Victoria nods encouragingly, apparently expecting more.

'Er … we just had a small wedding in the local village church. We decked it out with dozens of pink and white roses and filled it with candles. It was heavenly. And then we had a drinks reception in a marquee outside. We had balloons everywhere, canapes, cocktails, even a steel drum band. And the weather was *perfect*. It was wonderful,' I tell her.

Victoria's eyes have lit up. They're sparkling. Even I feel a bit swept away in the fantasy. It's actually really clear in my mind, since it was pretty much the dream wedding I'd planned for myself and Leroy – a simple and yet charming day. I'd done a mood board on Pinterest and everything.

'It sounds wonderful,' Victoria comments, and I can tell I'm stoking the flames of her own daydreams. I find myself wondering whether she has a boyfriend she's hoping to marry, or whether she's single and dreaming of falling in love.

'It was a beautiful day,' Will remarks, having finally popped the cork from the bottle. I must have been so swept up in my wedding fantasy that I completely failed to notice. He pours the bubbles into a glass. 'It was the best,' he adds, gazing lovingly into my eyes as he hands me the glass.

I gaze back, aware that Victoria is looking on and making an 'Aww' noise. Even though this whole thing is ridiculous, I can't help admiring Will's eyes a little bit as I gaze into them like a loved-up newlywed would. His eyes are just so striking. No wonder I used to draw them in the privacy of my bedroom when I was a teenager. But it's not just Will's eyes that are appealing. His features are all so perfectly proportioned. His face has filled out a bit since school and he no longer has that boyish fresh-faced look but he has aged well, despite the stress of visiting war zones for work. He's not wrinkled or balding or saggy in any way. He looks a bit rugged now, with a dusting of stubble along his jaw line and on closer inspection, there's a tiny frown line between his eyebrows, but it's almost appealing; it gives him a slightly serious, intelligent vibe.

'I can see how in love you are,' Victoria says.

I look up to see her gazing at me, having clearly misinterpreted my examination of Will's face. In love?! I mean, really, that's a bit of a reach.

'Oh yes! We're so in love!' Will insists. '*So* very in love.'

I raise an eyebrow at him and take a hungry sip of my champagne.

'That's wonderful!' Victoria smiles from ear to ear, a dreamy look on her face.

Another customer pipes up – piercing Victoria's daydream by asking for a G&T in an irritable, impatient tone, clearly not appreciating our chinwag about weddings. Will and I thank Victoria for the champagne, and she rolls her trolley along.

'Have you ever felt more hashtag couple goals?' Will jokes once she's out of earshot.

I laugh. 'Nope. Never!'

I glance over his shoulder to see that our plane has now soared above the clouds. We're gliding through the clear blue sky.

Will holds his bubbling glass of champagne out in a toast. 'Cheers to a lifetime of happiness together,' he says, a cheeky twinkle in his eye.

I laugh and clink my glass against his. 'Cheers Will. To a lifetime of happiness.'

Chapter 8

'I'm so glad we don't have to pretend we're a couple anymore,' Will says as we collect our luggage from the conveyor belt at Marrakech airport.

'Oh …' I yank my suitcase onto the trolley, feeling a little hurt. Am I really such a terrible pretend wife?! I thought I was doing pretty well, quaffing champagne and chatting away.

'I was just worried Victoria would see through it,' Will remarks. 'Although our fake wedding was pretty convincing. The steel drums were a nice touch.'

'Oh yeah, they just popped into my head,' I fib. Will doesn't need to know all the details of the wedding I never ended up having.

'It sounds nice. Steel drums rippling over a gentle summer breeze. A relaxed reception,' Will muses as we head from baggage collection towards the exit of the airport.

'Yeah, I suppose!' I agree, trying to sound as casual as possible.

We emerge into the lobby of the airport, where a throng of excited friends and relatives wait to greet their loved ones behind a rope barrier, with a spattering of bored-looking hotel staff holding up signs emblazoned with the names of guests.

'You can't really be in a bad mood when you hear steel drums, can you?' Will continues as we start walking past the crowd. 'I mean, is it even humanly possible?'

I laugh. 'Probably not. You'd have to be in a really dark place.'

'Wouldn't you? They just sound so happy. Such a joyful sound,' Will says dreamily.

Suddenly, I spot a man waiting behind the rope barrier holding up a massive sign with 'Mr & Mrs Brimble' written on it in big letters surrounded by dozens of hand-drawn red love hearts.

'What the ...' I utter, stopping in my tracks.

Will's gaze follows mine. The man must sense us looking his way as he suddenly catches our eye and smiles broadly, his face lighting up. He's in hi mid-forties and he's wearing a black tunic embroidered with a logo for our hotel – 'Marrakech Palace'. Damn it, so there's definitely no way he's got the wrong people. Not that Brimble is a particularly common name.

'Mr and Mrs Brimble!' he shouts, grinning and waving enthusiastically.

I glance at Will. He looks back at me, his eyes wide and perturbed.

'*As-salāmu 'alaykum!* Welcome to Marrakech!' the man says, beaming at us. He's giving us an Arabic greeting that means 'peace be upon you'. I read about it online, along with a few other Arabic words I've memorised, like '*shukran*', which means 'thank you', '*naäam*' - 'yes', '*laa*' – no, and '*min faDlik*', which means 'please'.

'*Wa 'alaykumu s-salām,*' I reply, returning the greeting.

Will glances over at me, impressed.

'Hi,' he says to the man. 'Have you umm ... made a mistake?' Will asks, sounding faintly hopeful.

'No! No mistake. You are staying at my hotel, Marrakech Palace, yes?' the man says.

Will nods hesitantly.

'Great!' the man replies, his eyes sparkling with excitement. He has one of those wide enthusiastic smiles that are almost impossible not to mirror and I find myself beaming back at him,

75

despite the weirdness of the situation.

'I am so happy to welcome you to my hotel and to Morocco!' The man unclips the rope barrier to let himself through to our side.

'I'm Medhi, I am the manager of Marrakech Palace,' he says, shaking our hands. Will looks completely taken aback.

Medhi smiles and takes the trolley from Will, sliding his sign between our bags. He gestures for us to follow him.

'Our car is outside. We'll drive to the hotel. I wanted to come and welcome you personally since you are the first couple to stay in our new honeymoon suite! This is so very exciting for us.'

'Honeymoon suite,' I echo, glancing at Will.

'Yes, honeymoon suite!' Medhi grins, looking a little perplexed. 'We cannot wait to have you! We've been preparing for weeks. Everything is ready,' Medhi says, wheeling the trolley ahead, eager to take us back to the hotel.

'Many congratulations, by the way. I should have said that before! Congratulations!' Medhi exclaims.

'Thank you,' I reply in a small voice. Will seems to have been stunned into silence.

'Here is the car,' Medhi stops by a taxi and gestures for the driver to load the boot with our luggage. Despite being completely perturbed, Will tries to help but Medhi point blank refuses. He starts speaking in Arabic to the driver.

Will turns to me, a panicked look in his eyes. 'Do you think this is the prize? A *honeymoon*?' he whispers.

'I guess so,' I mutter.

'We should explain,' Will insists.

Explain? Oh God.

'But what if we lose out on the prize and have to go home?' I fret.

Even though having a honeymoon with Will Brimble isn't at the top of my list of dream holidays, I don't want to go home either. We've made it all the way here. I've packed a bikini and

sun cream and fun books to read. I even painted my toenails!
I'm not ready to go home.

'I know …' Will sighs. I can tell he really needs this holiday too.

'Let's just play along. It won't be that hard!' I insist, as brightly
as possible.

Will raises an eyebrow, looking unconvinced.

Medhi thanks the driver, who closes the boot.

'Ready?' he says, smiling enthusiastically.

Will stares back at him blankly.

'It's just for a few days,' I remind him under my breath, fixing
him with a meaningful look.

I'm worried he's going to 'fess up, burst Medhi's bubble and
send us home on the next flight back to London. I can't exactly
have a honeymoon alone and I'm not having my holiday ruined
– honeymoon or not. I need some sun. I need some time off
from being a stressed-out single mum.

'Yes, absolutely!' I beam back at Medhi, placing my hand on
Will's shoulder and steering him towards the car door. 'We are
definitely ready!'

Will shoots me a look as I pull the door open for him and
silently urge him to get in.

* * *

By the time we get to the hotel, I know so much about
Medhi's family that I almost feel like a distant relative. As we
drove to Marrakech Palace, he explained how the hotel came to
be. Apparently, Medhi grew up in a tiny village in the mountains and moved to Marrakech without a penny in his pocket
when he was just 14. He got a job at a shop selling handbags to
tourists and then became a tour guide, taking groups on trips
from Marrakech to the Atlas Mountains, and began offering the
trips through hotels. He befriended one of the hotel managers
who saw his potential and gave him a job managing one of his

77

properties – a struggling hotel on the outskirts of Marrakech. Having impressed the manager by turning it around from a neglected unloved hotel to a popular boutique destination, Medhi asked the hotel manager for a loan to start his own hotel, the Marrakech Palace. He now lives there with his wife, Amira, and their son, Mohammed. His rags to riches story is really impressive and his enthusiasm is infectious. It reminds me of my own spark of ambition – the drive and hunger that inspired me to set up my own business.

Medhi explains how his brother, who also entered the tourism industry, recently went on a honeymoon to Dubai. He says that seeing the pictures of his brother's honeymoon inspired him to launch his own honeymoon offering. Will and I both go a little quiet at this point. I text Mick.

Me: We seem to be on a honeymoon!! Do you know what's going on?

I message my mum to let her know that we've arrived safely and to get an update on Hera. I can't bring myself to tell my mum that Will and I seem to have been booked onto a honeymoon. She'd be delighted. My mum replies to let me know that Hera's having a nap, with an adorable picture that momentarily distracts me from the strangeness of mine and Will's situation, when my phone suddenly buzzes again, with a text from Mick.

Mick: Maybe Hannah made a mistake. Sorry about that. Hope it works out. Have fun! M.

Maybe Hannah made a mistake? His niece must have accidentally booked the wrong package as the raffle prize. Oh God. What does Mick mean that he 'hopes it works out'? Does he also expect Will and I to just ride it out and play along?

'You are my first honeymoon booking!' Medhi enthuses. 'I am so happy to have you stay!' He beams at us.

I smile back. 'We're so happy too!' I insist, glancing at Will, who does a sort of half-smile, half-grimace.

'We're not far now,' Medhi says. 'This is Marrakech.' He gestures out of the window at the streets lined with palm trees, one even has a camel tethered to it. I nudge Will and point. Will smiles, but he still seems a bit perturbed by the whole honeymoon thing.

The driver pulls into a driveway. I spot a sign for 'Marrakech Palace'.

'We're here!' I point out, craning my neck to take in the hotel. It's incredibly grand with dreamlike Arabian architecture – a domed vaulted roof, tall engraved archways, marble pillars and more tall lush palm trees.

'Yes!' Medhi grins, turning to us. 'Welcome!'

'Wow!' I utter, in shock. When Medhi said he'd done alright for himself, he really meant it. The hotel is stunning. I'd seen pictures online, but they didn't properly capture the sheer magnificence of the place. Even Will looks completely awe-struck, having momentarily forgotten about our honeymoon predicament.

We stop outside the entrance and the driver parks the car.

'Wait … is that … confetti?' Will says, as he gets out and eyes the steps leading up to the hotel.

'Oh yes! We pay attention to the small details here at Marrakech Palace,' Medhi says.

I laugh as I take in the tiny love heart confetti in pink and red. It actually looks really cute, but you'd think the confetti featured tiny swastikas judging from the look of horror on Will's face.

A young boy of about 12 or 13 comes bounding up to Medhi, enveloping him in a hug before helping bring our bags into the hotel. Both Will and I try to help, but Medhi isn't having any of it.

'This is my son, Mohammed,' he says, ruffling the boy's hair.

'As-salāmu 'alaykum,' the boy says, smiling shyly.

'Wa 'alaykumu s-salām,' Will and I return the greeting.

'Natalie and Will just got married!' Medhi enthuses.

'Cool!' Mohammed replies.

As we walk over the confetti, I glance at Will, who looks back at me with a slightly desperate squirming expression. He clearly hates lying to Medhi and his family. A woman in a stunning embroidered kaftan comes rushing up to us as we walk into the hotel's reception, which is just as beautiful as the outside with an intricate rug laid across the marble floor and a decadent carved stone fountain in the centre.

'Welcome to Marrakech!' she says, throwing confetti over me and Will. 'I'm Amira!'

She pulls me into a hug. 'You must be Mrs Brimble!' she says.

I laugh. 'You can call me Natalie,' I reply, sweeping some confetti out of my hair.

I can feel Will watching me. He must find this whole Mrs Brimble stuff a bit uncomfortable seeing as the last Mrs Brimble ended up a divorcée. Definitely worth sticking to Natalie.

'And you must be Mr Brimble!' She shakes Will's hand.

'Yes, I am,' Will replies, smiling politely.

I don't think he realises he has a few pieces of love heart confetti on his shoulders and in his hair.

'We are so happy to have you here!' Amira is just as enthusiastic as her husband.

She briefly shows us around the hotel, which is absolutely spectacular, from the enormous restaurant decked out with pillars and drapes and shimmering chandeliers to the sparkling aquamarine pool hat is just as beautiful as the pictures Mick displayed on the projector screen back at the raffle. It's lined with deck chairs and a few guests are sipping drinks and soaking up the sun. It looks heavenly. One guest, a suave-looking man who appears to be in his forties, places his newspaper down on his lap and eyes me over the top of his sunglasses. I can't tell if he's checking me out or what, and before I can figure it out, Amira leads me and Will back to reception, where she gestures for us to take a seat at some comfy-looking chairs around a coffee table laden with a pot of steaming tea and a plate of pastries. Medhi sits down with us.

'Here, help yourself,' she says, gesturing at the pastries. Amira picks up the dish and offers them to us.

We both take one, thanking Medhi and Amira profusely.

Amira begins pouring us cups of tea. It smells delicious – of fresh mint.

'So, you came all the way from London! How was your journey?' Amira asks.

We tell them about our flight and our upgrade. Will's a little quiet and it's mostly me carrying the conversation. I find myself effortlessly playing along with the whole couple thing. I even reach over and give Will's knee a squeeze at one point. His eyes widen, a little shocked, but I don't think either Amira or Medhi notice.

Amira echoes some of what Medhi was saying in the car, telling us how incredibly excited they are to have us staying in their new honeymoon suite. Will and I exchange a look at one point, over the rims of our teacups, and I can tell from the slightly skittish, unnerved look in his eyes that he's not enjoying lying to them. But surely, he realises that if we were to 'fess up, we'd only massively disappoint them both. We faked being a couple on the plane, what's another couple of days? I give him an encouraging look.

'You probably want to go up to your room and relax,' Medhi says after we've eaten another pastry and the tea has run out. 'Let me take your passports and I'll give you your room key.'

Medhi gets up and we head to the reception desk, thanking Amira once more for the lovely welcome.

I open my bag and pull out my passport. I hand it to Medhi. As lovely as he and his family are, and as delicious as the pastries and mint teas are too, my head is beginning to pound a bit from the Dom Perignon Will and I necked on the plane. Keeping up the pretence of being a married couple when you've had half a bottle of champagne and flown from England to Africa is a bit exhausting.

Medhi studies my passport and frowns. Oh no. What now?

'Natale Jackson?' he says. 'Not Natalie Brimble.'

Oh crap. How did I not anticipate this moment? Will and I even talked about names on the plane!

I glance at Will. He pulls a face, looking completely awkward about the whole situation. He opens his mouth as though to speak, and I'm suddenly sure he's going to say something to give us away.

'I kept my own name,' I blurt out. 'I'm progressive like that. Modern!'

Will shoots me a look.

'Right,' Medhi replies. 'So you have different names?'

'Yes, it's quite common in England,' I tell him.

'Oh, I see.' Medhi smiles politely. 'May I take your passport, Will?'

Will hesitates and for a moment I'm worried he's going to just keep his passport, turn around and get a taxi back to the airport, but he reaches into his pocket and hands it over, shooting me a weary look as he does so. I pretend not to register it.

Medhi checks us in, handing back our passports along with our room keys.

'Where is your wedding ring?' he asks suddenly, eyeing Will's ring finger, which is, of course, completely ringless.

'Oh …' Will's face goes blank.

The phone at reception suddenly rings, with a loud piercing tone and I feel like Will and I have been saved by the bell, but Medhi raises a finger as though to indicate that we'll return to this conversation in a minute. He starts speaking in Arabic to whoever is calling.

'We should tell him,' Will whispers, taking a few steps closer to me.

'No, Will. I need this holiday, okay? I *really* need it. And they really want us here, too. They're so excited. Please don't ruin this for everyone. Please,' I whisper back, imploringly, surprising myself with my own intensity. Tears have even sprung to my eyes. I guess motherhood has made me more tired over the past year than I've been letting on, even to myself. I do really need this holiday. I want to stay in a nice suite and just have a break from reality. Medhi and his family seem so thrilled to have us, what harm does it do to play along and pretend to be married for a few days? They'd probably be incredibly disappointed if they discovered at this point that we're not married. Playing along really would be better for everyone.

'Okay, okay,' Will sighs, taking in my desperate expression.

'Thank you, Will. I owe you,' I say, reaching up and taking his hand. I give it a squeeze.

Medhi hangs up the phone and turns to us, spotting me squeezing Will's hand – convenient! Hopefully, my hand squeezing will only add to the impression that we're married. Married couples squeeze each other's hands all the time, right?

'So,' Medhi sighs, and for a moment, I think he's forgotten all about the rings, but he lasers in on mine and Will's hands on the counter. 'You don't have a ring either! Surely this isn't a progressive thing?'

'Haha!' I laugh. My laugh comes out more than a little high-pitched. I may have successfully managed to convince Will to play along as my husband but I'm no closer to explaining why we're not wearing rings. Medhi's right to be surprised. If we were married, surely we would be wearing them, so why aren't we? Why the hell aren't we? My mind is blank. Medhi is looking between me and Will, waiting for a response.

'Err ...' I glance at Will, my mind racing. Could they have been stolen? Or lost? But why would we both have lost our rings at the same time? We wouldn't have both been simultaneously that ditzy. Crap, I can't think of anything. I look at Will with pleading eyes, willing him to come up with something. He's the journalist. Aren't they meant to be good at thinking on their feet? But Will stares back at me, looking equally stumped.

'Umm ...' He looks towards Medhi, who raises his brows expectantly.

The silence is deafening. Our bubble is about to burst. Damn it. So much for my pretend marriage. Over before it even began.

'They're in our luggage,' Will says finally.

Phew. Yes! Go Will.

I nod enthusiastically. 'Yes, they're in our luggage,' I reiterate dumbly.

'But … why?' Medhi asks. Good point. I look to his ring finger. Gold band on it, naturally. In the place that normal married people wear them. Not stashed away in a bag somewhere.

'Umm …' Will squirms, chewing his lip. Then his eyes flash with inspiration and I can tell he's had a brainwave. 'We, er, set off the metal detector at the airport when we were checking in so we put our rings in our hand luggage.'

Nice one. I smile proudly at him.

'But why didn't you just put your rings back on after?' Medhi asks.

Jeez. Is Medhi obsessed with rings or something? What is this? The Spanish Inquisition?

Will glances at me. He looks so uncomfortable. His cheeks are a little flushed. I wish I could step in and help but I have absolutely no idea what to say. Plus, Will's the one who's been married before. Surely, he knows a bit more about what it's like to wear a wedding ring than I do?!

'We thought there might be another check-in point, so we just kept them off. Didn't want to keep taking them on and off in case we mislaid them. They're obviously really important to us,' Will says.

I nod enthusiastically, feeling so impressed with Will. I knew he'd be able to lie.

'Ah, I see,' Medhi sighs with satisfaction. 'Very wise.'

Very wise indeed.

'Yes, you know what it's like! Being married!' Will tuts, rolling his eyes indulgently.

I kick his ankle, urging him to stop. Enough already.

'Well, thanks so much, Medhi,' I interject, before Will can ruin things. 'We're so delighted to be staying here. We'd better head up to our room and unpack.'

'Of course,' Medhi says, before calling over to his son to get him to show us the way.

Mohammed leads us to the lift and we head up to the second floor. He shows us down the corridor to our room.

'This is your suite,' he mutters, gesturing towards the door.

'Thank you!' I reply, but he's already hurrying back along the corridor. He certainly has a long way to go if he's going to ever become as ebullient as his dad.

'We need rings,' I hiss at Will once Mohammed is out of earshot. Will slides the key into the hotel room door.

'Yeah! I know,' Will sighs, shaking his head as he twists the key in the lock.

'Do you think Medhi bought all that ring stuff?' I ask, hoping Will is going to assure me Medhi he bought it hook, line and sinker.

'I'm not sure,' Will sighs. 'We should definitely get rings to be on the safe side,' he says as he finally manages to turn the key in the door and get it open. He opens the bedroom door to reveal a huge, wide room. The walls and ceiling are painted a soft terracotta with a brushed texture that makes it look rustic and dreamy – a far from my hedgehog wallpaper back home. Ornately carved silver lanterns hang from the ceiling, each adorned with pieces of coloured glass. I flick the light switch on and the room is showered in tiny diamond-shaped shards of light.

'Wow!' I utter, glancing at Will, who looks equally impressed.

The room is shaped like an octagon, and arched doorways with intricately carved wooden doors lead out to a balcony. One of the doors is open, revealing a view of tall palm trees soaring above the stone fortress-like walls of the hotel, and beyond, the Atlas Mountains, the same reddish terracotta shade as the walls stretch into the distance. The view is spectacular.

'They brought up our luggage already,' Will says, gesturing at our bags which have been left by the side of the bed. The bed. I somehow skimmed past that part of the room. It's enormous. A massive, sumptuous, king-sized bed piled high with heart-shaped cushions and surrounded by a cocoon of luscious red and pink drapes, with crisp white sheets covered in sumptuous satin cushions, red foil-wrapped heart-shaped chocolates, and pink and red rose petals.

'Oh, lovely!' I say weakly.

'Yes, lovely,' Will replies through gritted teeth.

Chapter 9

'So …' I utter, picking up a rose petal from the crisp white bedsheet and holding it between my fingers. I give it a sniff, but I can't smell anything.

'So …' Will echoes.

I drop the petal back on the bed and perch at the end. 'What exactly do you do on honeymoons then?' I ask.

He feigns a serious expression and sits down next to me.

'Well, Nat, ever heard of this thing called the birds and the bees? Or do we need to have a little talk?' Will jokes, a smile playing at his lips.

'Oh, shut up!' I retort, giving him a shove.

'Ouch!' Will recoils, clutching his arm as though I've hurt him.

A silence passes between us and I suddenly become aware of the air-conditioning fan whirring overhead. 'I mean, obviously we're not going to do *that* so what are we going to do?' I ask.

'Tricky one …' Will muses.

'We can't exactly go downstairs and start exploring, can we? Wouldn't a normal pair of newlyweds be tearing each other's clothes off right now?' I ask.

Will smiles. 'Yes, they probably would be. It's one thing faking wedding rings, but you're not going to suggest we fake sex, are you? Banging the bed and crying out in ecstasy?'

I roll my eyes and pick up one of the pink satin love heart shaped pillows. 'No, Will, I wasn't going to suggest we fake sex!'

'Phew.'

'But what are we going to do up here?' I ask.

'I saw a mini Scrabble at the airport, should have bought it.' I can't tell if he's joking.

'Mini scrabble?' I echo, deadpan.

'It would have passed the time,' Will points out. I have a strong feeling he's not joking.

'Talk about unromantic!'

'Okay ...' Will looks around the room, as though for inspiration. His eyes land on a small fridge in the corner of the suite. He gets up and wanders over to it.

'What's that?' I ask as he pulls open the door.

'Mini bar,' Will says, peering inside.

From where I'm sitting, I can just about make out a few bottles, but I can't see what they are.

Will pulls out a bottle of champagne from the fridge that has a ribbon tied around the neck and a note. He inspects it.

'"Congratulations! Wishing you a lifetime of love and happiness",' Will reads out. He looks over and raises an eyebrow.

'Wow! Are all honeymoons like this? I feel like we're getting a hero's welcome when all we did was get married – at least that's what they think,' I say.

Will closes the fridge door and comes back to the bed, holding the bottle of champagne by the neck.

'Well, my honeymoon wasn't like this at all,' he says, perching at the end of the bed.

'Oh really?' I ask in a deliberately casual tone, even though my interest is suddenly piqued at the prospect of Will broaching the subject of his marriage.

'What was it like?' I ask.

'Well ...' Will pauses, as though searching for the right words

88

to describe it. 'There were a lot of horses involved,' he says.

'Horses?' I balk.

'Yes,' Will grumbles. 'I was pretty much third wheel to a Mustang called Bernie.'

I snort with laughter. 'Okay, you need to elaborate!'

'My wife was really into horse-riding and persuaded me that we should have our honeymoon in Cornwall. She chose a lovely hotel and I thought we'd relax, enjoy the beach, unwind, but little did I know the hotel was five minutes from a stable and she'd already arranged to ride one of the horses pretty much every day,' Will recalls, rolling his eyes at the memory.

'When she was meant to be riding you,' I tease, trying not to laugh.

'Exactly!' Will agrees.

'That's tragic. Usurped by a horse,' I comment.

'I know. I guess that was a red flag right there!'

I want to know more, but I'm suddenly hit with the urge to pee.

'One sec,' I say as I dash through a door leading to what must be the bathroom.

I'm expecting a toilet, a bath, maybe some nice towels, but I certainly wasn't expecting a jacuzzi. The bathroom is ridiculously and unnecessarily large. All the fittings are a matching textured brown stone and everything looks brand new. It's completely gorgeous with a huge jacuzzi in the centre. Like the bed, the floor and the jacuzzi have been scattered with rose petals.

'Oh my God,' I utter, taking it in.

'What?' Will calls out.

'One second!' I call back, my bladder busting.

Even the toilet is five-star, so sparkling clean I could probably eat my dinner off it. Once I've relieved myself, I wash my hands in the massive sink using rose-scented soap from a glass dispenser.

I head back into the suite. Will is looking out of the window, an intense and pensive expression on his face. I'm tempted to ask what he's looking at or what he's thinking about, but I'm also dying to tell him about the jacuzzi. The jacuzzi wins.

'Will, the bathroom has a jacuzzi!' I gush.

Will immediately spins around. 'A jacuzzi?!'

'Yeah!' I reply.

His face lights up and he comes over to the bathroom, taking it in. It truly is an incredible bathroom, aside from the beautiful appliances and the incredible jacuzzi, there are other gorgeous details too, like potted orchids, antique mirrors and even chandelier lighting.

'Wow!' Will gazes at it in wonder.

'I know! Let's get in the jacuzzi! We can be in the jacuzzi while other newlyweds would be having sex,' I comment, impressed by my own plan.

'We might end up quite prune-like,' Will points out.

I shrug. 'I can live with that!'

Will is still holding the bottle of champagne. 'I'll put this back,' he says, glancing down at it.

'Why? Champagne in a jacuzzi! Isn't that the kind of thing you're meant to do on holiday?'

Will smiles. 'It's been so long since I had one and back then it was more like Jägerbombs in a nightclub, but yes, champagne in a jacuzzi is totally holiday worthy.'

I smile, pleased with his reaction. 'Almost as good as sex. Probably better, actually,' I joke.

Will laughs. 'Hmmm … depends who you're having it with,' he says, smiling flirtatiously.

I laugh, feeling my cheeks reddening ever so slightly. I can already tell this holiday is going to be full of moments like this – awkward, intimate, and vaguely flirtatious – and even though part of me secretly enjoys it when Will flirts, another side of me feels like a scared little mouse. He's hot and everything but sex, men, relationships, even holiday romances – they're just complications I really don't need right now.

'Well, I'm going to get changed into my bikini,' I say, looking back towards the suite and styling out his comment. 'Erm ... shall I get changed in the bedroom and you in here?'

'Sure,' Will replies.

He heads back to the suite and while I'm getting my bikini out of my bag, Will opens his suitcase and retrieves a pair of swimming trunks, which he takes back to the bathroom to put on.

I take off my jumper and jeans and then quickly whip off my underwear, rapidly swapping it for my bikini briefs and halterneck bikini top. I know Will's hardly going to just burst into the room but I can't help feeling awkward regardless. I'm still aware of his presence. I can hear him shuffling about in the bathroom: the wheels of his suitcase against the stone floor and a rumbling bubbling sound, which I guess is the jacuzzi being turned on. I take a look at myself in the mirror on the wardrobe door. I look better than I expected. I haven't worn a bikini for years. I think the last time I wore one was when Lauren and I went on a long weekend away to Malta and spent pretty much the whole time lying on the beach soaking up the sun. I was slimmer back then, but as I take in my reflection, I still feel good about myself. I may not be a perfect size ten anymore but these days, I feel more myself. I know what suits me, like now I'm wearing a high-waisted polka-dot bikini with a matching top. It looks good with my curvy figure, almost like one of those Fifties' pin-up pictures, from the right angle, maybe. And unlike back when I was on holiday with Lauren, I don't feel self-conscious either. I may have had a better figure back then, but a figure's nothing if you don't have the confidence to match. I know what suits me now too. This polka-dot bikini is so much more flattering than the flimsy crochet thing I remember wearing on that holiday. I didn't even like it when I bought it, I just saw a model wearing it and thought it looked good on her. It was tiny, barely covering my modesty and it was useless to swim in too. By the end of the trip, it had practically unravelled.

'You ready yet?' Will calls out through the bathroom door, his voice snapping me out of my reverie.

'Yeah,' I call back.

I walk over to the bathroom door. 'Are you decent?'

'Yep!' Will replies.

'Just checking,' I reply as I push the door open.

Will is sitting in the jacuzzi with a smug, blissed-out smile on his face. The water bubbles around his chest, which looks hairier than I remember it from school. He looks over at me and I'm not sure if I'm imagining it, I don't think I'm imagining it, but I swear his eyes widen a little as though he likes what he sees.

'Are you, umm … Are you …' he stammers as though the sight of me in a bikini has tripped him up somewhat.

'Am I?' I coax him, taking a step forward.

'I was going to say are you getting in, but could you get some glasses actually?' Will says, clearing his throat and recovering his composure. I glance over his shoulder and spot the bottle of champagne on the side of the jacuzzi. I must have been so busy looking at Will that I completely failed to notice it there.

'I feel like such a pimp right now,' Will jokes. 'Got my champagne, my jacuzzi, my hoes, or hoe, rather.'

'Hoe?!' I balk, feigning indignation even though I can't help laughing. Will is such a far cry from the kind of rap star baller he's talking about that it's just hilarious. With his well-spoken voice and slightly pasty chest, he really doesn't fit the bill.

'Arghh, humour me!' Will laughs.

I roll my eyes, although I can't help smiling. 'I'm getting some glasses!'

I nip back into the suite and head over to the fridge, hoping there'll be some champagne flutes nearby and sure enough, there are. Right next to the fridge is a selection of glasses, even a kettle, some teabags, instant coffee and some biscuits. I hadn't spotted them before from where I was sitting. I pick up two champagne flutes and head back to the jacuzzi, with a spring in my step.

Will is decanting a bottle of pink liquid into the jacuzzi as I get back in.

'Oh my God, Will, what is that?' I gawp, worried it's bubble bath and we're about to flood the entire bathroom with bubbles.

'Don't worry, it's rose oil,' Will says. 'Found it by the bath.'

'Oh great!' I reply as I place the glasses on the side of the jacuzzi and get in. I glance at Will as I climb into the jacuzzi, lowering myself into the warm bubbling water. I can tell he's making a deliberate effort not to check me out. He seems to have glued his gaze to the wall. His effort not to make me feel perved upon is actually quite cute. I lower myself in.

'You can look now!' I joke.

Will looks back around. 'Oh, I was trying to be, you know, I didn't want to look like I was checking you out.'

'I know.' I smile.

'Haha, great, well!' Will reaches for the bottle of champagne. 'Shall I pop it or do you want to?' he asks.

'You do it.'

'Sure.' Will starts unpeeling the foil wrapping from around the neck of the bottle, cupping his hand around the cork. I'm not one for flying corks and I cower behind my hands.

'Point it to the wall!' I urge Will as the cork suddenly pops off into his hand. The champagne starts bubbling out. I grab a glass and try to catch some of the bubbles. They subside and Will pours me a proper glass. I reach for the other empty one and he decants some of the champagne into it too. He places the bottle back on the side of jacuzzi and I hand him one of the glasses.

'Cheers!' I say, and we clink glasses.

I take a sip. The cool champagne and the hot jacuzzi is a great combination and I can't help feeling totally relaxed. The bubbles are rippling over my back, taking away any stiffness or tension from the flight and they smell delicious too, the rose fragrance adding yet another layer of blissfulness to the experience.

'God, this is so nice,' I muse, although I can't help feeling a little guilty. I'm having such an amazing time and since I arrived at the hotel, I've barely thought about Hera once.

'It really is,' Will sighs, closing his eyes and lowering himself further into the bubbles.

'I just realised I hadn't thought about Hera, is that bad?' I pipe up.

'Nah!' Will opens his eyes a fraction and on seeing the worried look on my face, he straightens up.

'It's really not. You're in a whole new environment taking everything in. Nothing here reminds you of life back home. Just because you haven't thought about her for five minutes, doesn't mean you don't love her,' Will says, giving me a kind, encouraging smile.

'I guess,' I relent.

'Honestly, it's fine,' Will insists. 'The fact that you're even worrying about it shows how much you care.'

'I suppose.'

'You need some time off too, Nat. And don't beat yourself up for enjoying it. You have four days to let your hair down and have fun, then it's back to all the stuff that being a mum entails. Just make the most of it, because if you don't, you'll regret it. I still have worries at the back of my mind, but I'm just not going to let them get to me while I'm here. Four days off from real life, it'll all be waiting for us when we return,' Will says, taking a sip of his champagne.

I hate to admit it to myself, but he's right. I do love Hera and of course, I miss her, but if I spend this whole holiday fretting and pining for her, it won't achieve anything other than making me miserable and bringing both me and Will down. It won't get me home any quicker and will just be a waste of a totally brilliant holiday.

'You're right, Will,' I admit.

A silence passes between us, filled by the sound of the bubbling jacuzzi.

'What are you worried about?' I ask him. 'Or would you rather not talk about it?'

'Oh, just job stuff, really,' Will replies. 'The freelance life is a bit stressful, especially after having been working full-time for pretty much my whole career. I find the insecurity a bit much, but you know, those are England worries. While I'm here, I'm just going to put it out of my mind.'

He smiles and he does look completely relaxed. His face suddenly brightens. 'Hey, I have an idea,' he says.

'What?' I reply hesitantly.

'Let's play a game!'

'A game?' I echo.

'Yeah, a drinking game.'

'Oh God!' I laugh. 'Which one? I can barely remember any of them.'

'Never Have I Ever. Classic!' He grins his boyish smile and his enthusiasm is infectious.

'Okay, let's do it,' I reply, figuring we may as well. I probably haven't played a drinking game since back when I originally knew Will, at school. Even though it's a bit childish to play drinking games, it'll be a laugh and a great way to get to know a bit more about Will and what he's been up to over the years.

Will reaches for the champagne and tops up our glasses.

'I'll go first,' I comment, holding my now full glass of champagne.

'Okay, hit me,' Will says, as he places the bottle of champagne back on the side of the jacuzzi.

'Never have I ever ...' I look at Will and try to think of something. '... Had sex in a jacuzzi,' I suggest, plucking the first thing that comes to mind.

Will grins. 'Nope! 'Fraid I haven't!' he says.

'Really?'

'Yeah.' Will shrugs. 'I was married for six years, we barely travelled and it's not like we had one at home. Why? Have you? Do you want to?' he asks, with a cheeky smile.

'No!' I laugh his suggestion off. 'I thought you might have done before you were married, back when you were mingling with celebs!'

'Nope, not even back then. But I might add it to my bucket list now,' he says, giving me a flirty look again.

I smile, glancing away a little shyly. 'Your turn!' I say.

'Okay, never have I ever …' he casts his eyes up as he tries to think of something. '… Had a vajazzle!'

I raise an eyebrow, eyeing his glass, willing him to drink it. I take a sip of mine. 'Low blow, Will! I had to have one when I was representing my client! She offered me one so I could see her work first-hand.'

Will takes a sip of his champagne.

'Oi, you're not meant to drink unless you've done the thing!' I point out.

'And?' Will comments wryly.

'You've had a vajazzle?'

Will grins. 'I didn't think I had at first, but then I remembered when I was in Ibiza after uni, I got one when I was drunk. It was a dare,' Will recalls.

'You got a vajazzle!' I giggle. 'What the hell?!'

Will laughs. 'Yeah! They were all the rage back then!'

'For women! It's called a va-jazzle, coming from va-gina. It's not a pajazzle for your penis!' I point out, unable to stop laughing at him.

'That's so discriminatory, Natalie. If I want a vajazzle, I'll get a vajazzle,' Will says, with mock indignation, which only makes me laugh harder.

'Clearly!' I point out. 'So what was your vajazzle, or should I say, pajazzle of?' I ask.

Will sinks further into the bubbles, deliberately looking away, pulling a face. 'Never mind.'

'What?' I kick him through the bubbles. 'You brought this up! You have to tell me now!'

Will grimaces. 'I wish I had never brought this up.'

'Too late for that now!'

'Oh God …' Will sinks even deeper.

'Come on!' I coax him, giving his leg another nudge with my toes.

'Okay, okay!' He straightens up. 'Bear in mind, it was a dare and I was drunk. Very drunk.'

'Was it a girl's initials or something? A conquest? Someone you shagged somewhere other than a jacuzzi,' I tease.

'No, it was Nathan's idea. There was this girl doing them at our hotel and he paid her to do it.'

'Uh-huh … so what was it? A star? Lips?'

'It was, erm …' Will coughs and looks away. 'It was a penis.'

'Did you just say "a penis"?'

'Maybe.' Will grins.

'You got a pajazzle of a penis. Oh my God, I'm dying!' I crack up.

'It wasn't the best look,' Will remarks. 'It's Nathan's fault, he's really puerile.'

'Nathan's fault?! You were the one rocking the sparkly penis on your man parts!'

'Why did we decide to play this game again?' Will grumbles, a smile playing at the corner of his lips.

'It was your idea.'

'Definitely not my finest!' he jokes. 'Anyway, it's your turn.'

I sink back into the bubbles, trying to think up a good question. Something Will's probably done that I definitely haven't. Although he had a few dalliances with minor celebrities before he got married, I can't imagine he got up to that much mischief when he was married and if he did, it's probably not the best topic to broach right now. I still don't know exactly why he got divorced and I should probably let him come out with that in his own time, if he even wants to talk about it at all. Yet despite being married for a good chunk of his twenties, he has been

97

single for the past year or so, and I can't help wondering if he's had much action.

'Never have I ever … been on a Tinder date?' I say, eyeing Will, expecting him to drink, but he eyes me back and doesn't take a sip.

'You've never been on a Tinder date?' My mouth has dropped slightly open.

'No. What makes you think I would have?' Will says.

'Because you're single …' I point out.

'And so are you and you're not drinking,' Will retorts.

'Yeah, but I have a baby to worry about,' I remind him.

'True,' Will admits. 'I contemplated it at one point. Downloaded it at a low ebb and swiped on a few people but that whole swiping thing, I just don't like it. It feels like a really shit computer game or something, just with people. I just don't think that's how I want to meet someone. It feels a bit hollow.'

I eye Will as he speaks, relating to every word.

'So you've never had a Tinder date then? Not even before Hera?' Will asks, giving me a shrewd look.

'Nope!' I cast my mind back over my dating history. 'I mean, back when we were at university, dating apps weren't really a thing and really, anyone who needs an app to date at uni probably isn't getting out enough. Then after, I met a few guys through friends, dated one guy I met on a night out. I met Leroy through the gym and since him, Tinder has been the furthest thing from my mind! So no, no Tinder dates for me.'

'Maybe we should download it in Marrakech, see what the Tinder scene's like over here, cross it off the bucket list,' Will jokes.

'Shut up, Will!' I splash him and he squints, shielding his eyes.

'Okay, my turn. Never have I ever …' He puts a finger to his chin and does a mock thinking face. 'Never have I ever … had a baby,' he lands upon, grinning.

'Oh, come on! Cheap shot!' I take a sip of my champagne.

'I know, but this champagne's not going to drink itself, is it?' I laugh, rolling my eyes.

In the end, the champagne doesn't drink itself. We sit in the jacuzzi until our skin resembles ET's and we know more about each other's sexual history than I think either of us had bargained for. I've found out that yes, Will has sexted and that he and his ex-wife used to do it quite regularly when he was overseas, in fact, and that he has had sex outdoors (in a stable, FYI) and that yes, he has slept with someone from the village in recent years (a fling with Rowena of all people, which they both apparently decided would be nothing more than a one-night thing. Rowena apparently prefers women, which might explain why she was so keen for me to come over to do cross-stich). I've also established that no, he's never slept with anyone from work, and yes, he has kissed another man (another dare from his Ibiza trip). Embarrassingly, Will has discovered that I once dabbled in S&M (an awkward spanking incident with Leroy), I've never had a threesome and I did once have a dalliance with a co-worker (a fumble with a bearded hipster entrepreneur at the Camden office back before I met Leroy).

'Not even Lauren knows this much about me,' I comment as I climb out of the jacuzzi, my skin rubbery and wrinkled.

The floor's slippery and I'm a little tipsy. Will gives me a hand, helping me out.

'Well, if we're going to be a married couple, we need to know each other inside out!' he says.

'I guess.' I laugh, wondering just how intimate this holiday is going to be.

Chapter 10

You know those pictures you see in guidebooks of Marrakech with the pretty spices in colourful peaks, a stalls adorned with glowing lanterns, silver teapots, curled toe leather slippers and woven rugs? Well, it's like that, it's absolutely gorgeous, but those pictures don't capture the smells, the noise and the commotion. They don't capture the full sensory overload. The air is fragrant with the rich scent of spices, leather bags fresh from the tannery and sizzling meat from kebab stands. Every three steps, a vendor tries to tempt us into checking out their wares. A few of them have called out 'blue eyes' to get my attention. One even called me 'Miley Cyrus', which I was actually quite chuffed about. Will and I have been walking for five minutes and I've already had a handbag thrust into my arms, an embroidered kaftan, a hand-painted plate, even a painted ladle. The pictures don't capture the stray cats that prowl along the streets, slinking past your legs. They don't capture just how winding and labyrinthine the souks really are.

'So, what we need is something that looks like gold, but is actually really cheap and rubbish. And we'll haggle the seller down as much as possible,' Will says, weaving through the crowd. Unlike me, he seems completely at ease in the intense environment, despite having been lounging in a jacuzzi quaffing champagne only half an hour earlier.

'Yep. Cheap and rubbish. Got it,' I reply, as we wander down a narrow passage lined with stalls.

I never pictured myself wedding ring shopping in Marrakech and 'cheap' and 'rubbish' were hardly the adjectives I thought I'd be using if I did ever go shopping for a ring, but when you're faking marriage, this is how it goes. Will and I are hoping that if we get gold bands, Medhi will be off our case and we'll be able to fly under the radar as a married couple during our stay here.

Suddenly, I feel something on my back and yelp, spinning around. It's a monkey. A literal monkey. A man is trying to put a monkey onto my back. Will pulls me out of the way as I shriek. The monkey is wearing a little hat with a bell on it and a tailcoat.

'What the hell?!' I cry as we hurry away.

'They put the monkey on you and try to charge you for a picture,' Will explains.

'Right …' I utter, brushing dust from my shoulder. I couldn't feel further away from Chiddingfold right now.

Will and I pass another dozen stalls, but I think we must be in the apparel part of the souk, because all they seem to be selling are robes, slippers and bags.

Will pauses to examine some sparkly pink slippers with a curly upturned toe. Surely, he's not getting them for himself? A present for his mum, perhaps? I'm about to ask, when something catches my eye. It's a jewellery shop, its gold wares glinting in the sun. I wander over to it and spot rings.

'Will!' I call out. He looks over.

'They've got rings here,' I tell him.

'Great!' Will puts the slippers down and wanders over.

We both eye the gold rings on display in a glass cabinet by the counter. They're perfect – simple, classic and earnest-looking. Just like wedding rings ought to be. The seller, who seems to have a personal penchant for gold, with gold chains around his neck and hoops in his ears, eyes us checking out the rings.

'They look like wedding rings, don't they?' I say to Will.

'Yeah, they really do,' Will replies.

I ask to see them, and the seller opens the cabinet and takes out the tray of rings. I reach for one and slip it on my wedding finger. It feels odd to slide a ring on a finger I'm so used to avoiding when it comes to jewellery. The ring I've chosen is a perfect fit and I hold out my hand, admiring it.

'Looks good, eh, Will?' I say, nudging him.

For some reason, his face has misted over. He looks miles away.

'Yeah, yeah.' He springs back to the present, clocking my ring. 'Yeah, it looks great.'

'Aren't you going to try one on too?' I ask, narrowing my eyes at him. He has an oddly distracted look about him that I can't figure out.

'I ... actually, I have one with me already,' Will says.

'You have a wedding ring?' I raise an eyebrow.

'Yeah, I'd forgotten about it, which is kind of bad, but I just remembered. It's in my wallet.' He reaches into his jacket pocket and pulls out his wallet. He flips it open and pulls a ring out of a small pocket inside.

'Oh ... You carry your old wedding ring around?' I appraise the gold band, which Will is now sliding onto his ring finger.

'It's actually not my ring,' he says, holding his hand up to admire it. It seems to fit perfectly.

'Then whose is it?' I balk.

'It was my dad's. I started carrying this around with me after he died. It's been in my wallet for years. Literally years! So long that I'd practically forgotten about it, but looking at the rings, I suddenly remembered about it and it occurred to me that I could wear it,' Will remarks, his faraway distracted expression now making complete sense.

'Are you sure, Will?' I say gently. It's one thing buying cheap rings for the sake of a fake honeymoon, but I don't want Will to think he has to do something that's going to make him genuinely upset.

'Yeah.' Will smiles, looking at the ring. 'It's funny, all this time, I've known it was there, but I haven't really looked at it. I was a bit scared to in a way, in case it would bring back memories and get me down, but now I'm looking at it and wearing it and I don't feel bad. It feels surprisingly nice, actually. Sort of comforting.'

I smile sweetly at him and place my hand on his back, giving him a gentle rub.

Will looks over and smiles at me tenderly. I feel a stab of affection for him. The closest interaction I've had with Will over the last decade has been seeing him on TV, in a suit, looking slick and professional, yet the man standing here now, the man in his red check shirt, with messy hair still ever so slightly damp from the jacuzzi, gazing at his father's wedding ring, is worlds away from that man. Will isn't the corporate suave media guy I thought he'd become, he's still Will the sweet, emotional soul I fell for so many years ago.

'So, what's the cheapest price you can do for this ring?' Will asks the vendor, gesturing at my hand.

We haggle the vendor down to a fiver. I know the ring isn't gold, but who cares? It looks real enough, and I know I shouldn't, but I can't help feeling a tiny thrill of excitement as I wander out of the shop with a gold band on my finger. A simple gold ring. I never wear jewellery as understated as a wedding ring. If I wear rings, they're usually blingy with a massive costume jewellery rock in the middle or something, but mine and Will's fake wedding rings feel so simple, so serious, so mature. I can't stop staring at the gold band on my finger, even while we're walking out of the shop back into the souk.

'How do I look, hubby?' I ask, pouting at Will, while holding my ringed hand to my face and wiggling my fingers.

'Beautiful,' Will laughs.

I glance at his ring, sparkling on his finger. 'Are you really sure you're okay wearing that? We could always get you one, they are only five quid, after all.'

Will holds up his hand and takes in his ring. 'Yeah, do you know what? I actually quite like wearing it,' he insists brightly.

I think back to Will's dad, Gary. One thing I'll always remember about him is the way he used to have a nickname for everyone in the village. He had this easy-going, naturally matey way with people. I've never met anyone else quite like that. He used to call me 'Picasso' because of my interest in art and while coming from some people, a nickname like that might have seemed a bit annoying, when Gary said it, it was just funny and sweet and chummy. He could get away with it. He even called my mum 'Lashes' on account of a phase she went through of wearing false eyelashes. The way he came up with nicknames for everyone just showed how well he tried to get to know each person. He was so good humoured, and his nicknames were his way of being friendly, breaking the ice and putting people at ease.

'Do you remember how your dad called me "Picasso"?' I remark.

Will laughs. 'Oh God, yeah. Or "Frida",' Will recalls. I suddenly remember how his dad also called me 'Frida' after Frida Kahlo.

'Only Gary could pull that stuff off!' I say.

'Yeah, he had a knack about him,' Will says fondly. 'I've lost track of the number of nicknames he gave me. Must have gone through dozens, everything from "Peter Pan" when my growth spurt came on late to "Beckham" during my football phase.'

'Brilliant!' I laugh. I know Will adored his dad and that his death can't have been easy for him, but it's nice to see him joking around like this, remembering the good times.

'Shall we get some food?' Will asks as the air becomes increasingly fragrant with the smell of spices. 'There are tons of outdoor restaurants in Jemaa el-Fna,' Will tells me as we walk in the direction of the smell of food coming from the main square.

'Sounds good,' I agree.

'It can be quite full on though,' Will warns me as we get closer.

'Ha! I think I can handle it, Will,' I scoff. Just because I come from a tiny Surrey village doesn't mean I can't handle Marrakech. I mean, honestly.

We arrive at Jamaa el-Fnaa. It's enormous, with sellers spilling out of the souk onto the square, laying rugs on the ground to sell their wares. Many of them try to get my attention, brandishing the prettiest lampshades, handbags, and sparkling slippers at me as I pass. The sellers blend into pop-up restaurants, which are being set up across the square. The restaurateurs lay out tables and chairs, the legs of which clatter against the paving stones, while their co-workers fire up grills and chop up ingredients, getting ready for the night's trade.

I'm so busy checking out the enticing pop-up restaurants that I barely notice an oncoming donkey cart ploughing towards me at an alarming speed.

'Ahhh!' I shriek, jumping out of its path.

I catch my breath when a soft lilting tune distracts me. I turn to see a cobra. A real-life cobra. It's bobbing its head along to the sounds of a flute played by a skinny man with a lined face sitting next to it, blowing into his instrument which makes the most peculiar sound like a mystical bagpipe. There's a little dish next to them containing a few dirham notes. The cobra bobs and weaves its head in time to the music. I grab Will's arm, my hand slick with sweat, praying the snake can't sense my fear.

'Let's get away from here!' I hiss.

Will laughs. 'I told you it could be full on. Snake charmers are a bit of a thing in Marrakech, although I think there's a crack down on them. They remove the teeth of the cobra or sew their mouths shut so they can't strike anyone.'

'Oh ...' I reply, my fear suddenly replaced by sympathy for the snakes.

'Are you okay?' Will asks.

'I'm fine!' I reply, although my voice sounds a little tight.

Will's right, Jamaa el-Fnaa is quite intense. I'm a single mum who spends most of her time at home and in the space of five minutes I've been accosted by a man with a monkey, nearly been ran over by a donkey cart and come face-to-face with a cobra. I could do with a sit down.

We walk to the opposite side of the square, as far away from the cobra as possible and find a small outdoor restaurant selling tagines. We place our order and settle down at one of the tables, looking out onto the square. Of all the places in the world to people watch, Jemaa el-Fnaa is a fascinating spot. I take in the commotion of souk sellers, restauranteurs, snake charmers, even fortune tellers, hustling for business from tourists, many of whom look as bemused as I felt five minutes ago. A waiter brings over our tagines and we tuck in. They're delicious – succulent, spicy and steaming on a bed of fluffy couscous.

At one point a rowdy group of English guys walk up to our restaurant. One of them – a tall, bleary-eyed bloke – checks me out and I brace myself, worried he might try to talk to me. I really can't be bothered with some sleazy chat-up line from a boozy Brit abroad, but the man glances at Will, and then looks down at the ring on my finger, shrugs and walks away, immediately losing interest.

'Oh my God, these things really do work!' I stare at my ring in wonder.

I explain what happened to Will and he laughs.

'Yeah, that's the idea!' he says, taking another bite of his tagine.

'I know, but it just felt like … magic!'

Will smiles.

I finish my tagine and we make our way back to the hotel. Marrakech doesn't have as many streetlights as Surrey or London and the streets are much darker now the sun has set, the only light as we walk to our hotel being the glow that spills from a couple of shops shutting late. There's a chill in the air now and I pull my cardigan tight around my body.

'Come here,' Will says, holding his arm out to me and beckoning for me to cosy up to him.

'Is this part of the marriage act?' I ask, eyeing Will's open arm. I look down the road. The hotel isn't even in sight yet.

'No, I just thought you looked cold,' Will says.

'I am actually,' I reply, shivering.

'Well, come on then!'

'Okay.' I take a step closer to him. He wraps his arm around my shoulders, and I can immediately feel his body heat. His body is like a radiator. He must be one of those naturally hot-blooded people. Leroy was a bit like that. He'd sleep naked night after night with just a duvet over him, while I'd wrap up in fleecy pyjamas, fluffy socks and create my own warm cocoon on my side of the bed with a blanket. I'm sexy like that.

Walking alongside someone while they've got their arm slung around your shoulder is actually harder than it seems unless you put your arm around their back. I try walking with my arm just sort of flapping between mine and Will's bodies, then I try holding it up behind Will's back, kind of suspended in mid-air, but that just looks ridiculous and it's not exactly comfortable either. Plus, we're a little bit out of step and I'm pretty sure that would be corrected if I just latched onto him.

Will grabs my hand and clamps it to his hip. 'That's better,' he says.

I smile, a little awkwardly, feeling Will's taught hip under my palm. The tragic thought hits me as we walk that this is the closest I've been to a man since Leroy. It feels strange, but in a good way, like a feeling I hadn't realised I was missing. There's a certain innate sense of comfort to being close to someone, to walking down the street, arm-in-arm with another individual. It takes me back to the good aspects of being in a relationship, when you're with someone who loves and supports you and everything feels just that little bit less stressful, from the small things, like walking down a cold street together and sharing body warmth to everything else coupledom entails, like talking over problems and going halves on bills. A good relationship is like a coat of armour, protecting you against the hardships of life, but a bad one is like having your skin torn off and being even more exposed than ever. I've been so raw from the whole Leroy thing for so long that I've barely even remembered the good aspects of relationships, and even though there's nothing particularly romantic between me and Will, it's nice to be reminded, nonetheless.

I glance over at Will as we get closer to the hotel. He looks as pensive as I feel, and I can't help wondering what he's thinking. It feels strange that today is only the first day of our holiday, it feels like ages ago that we were getting into the taxi in Chiddingfold.

We walk up to the entrance of Marrakech Palace.

'Good evening!' Medhi says, as we pass reception. He looks between us, smiling broadly. It's only then that I realise how couple-like we must actually look, walking arm in arm. For once, we're not faking it.

'Hi Medhi,' Will and I both reply. We chat to him for a while about our evening, mentioning having dinner in Jemaa el-Fnaa. Naturally, we leave out the bit about bartering for cheap rubbish wedding rings.

The reception counter is quite high and so I rest my hand on it, hoping Medhi will spot my ring, but despite having been obsessed with our lack of wedding rings earlier, he doesn't glance towards my hand once.

I fake a cough, mid-conversation, bringing my ring hand up to my face in the hope that maybe now, Medhi will notice my wedding band, but he still doesn't appear to register it. He doesn't look once at Will's hand either, even though he's placed it prominently on the counter too.

Will and I exchange a slightly exasperated look.

'Breakfast is between 7 a.m. and 10.30 a.m. We serve a traditional Moroccan breakfast as well as continental,' Medhi says, still completely oblivious to our rings.

'That sounds brilliant,' I reply, meaning it. Breakfast these days tends to consist of one of Hera's rusk biscuits washed down with strong coffee. I used to be the kind of person who enjoyed leisurely breakfasts all the time. I used to have business meetings over breakfast. I haven't been out for a proper breakfast since Hera was born. It'll be really nice to have a decent one in gorgeous surroundings.

'See you in the morning then,' I say, waving with my ring hand, but Medhi still doesn't seem to notice my ring. Oh well, at least I can flash it over breakfast.

Chapter 11

Funnily enough, honeymoon suites aren't really designed for one person sleeping on the sofa, but somehow Will and I have made it work. We found a spare blanket in the wardrobe and Will huddled up on the couch, letting me have the king-sized bed to myself. It felt a bit strange to neatly pick off the rose petals and chastely tuck myself in, rather than be thrown on the bed in the throes of passion as it was clearly intended. I couldn't sleep for a while, I kept thinking of Hera. Even though my mum and I exchanged a ton of texts before bedtime featuring lots of pictures and updates on everything from what Hera had for dinner to what pyjamas she was wearing, I still missed her so much. The awkwardness and unfamiliarity of having Will in the same room as me also proved annoyingly distracting, but eventually, tiredness took hold and I fell into a deep restful sleep. So restful in fact, that Will and I have had to hurry out of the room to catch breakfast before the hotel stops serving.

The breakfast at the hotel is everything I'd hoped for and more, with an array of options from croissants and pastries to sausages and beans to Moroccan pancakes and jam. I decide to opt for a traditional Moroccan breakfast, with several pancakes and an apricot compote.

'This place is heavenly.' I sigh contentedly, gazing out over hotel restaurant with its marble pillars and lantern lampshades as I tuck into my second pancake.

'It really is,' Will replies as he sips his coffee. 'It couldn't be more different to my last experience in Marrakech. We stayed in a hostel right by the site of the bombing. It was completely chaotic. There were sirens blaring through the night. Police everywhere. Total panic. Not to mention the horrible thin mattresses and shared bathrooms, although they were the least of my worries at the time.'

'It sounds awful. You can have the bed tonight,' I insist, feeling a little guilty.

'Thanks,' Will replies, before biting into his croissant. He glances down at my hand, and more precisely, my ring finger.

'Oh no …' he mutters, staring at it.

'What?' I place my coffee cup down. 'What is it?'

Will reaches over, takes my hand and scrutinises my finger, pulling a face. 'Our rings really are cheap crap. It's left a green mark on your skin already,' he says, twisting my ring up to reveal a repulsive greenish stain.

'Oh God,' I sigh.

'Good morning!' Medhi greets us with his signature broad beaming smile. I quickly pull my hand away and place it under the table, out of sight. I'm hardly going to look like a newlywed with my cheap disgusting ring! I need to clean my finger as soon as possible. Maybe we should have splashed out on real gold after all.

'Morning!' Will and I reply.

'Did you sleep well?' Medhi asks.

'Oh yes, amazingly!' I enthuse.

'Great night's sleep, thank you,' Will concurs.

'The petals and the pillows were a lovely touch,' I add.

Medhi smiles proudly. 'I'm so glad you were comfortable. I wanted to check because housekeeping just came down and they said it looked like someone had slept on the sofa.'

111

What?!

Will and I exchange a panicked look. Damn it. We both slept in and in our hurry to make it to breakfast in time, we forgot to clear the sofa, or hang the 'Do Not Disturb' sign on the door handle. Great. Just great. We hardly look like newlyweds now.

'Err ...' I utter.

Medhi stares at me, waiting for an answer.

'Oh, erm ...' Will is visibly squirming. His cheeks flush pink.

'I, erm ...' I try to think of a plausible excuse for why, on what is supposedly the first night of our honeymoon, my husband would have slept on the sofa, but my mind is blank.

'Well, err.' I glance down at the crumbs of my pancakes, as though they'll give me the answer, but my brain is like tumbleweed rolling across the Moroccan desert. I glance up at Will, urging him to say something. After all, he saved our skin with the lie about the rings and luggage last night.

'Natalie, err ...' A flash of something passes across his eyes – inspiration has struck! I'm beginning to recognise that look. 'Natalie wasn't feeling well,' he says, meeting Medhi's gaze. 'I think the tagine we had in Jemaa el-Fnaa was a bit too spicy for Nat so I, erm, thought I'd give her some space.'

What the hell?!

'Oh,' Medhi replies, with a look of concern. 'It sounds like it must have been very serious.'

'Yes, exactly. You know what these things are like. Jumping up from the bed, running to the toilet. Getting gassy. The works. New cuisine – it can be hard on British stomachs,' Will says, smiling sympathetically at me.

I get that he's trying to embellish the lie to make it sound more convincing but *running to the toilet? Gas? Really?*

Medhi eyes me sympathetically too.

I smile tightly, flashing a glare at Will. I cannot believe this. So Medhi thinks I've been rushing to the toilet all night and probably farting so loudly and disgustingly that I've forced my husband onto the sofa. Great. Just great. While most new brides would be being passionately ravaged on the first night of their honeymoon, I can't even get through the first night of a pretend honeymoon without having the pretend shits. This is mortifying. I'm almost tempted to just blow our cover, but I can't now. We're way too far into the lie. Will's taking a sip of his orange juice with his wedding ring flashing right now.

'Yes.' I rub my stomach. 'It was a long night, but I'm okay now,' I tell Medhi.

A long night? What am I even saying?

Will's lips twitch and I can tell he's trying not to laugh.

'This is terrible. You need to be careful. Some of the sellers in the square, their restaurants are not so safe. You need to eat in the good places,' Medhi says, looking worried.

Will nods gravely, correcting his expression to strike a more serious note.

'Come to me next time. I will tell you where the good places are,' Medhi says.

'We will,' I reply, realising that I'm still rubbing my stomach.

'Are you in pain, Natalie?' Medhi asks, noticing.

'Oh, no. I'm fine.' I immediately pull my hand away and plaster a smile on my face. 'I'm good.'

Medhi eyes me sceptically. 'One second. My wife will have something to help you. She makes the best herbal teas. Remedies for everything! I will ask her.' Medhi turns to go and get Amira.

'No, honestly, I'm fine!' I insist, but it's too late, he's already off.

'So ill from my tagine that I got the shits and farted all night?' I hiss at Will the moment Medhi's out of earshot.

'Sorry,' Will replies, looking both guilty and amused. 'It sounded better in my head, then when it came out, it was a bit ...'

'Humiliating?' I suggest.

Will covers his mouth with his hand and I can tell he's trying hard not to laugh.

'I'm glad you find this so hilarious, Will. But now Medhi and his whole family are going to think I have the shits. It's hardly the five-star relaxing luxury experience I was expecting!' I moan.

'You're probably not the first person they've had staying here who's had the shits,' Will points out.

'Fabulous! I'll just join the cannon of guests who've had the shits then.' I slump back into my chair.

Will laughs, in spite of himself.

Amira comes over to our table, frowning, clearly fretting over my wellbeing.

'Come with me, Natalie,' she says. 'I will help you feel better. I have a remedy.'

'No really, it's fine. I'm feeling much better.'

'Please. Please let me help you,' she implores, fixing me with a look of almost maternal concern. I feel like I can't say no without upsetting her. I've finished my breakfast. It's not like I'm doing anything.

'Okay,' I reply. 'Thank you.'

She smiles, beckoning for me to follow as she turns to head back to the kitchen. I shoot Will a look as I get up to go.

The kitchen is full of pots and pans and jars of spices and herbs. There are shelves on the walls piled high with cookery books and old hand-written recipes pinned to the walls. A few other staff are milling about; one is doing the dishes, another is chopping onions and another is mixing some kind of dough. They look my way, and although they seem a little taken aback by the presence of a guest in the kitchen, they smile politely and continue with what they're doing.

'Take a seat,' Amira says, gesturing for me to sit down at a table where I imagine the staff eat their meals.

'Tell me what's wrong,' she insists, sitting down opposite with an intent look on her face.

Oh God, she truly cares about helping me. I make up some generic symptoms and Amira nods gravely, before setting to work mixing herbs, grinding them in a pestle and mortar.

'I will make you a tea my mother used to make me when I was sick. It will make you feel much better, I promise,' Amira says warmly.

'Thanks so much,' I reply, feeling grateful even though I'm not even remotely ill. Amira really does seem to want me to get better, taking me under her wing as though I'm not just a guest at her hotel, but family. It's so sweet and kind.

'You know, our housekeeper came downstairs, and she thought you and Will were fakes,' Amira tuts as she tips the herbs into a silver teapot.

I gawp at her. 'What?' I utter, with an awkward laugh.

'Yes. It is quite common around here,' Amira tells me, glancing over as she holds the teapot under the tap, filling it with water. 'Friends or couples book a room and then pretend to be married to get upgraded to the honeymoon suite. Quite a lot of hotels experience this problem. Some have even started asking to see marriage certificates.'

'Right ...' I squirm. 'I can't believe people would do that!' I add, feigning indignation.

'They want the nicest room. The champagne. The chocolates. It's a big problem.' Amira sighs, flicking the hob on and placing the teapot onto the heat.

'Oh no, how awful,' I say, plastering an appalled look onto my face.

'I know. I told her you and Will are not like that. I'm a good judge of character. I know you are good people. I knew you wouldn't do something like that. I was sure there was another reason, then when Medhi told me about your stomach problems, it made sense. I knew it had to be something,' she says, smiling kindly as the flames of the hob lick the teapot.

I nod, feeling like the worst person in the world. 'Yes. Just an upset stomach, nothing untoward!'

Amira smiles. 'I know.'

Amira tells me about her family's herbal remedies as the teapot begins to boil on the stove. I'm struck by a sudden urge to just confess. The way Amira is being so caring and seeing the best in me despite how much of a fake I am is making me feel terrible, yet every time I try to think of a way of explaining, the words don't quite come. Amira takes the teapot off heat and retrieves a cup from a cupboard, pouring the tea into it.

She hands me the cup. 'I hope this helps,' she says.

'Thank you so much,' I say, smiling gratefully as I take it from her.

I can't bring myself to 'fess up. The moment's passed. I need to force the guilty thoughts out of my mind and focus on something more constructive. So Will and I have lied? It may have been a pretty bad thing to do but we have to live with it now. I'll make it up to Amira and Medhi. I'll get them some press coverage or something – a nice magazine feature. I'll wave my PR wand and zap away the stain on my conscience. Yes, that'll do.

I take a sip of the tea, relishing its fruity medicinal taste. 'I feel better already, Amira.'

'It's no problem, no problem at all,' Amira says. Her kindness is so unnerving. Every caring comment highlights what a terrible person I am.

I gaze around her kitchen and try to think of something to say to lighten the mood. I take in the rows of spices, oils, herbs, but I've never been much good in the kitchen and they don't inspire a conversation starter. When I was in London, I pretty much lived off Pret sandwiches, sushi and M&S ready meals. My eyes suddenly land on a framed picture of Amira and Medhi on display on a shelf next to a stack of cookbooks.

'Aww, what a sweet picture,' I say, attempting to stand up to get a better look, but Amira insists I stay put.

She takes the picture from the shelf and hands it to me. Amira is wearing a gorgeous emerald-green jewelled kaftan with a gold headpiece and a magnificent flowing veil. She looks absolutely stunning. Medhi is holding her hand and gazing at her with a look of total adoration.

'It was a beautiful day – the day I married my soulmate,' Amira says, smiling fondly at the memory.

'Wow, you both look so happy,' I comment dreamily.

It's true, they really do. They're both smiling from ear to ear as though they want nothing more from the world than each other. It's a really sweet shot and looking at it, I can't help feeling a little sad. I've never had that all-consuming overwhelming love before. Love that makes you feel completely overjoyed and elated. Pretty much all of my romances have been fleeting. Since I broke up with Leroy, I've been able to see that what he and I had wasn't founded on unconditional love, it was mainly just lust and a bit of neediness too. At the time, the social pressure of turning 30 and being unmarried had started to get to me. I don't think I was even consciously aware of it, but I've always been someone who's kept up with the people around me, even achieving things faster than others. I didn't take a gap year and I was the first of my friends to graduate, I was the first to set up a business, the first to move into my own flat. I guess I didn't want to end up the last to get married. I wanted to settle down and fit in. But now I realise that settling down because all your friends are settling down is the worst possible reason and will always come back to bite you. Now I'm the first of my friends to be a single mum, the first to move back home and even the first to go on a fake honeymoon. I guess that's karma for you! What I should have looked for in a relationship wasn't convenience and good timing, it should have been this: what Amira and Medhi have – pure, heartfelt, joyful love.

'How old were you when you got married Amira?' I ask. She looks younger in the picture, but not especially young.

'I was 33. I'd started to wonder if I'd ever find anyone, then Medhi came along.' Amira smiles fondly as I hand the picture back to her.

'That's so inspiring,' I muse. A year older than me. Maybe I'll get there one day too.

'Inspiring?' Amira quirks her brow as she places the picture back on the shelf.

'Err … yes. Inspiring!' I say, sounding ridiculous. I really need to work on my lying skills. 'I mean love, isn't it just inspiring?' I smile moronically.

'Yes, of course!' Amira replies, looking a little perplexed. 'You'll have to show me your wedding pictures later too.'

Wedding pictures?

'Tonight?' Amira suggests.

'Tonight …?' I echo.

'You must have them? On your phone, at least? I'd love to see,' Amira says, her eyes twinkling. She's right, any newlywed would have snaps of their wedding on their phone. Why on earth did I not anticipate this kind of thing? I thought faking being married would be easy, but it's a nightmare.

One of the staff, the man chopping onions, glances over. He has warm brown eyes and a mysterious jagged scar on his cheek. The woman mixing dough also looks over her shoulder.

'Wedding pictures?' she chimes in.

Amira nods. 'Natalie and her husband Will are staying in our honeymoon suite. Such a beautiful couple!'

'Oh, an English wedding! I'd love to see the pictures too,' she adds. Even the male chef chopping onions seems interested, smiling enthusiastically. The guy doing the dishes doesn't seem interested. If only more people could be like him.

'Of course!' I reply in a slightly high-pitched tone. 'Yes! I left my phone in my room, but I'll show you tonight.'

'I can't wait,' Amira says, topping up my tea.

I take a sip, smiling brightly.

Chapter 12

'We have to do what?' Will balks, perching at the end of our double bed, which has been neatly made by the nosy housekeeper.

'We just need to fake a wedding photograph. It won't be that hard,' I insist.

Will eyes me like I'm crazy.

'You owe me, Will. After the whole shits incident.'

'Hang on a minute, I owe you wedding photographs?'

I explain the entire conversation with Amira – including the housekeeper's suspicions, Amira's wariness over fake honeymooners, and her sweet trusting motherly nature that made it impossible to admit that we'd been lying.

'Oh my God,' Will groans when I get to the end of the story.

'See? We can't get out of it. She asked to see pictures tonight,' I tell him.

'Can't we just pretend we don't have any on us?' Will suggests weakly, clearly knowing this doesn't ring true.

'Come on, Will. If we were really newlyweds, of course we'd have pictures. It would look so suspicious if we didn't.'

'I suppose you're right,' Will grumbles. 'But we told Medhi and Amira we got married in a little church in England. How the hell are we going to fake that in Marrakech?' Will asks.

'I guess we should just leave out the church bit? We said we had an outdoor reception. Let's just take an outdoor shot. A garden's a garden after all, right? Whether it's in England or Marrakech.'

'As long as you crop out the palm trees,' Will grumbles.

I roll my eyes. 'Come on, it won't be that hard. It might be fun!' I suggest.

'Hmm …' Will raises an eyebrow, not entirely convinced.

* * *

'So, where shall we take these pictures then?' I ask as Will and I wander down the street, away from the hotel.

It's just as lively and chaotic as it was last night, with donkey carts, stray cats and vendors trying to get our attention like paparazzi, calling me 'blue eyes' and Will, 'Tom Hiddleston'.

I Googled wedding pictures before we left the hotel, while Will was in the shower. Far too many of them feature couples walking down the steps of a church while ecstatic friends and relatives throw confetti over them. I mean talk about setting the bar high. Fortunately, I found another style of shot which is equally charming, almost more romantic in fact, which I reckon Will and I can fake. It's the walking through a garden, holding hands, gazing into each other's eyes shot. Or if not gazing, whispering sweet nothings into each other's ear. Basically, you just have to look like you're having a private moment, oblivious to the world (apart from the photographer snapping away, obviously). Will and I have decided that our fake wedding had a boho vibe, not because either of us is particularly into the boho vibe, but because the closest thing I've packed to a wedding dress is an embroidered white lace flowing maxi dress that just about passes as a boho wedding gown. And at least with a boho vibe, I can wear my hair down and to complete the look, all I need is a bunch of flowers. Will happened to pack a white shirt and smart trousers to wear in case we were going to any fancy restaurants, and we figure with a few tweaks on Photoshop, we might just be able to get away with it.

'I can't believe I'm doing this,' Will comments as we weave through the souk. 'Obviously, we can't take the pictures in a well-known garden because Medhi and Amira might recognise it. We need to find somewhere they probably won't know about. Somewhere private or really non-descript.'

Will looks into the distance as though the perfect park might present itself, but we're deep in the souk and it's just rugs and spices and pots as far as the eye can see. I nod.

'Good point. But where?' I ask, in case Will might know somewhere from his last trip here, even though I don't think he spent much time during that trip in gardens.

'Let's just wander around until we find a park. Somewhere that might work,' Will suggests, as we make our way through the bustling crowds.

We wander through the souk, trying to find a street that might lead to a park, but it's a maze of shops with each stall-lined street seemingly leading on to another. Eventually, we stumble upon a market, which seems to be aimed more at locals selling household supplies rather than tourist souvenirs. One of the vendors is selling rolls of fabric. I spot some embroidered white lace and Will and I both agree that it would make a good veil. We buy a couple of metres from the vendor. I figure I can pin it to my head with bobby pins and with a few artful tweaks on Photoshop, it should look just about passable.

We stop at a bakery and buy a selection of ridiculously cheap pastries. For the cost of one pain au chocolat and a loaf of bread at a London bakery, we manage to buy a couple of dozen bite-sized pastries and two bottles of water. We're so busy exploring the market that I almost forget about what we actually set out to do: find a park to take wedding pictures. We resolve to stop shopping and concentrate on our mission, wandering further away from the market. Eventually, we emerge into a less bustling chaotic part of Marrakech. It's more suburban, with homes interspersed with banks, pharmacies and mosques. We keep a lookout for a park, walking street after street. I'm beginning to get tired, and I'm about to suggest that we just give up on this whole silly idea when we stop by some railings to get our bottles of water from my bag. I peer through the railings and spot a boring-looking park. There are no exotic plants, no palm trees, no unique features. It could easily pass as a park in England and it's pretty much empty, too. It even has a public toilet where we can get changed. It's perfect.

'Will, what about this place?' I ask.

Will looks up from unscrewing the cap on his water bottle and peers through the railings.

'It's so boring!' he says, his eyes lighting up. 'It's ideal.'

'I know!' I grin, clapping my hands together.

'So, erm, who are we going to get to take the pictures?' I ask.

'You don't have a tripod?' Will gawps.

'No! I only have my phone, Will!' I say, waving my iPhone at him.

Will slumps against the railings. 'So not only do we have to dress up and pretend to have just got married, but we have to do so in front of another human being?' he groans.

'Umm ... yes?' I venture in a tiny voice, smiling awkwardly. 'It'll be fine! We'll just ask someone.' I smile optimistically, determined to make these shots work. Once we've got Medhi and Amira off our back, we can start to relax.

'Okay ...' Will relents.

We head into the park. It's really not the nicest place. A bin in the corner is overflowing with rubbish. The park is teeming with pigeons and the pathway where I imagined Will and I taking our shots is covered in pigeon shit. I pull a face at Will, who looks equally uncomfortable. I wouldn't be surprised if there were a few rats under the bushes. The whole place feels a bit wild and abandoned and I can immediately see why there are absolutely no locals relaxing on the park benches. All I can think as we head to the cobwebby toilets is, thank God for Photoshop. Lauren's an absolute pro at it. I get her to do bits and pieces for my clients from time to time. I'll send her the pictures this afternoon and I bet with a few clicks, she'll probably be able to make this crummy old park look like a palace garden. I'm sure she'll be up for helping, she does kind of owe me a favour with all the freelance work I've sent her way over the years.

I venture tentatively into the disused bathroom and change into my wedding dress, or more accurately, my River Island lacey maxi dress. I brought some silver sandals with me that I'd planned to wear by the pool, and they just about pass as wedding shoes. I did my make-up and curled my hair back at the hotel, but I add a bit of blusher for good measure, apply a slick of lipstick and preen my locks a bit. I check out my reflection: nice, but not quite bridal. I add my makeshift veil and end up looking like a child dressing up for a school play. It's a far cry from the kind of thing I imagined I'd wear at my wedding to Leroy. I picked out my perfect dress for that wedding. I spent ages flicking through bridal magazines trying to find one, but they were all either too sparkly or puffy or whimsical or tapered or chic. I couldn't find something that felt me, then finally I landed upon this dress that had a sort of asymmetrical fishtail style and it was just so cool and striking and different that I knew it was the one. I started saving for it since I knew Leroy wouldn't be able to help with the cost and the dress didn't exactly come cheap. When our wedding fell through, I ended up putting all the money into my deposit savings account. I guess houses make better investments then dresses anyway.

I come out of the loo, and find Wil, already standing, leaning by the wall in his suit, gazing off into the distance, people-watching passers-by on the street beyond the park railings. I pluck a few tulips from a nearby flowerbed to use as my wedding bouquet.

'Natalie!' Will says, taking me in, his eyes lighting up. 'You look ...' He pauses, searching for the right word. He smiles, a little awkwardly. 'You look really g- g- good. Gorgeous. You look gorgeous.'

I raise an eyebrow. 'Not good?'

'I was going to say good but what I meant was gorgeous. I just wasn't sure if I should say that. Is that appropriate?' Will asks, smiling almost shyly. What is this?

'Gorgeous is much better than good, Will. Thank you,' I comment, laughing casually, even though I can't help feeling a little twinge of something. What is it? Attraction? Flirtation? Hope?

'You like the veil?' I ask, fingering its edges.

'Yeah, I love it! It suits you!' Will remarks, smiling affectionately.

I laugh. I'll never get my head around what men find attractive. I take in Will's attire. He's wearing his black trousers and white shirt. He's even added a red tie. He looks incredible. The last time I saw Will in a suit, he was being interviewed about politics on Sky. He looked good then and he looks even better now. He looks so tall and dapper, his broad shoulders and fine form accentuated by the sharp tailoring and neatness of his outfit.

'You look good too. Gorgeous,' I add, genuinely meaning it.

A moment passes between us, when we're just gazing at one another, taking each other in. Will is seriously handsome. Obviously, I knew that already, but seeing him now, it really hits home. He was always attractive, but he's masculine now in a way he wasn't back at school. His body's strong and imposing, and he has an air of suaveness and authority in his smart clothes that he never had back when he was trying to be a skater boy. He's hot now. A head-turner. A bird chirps in the tree overhead, interrupting my thoughts and bringing me back to the task at hand.

'Okay, umm, I'm just going to go and, umm, find a photographer,' I say, scurrying off, hoping my face hasn't revealed the adoration I've been feeling. I can't help wondering what Will was thinking as he looked at me. His eyes had a faraway look about them. I wonder what he thinks of me now compared to the 16-year-old girl I used to be.

Feeling a little flustered, I walk out of the garden towards the street. People immediately start pointing and staring. I smile weakly and walk towards a pair of tourists looking a little lost. They're a middle-aged couple and they appear fairly ordinary and approachable.

'Hi!' I beam. 'I'm Natalie. How are you? I just wondered if you might be able to take my picture?' I ask. A reasonable request. Tourists ask people to take their picture all the time.

'Umm, sure,' the woman replies in an American accent, lifting her sunglasses to get a better look at my dress. She looks me up and down, taking in my veil and my white lacey dress, her face a picture of confusion. Her husband appears equally perplexed.

'Is that … a veil?' he asks.

'Umm, yes!' I reply brightly, pleased that my makeshift veil looks convincing.

Will appears by my side and introduces himself. It turns out the couple are called Susan and Geoff. They're from Ohio, and they're on a trip across Europe but they thought they'd make a detour to Marrakech.

'So, why are you wearing a veil? Are you getting married?' Susan asks.

A reasonable question.

Will gives me a pointed look as he awaits my response. I can tell he isn't going to step in and save me this time. Not that I'd want him to. He'd probably make up some awful excuse about how I'm wearing this get-up because I got the shits in my regular clothes or something.

'We, umm, it's just our thing, really,' I say.

Will raises an eyebrow.

'Your thing?' Geoff echoes.

'Yeah, we, umm, go around the world and take pictures in wedding gear. Bit different, eh?' I laugh.

The man and woman look at me like I'm completely insane

and I'm almost worried they're going to do a runner. I need to make this sound less crazy.

'Why would you do that though?' the woman asks.

'It's um, it's a project. About love and travelling. We're Instagrammers and you know how competitive it is on there,' I tell them, getting into my stride. 'We basically travel the world, taking pictures at sites all over the place, but we make it different by wearing a suit and gown. It makes us stand out. You need a USP on there.'

'Ah, I see …' Susan nods, as though it's all making sense.

Even Will's nodding. In fact, he looks quite impressed. Ha!

'What's it called?' Susan asks. 'Your Instagram account.'

'Oh, umm …' Shit. Shit. Think of something. I gaze across the road for inspiration and spot a billboard for a brand of toothpaste featuring a crest of a wave in the arctic and a slogan about the toothpaste being 'ice cool'.

'It's called Groom and Bride, Cross the Tide,' I tell her.

'Awesome!' Her face lights up. 'I love that.'

Geoff nods, impressed. 'Nice.'

Even Will is smiling, although I think he's just trying not to laugh.

'I'm going to look it up,' Susan says, reaching into the pocket of her trousers for her phone.

'Oh, could you take our picture first?' I urge her, my voice a little desperate. The last thing I need is for her to go on Instagram and realise Will and I are complete frauds. 'We're just in a bit of a hurry,' I add.

'Of course! No problem,' she says, shrugging off the thought. I feel a palpable wave of relief.

We all head into the garden.

'You could have just told her your veil was a headscarf!' Will whispers as we walk along the path.

Damn it. He's absolutely right. I could have just passed it off as a cultural thing, but no, I had to go and make up an entire

Instagram backstory.

'Oh God ...' I grumble.

'It's okay! We can do this!' Will reassures me.

'So why this garden?' Susan pipes up, her lip curling in disgust as she takes it in.

'We just thought it was a nice spot,' Will says, in an authoritative tone.

Susan and Geoff exchange a perplexed look, that Will and I choose to ignore.

I hand Susan my phone.

'We're just going to walk down this pathway,' I tell her. 'If you could take a few pictures, that would be great.'

'Sounds good.' Susan smiles, holding up the camera.

Will and I get into position, standing on the pigeon shit-spattered path.

'Act like you're whispering something to me,' I tell him.

'What? Why?'

'To make it look intimate. Obviously.' I roll my eyes.

'Okay.' Will sighs.

'Ready?' Susan says, looking at us through the camera screen on my phone.

'Yes! We really appreciate this,' I say.

'No problem,' Susan replies, gearing up to take the first few pictures.

Will and I start walking. I pretend to laugh at something he's said. He smirks. Then I poke him in the side.

'Um ...' Susan utters. 'These aren't coming out that romantic. Is that okay?'

'No, it's not,' I hiss at Will.

Susan looks up from the camera, a worried expression on her face.

'Sorry Susan. I was telling Will off.'

Will's still smirking.

'How about you kiss?' Geoff suggests, glancing between Susan and me and Will with a helpful expression. 'That would look romantic.'

Kiss?

'Um …' Oh God, I can't think of an excuse as to why we wouldn't kiss. We're meant to be bride and groom Instagrammers for goodness' sake, of course we would kiss.

'We could,' Will says, catching my eye.

What's got into him? One minute, he's making up embarrassing stories about how I've got the shits and the next minute he's calling me gorgeous and wanting to kiss me.

I eye him. He really does look good in his suit. It's no wonder he was invited on TV all the time back when he was a journalist, he's just so easy on the eye. You wouldn't change the channel away from him in a hurry. But beneath all that, he's still Will – the teenager I fell for so many years ago with his gorgeous jade and amber eyes and his endearing sweet nature.

'Okay, let's kiss,' I say. 'In the interest of authenticity,' I add under my breath so that only Will can hear.

'Exactly,' Will agrees, with a firm nod. 'In the interest of authenticity.'

'Okay, whenever you're ready,' Susan says, holding the camera up, poised to take a shot.

Will takes a step closer to me and places his hands on my waist. I look up at him, feeling nervous as I rest my hands on his hips. He's so close. His lips are only inches away from mine. He gazes into my eyes, smiling gently. An affectionate smile, full of warmth. God, he's a good actor. Or he actually wants to be doing this. I can't tell. I smile tentatively back and let my gaze wander down to his lips – thin, masculine, lightly pink, inviting, before looking back into his eyes. Will's hand moves across my back and he pulls me closer, closing his eyes as his lips meet mine. I close my eyes and kiss him. His lips are cool and soft, but the moment our lips meet, something happens. It's like we're two magnets snapping together and neither of us wants to let go.

Will kisses me properly, moving his lips against mine and before I know it, I'm enthusiastically kissing him back, our tongues are intertwining, his hand cups my face, drawing me even closer. I feel his warm hard body under his shirt. It's the most delicious passionate kiss. Far less clumsy than our kisses back at school. Will's confident now. An assured and skilled kisser.

'I think I have some decent shots,' Susan says, interrupting, coughing awkwardly.

Bloody Susan. Totally ruining the moment. Will pulls away, his eyes still on mine. They look tender even though Susan's no longer taking pictures. She may have put an end to the kiss, but it doesn't quite feel like the spell has been broken.

'Thanks Susan,' Will says, turning to her with a sheepish smile.

'No problem!' Susan replies, a little too brightly. She's acting like she's just seen a live sex show when it was only a kiss. Although it was a passionate one. I feel hot and flustered.

'Do you need any more pictures or is that it?' Susan asks.

Will and I flick through the shots. Our embrace looks spectacular. Eyes closed, lips locked.

Will looks incredibly handsome. I look pretty nice too. We do look good together. The picture really does look like a wedding day snap of two totally loved up newlyweds unable to keep their hands off each other, their love and excitement evident to all. It rivals Amira and Medhi's with its passion and romance. Aside from the pigeon droppings, this is the kind of wedding photo that I used to dream about as a little girl. A happily ever after type shot. It's beautiful. Pinterest, eat your heart out!

'These are perfect. Thanks so much!' I gush.

'No problem at all,' Susan says. 'I'll look up your account later.'

Will smiles, his face strained. 'Brilliant!' he says.

'Yes, great!' I add.

We thank Susan again and she and Geoff set off down the road back towards the centre of Marrakech.

'The poor woman's going to be completely confused when she

can't find our account later,' I mutter as we watch them retreat into the distance.

'I know!' Will replies guiltily.

I look at him, trying to think of something to say, something to acknowledge that kiss, but I don't know where to begin. I can't bring myself to ask him outright whether he was acting or if he felt something. And even if I did ask, do I even want to know the answer? Do I actually want something more with Will? I'd sworn off men before I came on this trip, and even though that kiss has just stirred everything up – my feelings, my desire, the past – I'm still not sure how I'd feel about getting involved with someone, even if they were my childhood sweetheart. And anyway, I have Hera to worry about these days, I can't just recklessly follow my heart like I used to.

'So, what shall we do now?' I ask.

Will is squinting at something in the distance. A small sign. He steps closer towards it.

'It's in Arabic, but I think it says something is a kilometre in that direction,' Will says, pointing into the distance.

'What's that way?' I ask.

'I don't know.' Will shrugs. 'Let's find out!'

'Okay,' I agree, figuring we have nothing better to do.

We grab our stuff and wander down the path, which grows increasingly less grotty the further away we get from the street. I suppose there are less scraps of food to attract vermin and fewer people coming in off the street to leave rubbish. After walking along the path, further and further away from the street, and talking about how much we both hope we never see Susan and Geoff again, the path finally gives way to a surprisingly beautiful lake. The water is a gorgeous chalky blue shade and it's surrounded by reeds and wild flowers.

'Oh my God, talk about a diamond in the rough!' I enthuse, taking it all in. 'Do you think this is what the sign was pointing to?'

'Must be! It's beautiful,' Will comments. 'We should've done the pictures down here!'

'Ah well,' I sigh. 'We can still take some. Wedding selfies.'

'True. Let's sit down for a bit,' he suggests. 'It's lovely here.'

He's right, it really is lovely. Butterflies dart between the flowers and dragonflies skim over the surface of the water. It's like a serene untouched enclave in the midst of a bustling city. I spot a grassy patch of ground beneath a nearby tree and suddenly remember the Moroccan pastries we bought earlier.

'I've got those pastries in my bag! Let's have a picnic,' I suggest.

We settle down on the grass, using my pashmina as a rug. I take the pastries out of my bag and tear open the bag they're in, laying it on the pashmina like a makeshift plate. I sit cross-legged opposite Will and take a bite of the crumbling pasty.

'So, what were your wedding pictures like? Must have been better than those,' I venture, unable to resist finding out a little bit more about Will's marriage.

'My wedding pictures!' Will leans back on his elbows as he gazes out over the lake. 'They probably couldn't have been more different to the ones we just took, that's for sure.' Will laughs.

'What do you mean? I guess you didn't go for the boho pigeon shit look?!'

'No, not at all! It was very fancy. We got married in an old seventeenth-century church in Cornwall, then had our reception in a five-star hotel nearby – a spectacular converted old castle. We hired a top photographer; he knew exactly how to get the right shots. We had so many pictures taken. It didn't stop, from the church to the reception, it was just constant. To be honest, I think we spend the whole reception taking photos, I don't really remember talking to many of our guests,' Will adds, a little regretfully. I take in what he's said. The Will I used to know was hardly the fancy five-star top photographer type. Was it his wife's influence or did he just want to make a big fuss out of his special day?

'Top photographer, eh?' I comment.

'Yeah, not exactly Susan and Geoff with an iPhone,' Will jokes.

'My ex was like that. Always wanted the best of the best. She came from a very wealthy family.'

'Right …' I utter. 'I was thinking that didn't sound very *us*.

I'd heard on the grapevine that Will's ex-wife was pretty posh, but I didn't realise just how posh. Most people who get married in Chiddingfold tie the knot at the local church with Blake – a barber from the village with a passion for photography – taking the pictures. We're not really five-star converted castle and fancy photographer type people.

'No, it felt a bit weird at the time, to be honest, but I just went along with it. It was like Elsa had all these ideas already of how she wanted the photo album to look and we just had to create that vision. It was a bit like the pictures were shaping us, rather than what we were doing and feeling shaping the pictures,' Will muses, reaching for a pastry.

'I shouldn't be hard on Elsa though,' he says, picking up a crumbly pastry with a glazed clementine on it. 'We're from Chiddingfold where people aren't really like that, but she was from a much more competitive world. All her friends were getting married and there was definitely an element of competitiveness about the whole thing: who had the best wedding, the best cake, the best dress, the best pictures. Even the best husband.'

I snort. 'The best husband?!'

Will laughs. 'Yeah, I'd like to think of myself as having been one of the best, if not the best, but she divorced me, so what can you do?'

He takes a bite of his pastry.

I try not to laugh, yet I can't help giggling. Will's attitude to his marriage is undeniably comical.

'Sorry Will, sucks to be you, eh?' I reach over and squeeze his arm.

Will laughs. 'It was mutual, but now she's with a millionaire finance guy. They seem like a much better match. They're getting married in the Bahamas!'

'Wow!' I comment. 'She can't really have just left you for an upgrade though?'

'No, it wasn't quite that ruthless! It's a bit of a sad story really, in the sense that it wasn't really very dramatic at all. I was working a lot, travelling a lot. Elsa was also really busy with work and we just became like ships passing in the night. And when we were together, we were just kind of ...'

Will pauses, searching for the right word. 'Flat'.

'Flat?' I echo.

'Yeah, I know this sounds bad, but it felt like we were bored. The spark had just gone.'

'God.' I pull a face. 'That is a bit depressing.'

'I know!' Will sighs.

'So you just drifted apart?'

'Yeah, basically, but we plodded along like that for far, far too long. Then Elsa got offered a really great job in New York and that was the catalyst for us splitting up. I was still working for the paper back then and we talked through the options – flying back and forth to see each other or me applying for a VISA and trying to find work in the States, but all of those ideas just seemed a bit far-fetched. In the end, we both admitted that the best thing to do was just part ways,' Will tells me.

'I see. I see what you mean about it being a bit of an anticli-mactic story,' I comment.

'Yeah. Sometimes a big external event just puts everything into perspective. It was for the best really. In retrospect, I kind of rushed into marriage after my dad died. A weird sort of panic set in. And I think Elsa rushed into marriage with me, but probably more for the sake of it than because of loneliness, like me,' Will says.

'Loneliness?' I echo.

'Yeah. I felt quite lonely when my dad died. Really lonely. That's why I'll always have a fondness for Elsa even if we are divorced. She was my companion. Through that time and even though it wasn't meant to be. She still helped me get through it,' Will says.

He wipes the crumbs off his shirt and casually reaches for another pastry as though unaware of how heart-wrenching his words are. The Chiddingfold grapevine never revealed to me just how cut up Will was after losing his dad, or that his grief might have influenced his urge to get married. He's been through so much and yet it's clear he's come out on the other side. He doesn't seem bitter about any of it – his dad's death, his failed marriage, even losing his job. He seems to have adopted a philosophical stance, learning from everything he's been through and being grateful for what he has. I can't help noticing how Will's emotional maturity is world's away from Leroy, whose idea of a heart to heart was a box of chocolates and make-up sex. He made the people on Jeremy Kyle look eloquent.

Will takes another of the clementine pastries. 'It's funny. If Elsa hadn't got that job in New York, we might still be together, pretending everything was okay while secretly being really quite unhappy together.'

'Oh well, it all worked out okay in the end. Now you're here with me!' I joke, trying to lighten the mood.

'Exactly! Thank God for my failed marriage,' Will jokes.

A moment's silence passes between us, while we watch fireflies darting over the surface of the water.

'How did you meet?' I ask, curiously, still feeling bemused at how different Will's life with Elsa must have been.

'At a press conference. I was covering a story on the collapse of a global bank and she was doing the PR. We swapped cards and the rest is history!' Will tells me.

'Swapped cards, so romantic,' I tease.

Will smirks. 'Beats Tinder though, I guess,' he says, rolling onto his front and reaching for another pastry. 'What about you and Leroy?'

'What about us?' I grumble.

'How did you two meet?' Will asks.

I tell him how we were both working out in the gym one

134

Sunday afternoon. The gym was deserted and as I sat on the rowing machine, Leroy caught me checking him out as he was weightlifting at the other side of the gym. Then he came over and we got talking. It's hardly the stuff of fairy tales and relaying the story to Will, it hits me how unsurprising it probably seems that Leroy would have eventually chatted someone else up the same way he approached me.

'And you were engaged?' Will says.

'Yeah. He proposed to me in Pizza Express,' I tell him. 'I think we even paid for the meal with a voucher.'

Will snorts with laughter. 'Sorry, I shouldn't laugh!' he says, covering his mouth.

'It's okay! You had high end, I had bargain bucket,' I joke.

Will sniggers. 'Oh my God. And what was the wedding going to be like? Do they do vouchers for them too?'

I poke him. 'It would have been like the wedding I described on the plane, actually. Steel drums, the village church, a summer's day,' I admit, a little sheepishly. 'It was my dream wedding to be honest, I just didn't have the dream guy to match.'

Will smiles, a sad sympathetic smile. 'One day, we'll get it right. Dream people and dream weddings,' he says sweetly.

'Yeah, fingers crossed!' I reply, reaching for another pastry.

Chapter 13

'You look wonderful!' Amira enthuses, taking in the photos, which thanks to Lauren have been artfully tweaked and now look like genuinely gorgeous album-worthy snaps.

They're so gorgeous, in fact, that I found myself sitting on the balcony of our hotel room earlier just gazing at them. The kiss Susan captured looks as intense as it felt and the whole vibe between me and Will is so romantic, with Will in his suit and me in my wedding dress, enveloped in his strong arms. I've spent so long, since Leroy, pushing down my romantic side and focusing only on Hera and my business, that it feels a little unsettling to be kissed and not only to be kissed, but to have photographic evidence of the kiss to pour over.

'Medhi! Come and have a look at this.' Amira beckons Medhi over, who seems equally enamoured with mine and Will's wedding shot.

'You can see the love between you,' Medhi says, smiling sweetly.

'Yes!' I laugh, glancing at Will, who has an awkward smile plastered over his face.

'Where is all this passion at the hotel?' Medhi asks, his eyes flickering with warmth and good humour. 'I know we are in Marrakech and we don't do public displays of affection, but you're allowed to touch! Especially at the hotel.'

'Oh, haha!' I look over at Will, who is also laughing awkwardly. We're clearly nowhere near tactile enough for newlyweds.

'Good to know!' he says, reaching over and giving me a bro-style slap on the back, like I'm his mate in the pub.

I raise an eyebrow. What was that?

Medhi and Amira exchange a glance. They must think we're the weirdest couple.

Amira hands my phone back to me. 'Thank you for sharing this. It must have been a perfect day.'

'It was,' I reply.

'Oh yes, definitely,' Will echoes.

I place my phone in my bag and slip my arm through Will's as we say goodbye to Amira and Medhi and head off to dinner. Our honeymoon package includes a romantic candlelit dinner for two at a fancy restaurant in the centre of Marrakech. Fortunately, the restaurant isn't run by Amira and Medhi, so we won't have to lie all evening.

'Why did you slap me on the back?' I laugh once we're out of earshot.

'I panicked!'

'You didn't panic earlier when we kissed?' I blurt out.

'No, I didn't,' Will says, giving me a tender, lingering look.

Suddenly, I'm acutely aware of his body next to mine. I've still got my arm through his and I can feel his body heat. I still want to ask if he wanted to kiss me or if it was all an act for the photos. I want to know, and yet at the same time, I don't. Part of me is enjoying believing that it was real. Maybe I'm starting to get seduced by my own lies because now I feel like I almost want to believe in the fantasy that Will and I are this loved-up couple.

Will reaches into his pocket, pulls a map out and peers at it, making sure we're heading the right way to the restaurant.

We walk down a few more side streets until we arrive at a tall, palatial building. The restaurant is unlike anything I've ever seen before. It's certainly worlds away from anywhere I've eaten in England. It doesn't feel remotely like a restaurant; it's such an architectural wonder that it could be a tourist destination in its own right. It's an ancient Mughal temple with intricately carved marble walls lined with pillars and tall archways. The walls are so tall that they defy ordinary dimensions. They must be at least forty feet high. The ceiling is covered in carved stars adding to the dream-like otherworldly feel.

Will looks equally awestruck as the waiter leads us to our table. It's been decked out with candles and even our napkins have been artfully folded in the shape of hearts. I glance at Will, who smiles wryly as we sit down.

The waiter hands us menus and even though we had tagines at Jemaa el-Fnaa, they sound so delicious that neither of us can resist ordering them again. We order a few salads too and a bottle of red wine and clink glasses.

'To fake marriages,' I joke, once the waiter is out of earshot.

Will laughs. 'To fake marriages, and old friends,' he says, clinking his glass against mine.

I echo his toast, even though I can't help feeling a twinge of unease as I sip my wine. Old friends? Is that really all we are? That kiss earlier didn't feel like a kiss between old friends, it felt like something much more. I place my glass on the table and force myself to stop obsessing over the kiss. Am I still 16 for goodness' sake?

'I thought we'd peaked with the Dom Perignon on the plane, but this is something else,' I comment.

'I know, I can't believe it,' Will replies, seeming equally stunned by our good fortune.

We sip our wine and chat away, taking a few pictures of each other in the beautiful surroundings before our food arrives.

I've opted for a vegetarian tagine. It's served in a traditional pointed tagine dish and I lift the lid to discover glistening aubergine, chickpeas, carrots, peppers with figs and black olives, adorned with a garnish of coriander. Will's gone for lamb, which looks equally good, served in a rich sauce garnished with flaked almonds and chopped herbs. The waiter tops up our wine, before heading back to the kitchen.

We tuck into our food and it tastes just as delicious as it looks. Even more so, in fact. My vegetables have been cooked in a spicy honey sauce that's both sweet yet tangy, with the black olives giving it a salty edge. It's fresh and simple but ridiculously moreish.

'This is so good,' I comment between mouthfuls.

'It really is,' Will agrees, taking another bite.

Once we've made a significant dent in our tagines, we finally start talking properly again.

'Who'd have thought we'd end up in a place like this, eating tagine together,' I laugh, reaching for my wine.

'I know, life has a funny way of bringing people together, doesn't it?' Will replies, glancing up from his tagine.

'Totally.' I meet his gaze. I take him in, viewing him as a stranger would. I don't know if it's the wine or what, but I appraise him as though I don't know him or the context of this holiday at all. I see a handsome man in a wedding ring. A man in a navy shirt with a strong-boned face, a content expression and slightly dishevelled hair. Looks-wise, he still ticks all the boxes. Perhaps he created the boxes. He was my first love after all, he probably defined the blueprint of what I go for in a man.

Will glances up. 'Why are you looking at me like that?' he asks, a little warily.

'I was just thinking,' I tell him, taking another sip of wine. 'Do you ever wonder what might have happened between us if everything hadn't gone so wrong when we were teenagers?' I ask, the thought tumbling out of me.

Will finishes the last bite of his mean and places his knife and fork down.

'Yeah,' he says, eyeing me with an almost unnerving intensity.

'I've thought about that a few times.'

A few times? What the hell?

'Really?' I utter.

The notion just popped into my head and yet apparently, Will's thought about it a few times. Despite having been married for the best part of his twenties. Ever since I was 16, I've pushed Will out of my mind and yet he's been thinking of me. I lean a little closer.

'Yeah, of course. I've often wondered what might have been. You know my parents got together when they were 15? They were childhood sweethearts. Stayed together until my dad ... passed away,' Will says, looking back down at his plate.

I reach over and squeeze his hand. It may have been eight years since his dad died but it's clearly still hard for him to say that out loud.

'It's okay,' Will says, taking a deep breath and reaching for his wine. 'My parents met at school too, and they got together and stayed together, so yeah, I have often wondered what might have happened between us. I've been going through all my old stuff since I got back to Chiddingfold and I found loads of things that reminded me of you. A little charcoal portrait you did of me in Art Club. An album by The Strokes that you leant me and I clearly never gave back. Pictures from that camping trip we went on.'

Will gazes at me, a sweet, nostalgic look in his eyes. I picture him, sifting through all these things from our past and I feel almost guilty. I shut the past away, literally and metaphorically. When Will broke my heart so many years ago, I either threw out or packed away everything that reminded me of him. I tried to forget everything that had happened between us, yet Will's revisited some of those mementos. I can't help wondering what he felt when he found them.

'I wondered where that Strokes album had got to,' I joke, trying to sound more casual than I feel.

Will laughs. 'The portrait you did of me was actually really good. I pinned it up on the noticeboard of my flat.'

'Really?!' I balk, thinking back to the portrait. I still remember it, after all these years. Namely, because I still remember how I managed to capture Will's likeness and that at the time, I really wanted to keep the portrait to pore over it in my forlorn teenage way, yet Will took a shine to it and I couldn't exactly tell him how much I wanted it for myself. But I can't believe he still has it, sixteen years later! Now, I really have to know how he feels. Doesn't that stuff make him feel weird given what happened between us? Or has he somehow been able to look at the past through rose-tinted glasses?

'But everything went so wrong between us,' I blurt out. 'I mean, we got on amazingly for a while, but then you went for Jo and everything was just ... over.'

Will sighs. 'I know. I guess I freaked out. What my parents had at school turned into something so serious and I suppose I wasn't ready. We were so young and yet what we had felt so intense. I wanted something serious in a way, but I was also just a teenager who wanted to fit in with his friends. And all my friends were pressuring me to have sex, play the field, go to parties. I know it's pathetic that I gave in, but I was just immature.'

'Wow. All this time, I thought you just didn't care. I didn't realise you freaked out like that,' I comment, thinking aloud.

Will nods. 'I really liked you, Natalie. I know it sounds stupid, but I don't think I was ready for all the feelings I was having so I screwed it up like a dumb kid.'

'God, I can't believe this.' I take another sip of my wine, my heart lurching. I feel like the lovestruck girl I once was.

Now it's Will's turn to reach over and squeeze my hand. His wedding ring glints in the candlelight.

'You know I adored you back then?' I admit.

Will nods, looking contrite. 'I know. I wasn't mature enough to handle it. I knew if we got together, it would mean something. I knew it would be serious.'

I nod. He's right, it would have been serious. I loved Will back then and even though we were young, it felt real. It felt like it could go somewhere, but I can see why that freaked him out. He was just a 16-year-old boy – the best-looking guy in school – with loads of admirers and a ton of peer pressure from his friends to play the field and do what everyone else was doing. I can't blame him for not wanting to settle down back then. He naturally would have panicked if he thought our relationship might end up being as serious or as long-term as his parents'. I can see how easy it would have been for him to have got unnerved and freaked out, screwing the whole thing up. If I'd have been in his shoes, I might well have done the same.

'I'm so sorry, Natalie,' Will says. 'I know it's long overdue, but I'm so sorry.'

'It's okay, Will. Honestly, it's okay,' I insist, and for the first time in years, I genuinely mean it.

I feel relieved that Will and I have spoken about this. It may have happened years ago, but it still kind of felt like the elephant in the room. I gaze out over the beautiful restaurant, observing the diners chatting away and enjoying their food, taking in the waiters weaving between tables carrying delicious dishes.

'I do have a confession to make though,' Will continues.

'What? I thought we'd cleared the air. What now?' I ask apprehensively, racking my brains for what Will be about to say. Surely there's nothing else to 'fess up to?! I thought we'd cleared the air. I reach for my wine and take a sip.

Will places his knife and fork down on his plate. 'I knew you were back in Chiddingfold,' he says, meeting my gaze. 'My mum ran into yours at the Co-op and your mum mentioned you were both going to the fundraiser so that's why I went. I wanted to run into you.'

I raise an eyebrow. 'Really?' I balk, feeling genuinely taken aback. 'But you seemed surprised to see me there!'

'I know. I was playing it cool. I knew you'd be there, and I was actually really excited to see you again,' Will admits, looking a little sheepish.

I try to take in what he's saying. Did he go to the fundraiser because he wanted to catch up like old friends or did he go because he wanted to rekindle something? Did seeing the portrait I did of him and rediscovering all those old trinkets reignite his feelings? Or was he just curious to see how I am? Suddenly, another thought hits me.

'Hang on a minute, don't tell me you slipped Edna a twenty to get her to pull out our tickets so we'd end up on this holiday together?' I'm only half-joking.

Will laughs loudly. 'No! I'm not that bad! But I have to admit, I wasn't exactly disappointed when our names got read out.'

I'm in such shock that I can barely think of how to respond. Will wanted to see me all along? He did a good job of hiding it. I thought he was just as surprised to see me at the fundraiser as I was to see him. And to think, he wanted to go on holiday with me ... I try to think how to respond, but I feel totally lost for words. All of a sudden, a waiter comes over to our table carrying a cake, grinning widely. I'm about to tell him he's got the wrong table when he places the cake down between me and Will.

'For the newlyweds!' he gushes. The cake is covered in white frosting with iced love hearts surrounding the word, 'Congratulations'.

I look in shock at Will, who is clearly trying hard not to laugh.

Chapter 14

'Good morning lovebirds!' Medhi booms as Will and I come down from our room the following morning.

'Morning Medhi!' I reply brightly.

'How did you sleep?' Medhi asks. 'No issues?'

By issues does he mean diarrhoea?

'Nope! None at all,' I reply firmly.

Will smiles cheekily. I shoot him a glare, which only makes him smile more.

Fortunately, the nosy housekeeper is going to find our bed looking like it's been slept in by both of us. When Will and I got back last night, we decided to just sleep together. Not actually sleep together, but we slept side by side. The sofa was untouched. I managed to have a surprisingly restful night's sleep, despite the strangeness of sleeping next to a man for the first time in well over a year.

'I'm so glad,' Medhi says. 'I told you Amira's tea would work.'

'Oh, it worked a treat,' I insist, trying to ignore the increasingly familiar twinge of guilt.

'Excellent.' Medhi smiles. 'So, you're taking a carriage tour today?' Medhi asks. I know newlyweds are meant to spend their honeymoon barely leaving their king-sized bed, but there's only so much time Will and I can spend in the jacuzzi and today we've decided to properly explore Marrakech, starting with a horse-drawn carriage tour. Although I have no idea how Medhi knows about it. I glace at Will, who seems equally perplexed.

'Your carriage awaits!' Medhi says with aplomb, gesturing across reception.

'It's here already?' I cross reception to get a better look. Medhi's right. Our carriage awaits! There's a horse-drawn carriage that truly looks like something from a fairy tale with its enormous wheels, fringed canopy and beautiful shiny horses.

'Oh, it's so pretty!' I enthuse, glancing at Will. Even he looks taken aback by how gorgeous it is.

We thank Medhi and step outside. It's a beautiful day. The sky is a bright, azure blue and it's warm, but breezy. It's the perfect day for a nice leisurely tour of such a fascinating city. I take a few pictures of the carriage to message to my mum – she would love something like this.

The guide sets off, the horses' hooves clip-clapping against the ground as we set off. We gaze out of the carriage window, which is framed with a cute curtain and take in the sights, from the souk to the crafts markets to ancient palaces and tombs. The sights are incredible, and I've already taken dozens of pictures by the time we stop at one of the palaces, Bahia Palace, and have a wander around. The palace is a sprawling nineteenth-century estate with a beautiful courtyard embellished with colourful mosaics, carved columns, intricate archways and coloured glass windows. It's stunning and as well as taking incredible Instagram-worthy snaps, we wander through, reading about the history of the landmark and discovering more about Marrakech as we do so.

We stop off at nearby tombs – the Saadian tombs – which date back hundreds of years, containing the graves of long-lost emperors. Despite being a little spooky, they're stunningly beautiful, with decadent carved stone pillars and frescoes. We wander through, taking it in, until the site gets crowded with an afternoon rush of tourists, and we decide to hear back to our carriage.

Eventually, our guide drops us off back at the souk and as we step off and re-join the hustle and bustle, I feel like I'm waking up from a daydream. The antiquated carriage combined with the otherworldly sights was just so surreal, and so different to the commotion of the souk. Will and I are both hungry at this point, so we head to a nearby café for a quick lunch to refuel before doing a bit of shopping. I pick up some spices and a nice hand painted tagine dish for my mum, a gorgeous little embroidered kaftan for Hera, a big beaded necklace for Lauren and some bangles for my assistant, Emma. Will and I go halves on buying two beautiful throws for Mick and his niece Hannah for sorting us out with this holiday and we get the same for Medhi and Amira to thank them for everything. Will gets the sparkly purple slippers he was admiring the other day for his mum.

We end up with so much stuff that we decide to take a taxi back to the hotel to unload everything and enjoy the rest of the day's sunshine at the pool. We leave our bags in our room and get changed into our swimsuits, still in the habit of one of us changing in the bathroom whole the other changes in the room. Our changing arrangements have become so routine that it goes without saying now that if one of us is undressing, the other will pop into the bathroom. Will's actually been really cool about it. The same's gone for our sleeping arrangements too. While we gave up on using the sofa thanks to the nosy housekeeper, we've managed to become respectful sleeping companions. The bed is large enough that we each have our own space and we've stayed respectfully on our chosen sides. Will doesn't even hog the duvet.

Once I've got my bikini on and a poolside robe, I reach for the book I've been meaning to read, which has so far remained unopened on the bedside table. I glance over at Will as I pick it up. He's already sitting at the edge of the bed in his trunks and a T-shirt, his book in his hand. It strikes me as a little funny how in tune Will and I are. Today has been a perfect day and we've both wanted to do exactly the same things at the same time, from happily exploring the palaces and tombs together to stopping for lunch and haggling over goods. And now we're both up for reading by the pool. There's been no discord or disagreement over what we do at all.

I decide to voice this thought to Will as we leave the room.

'Well, I like to think of myself as fairly easy-going,' Will says as we get in the lift.

'You are! Today has felt so easy. When I was on holiday with Lauren, she'd hardly want to sightsee at all. A holiday with Lauren consists of a lot of cocktails, a lot of time on the beach or pool or a lot of shopping. It's fun and all that but there are times when it would get a bit annoying,' I recall, thinking of one time when Lauren and I went on holiday to Majorca and she hadn't wanted to leave the hotel complex, since it had pretty much everything she could possibly want: a pool, a bar and attractive men.

'Yeah, I know what you mean. That sounds a bit like my holiday with Nathan and Jones. Lots of booze and the beach. And that was pretty much it.'

'And the pajazzle. Don't forget the pajazzle,' I joke as we arrive on the ground floor and walk down the corridor towards the pool.

Will pokes me. 'What happens in Ibiza stays in Ibiza! At least it was meant to,' he grumbles, the corner of his mouth curling into a reluctant smile.

I laugh as we emerge into the courtyard. The aquamarine pool, surrounded by sun loungers, and framed by palm trees, pillars and arches is a truly stunning sight. I feel a fresh wave of gratitude that Will and I are here, in this beautiful place.

Will and I settle down on sun loungers and immediately a member of staff comes along to see if we'd like to order a drink. I opt for a non-alcoholic cocktail and Will goes for the same. It strikes me as amusing that he goes for a mocktail too, as though we're on the same page with that as well, but I don't bother saying anything.

The weather is perfect. The sun bounces off the pool, making it sparkle prettily. It's perfectly warm without being sweltering. With the palm trees and the dreamy archways and pillars, I feel miles away from home yet perfectly content. I lower my sunglasses and open my book.

I read a few pages, feeling the sun warming my body. The waiter places my drink down and I take a sip, feeling utterly content.

A shuffling sound suddenly interrupts the moment and both Will and I look over to see Medhi's son, Mohammed, playing a card game at a small table underneath a palm tree. He's shuffling his deck and laying the cards out on the table. It looks like he's playing solitaire.

'He looks a bit lonely,' Will remarks in a hushed voice, his tone a little dreamy as though he's thinking out loud.

'I guess this is heaven for us, but even paradise must get boring if it's your daily life!'

'Yeah, no siblings to play with. Lots of strangers. Doesn't look like he gets to hang out with many kids his own age. Poor lad,' Will says.

I watch him playing solitaire, the sun beaming down on him. He looks pretty content from where I'm sitting.

'That's probably why he's a bit shy,' Will adds.

'Maybe,' I agree, studying Will's face as he watches the boy. He may have been sixteen years older than when I last saw him, but Will's still exactly the same person. He's still the same inquisitive, curious soul, the person who looks at the people around him – really looks – and tries to help them. He's frowning slightly and I can tell this 15-year-old boy's potential loneliness and shyness bothers him. While most holiday-goers would be concerned about the quality of their tan or whether they've got enough good pictures for Facebook, Will is worried about other people – strangers –and instinctively wants to help them feel better. Just like he saw me struggling with my Art Club all those years ago and helped with that too.

As I gaze at him, the sun illuminating his strong features. He's completely unselfconscious, wrapped up in thought. I feel a strange stirring – not the lustful butterflies I felt when we kissed in the park, but a raw tug in my heart. That pull towards him – a familiar and yet long-lost feeling. A feeling I haven't had since I was 16.

Will suddenly flicks his eyes over to me and I look away, embarrassed, as though he might have somehow been able to know what I was thinking. I turn back to my book and pretend to be engrossed, blankly reading a few lines before reaching for my drink. After a moment or so, I steal a quick glance at Will to see he's opened his book now too. Do I have feelings for Will? What is this? Lust is one thing. I can understand feeling lustful towards him, after all, it's been a while, but what I just felt wasn't lust. It was something much more concerning.

'You're right actually,' Will says, just as I try to switch from pretend reading to actual reading. I've managed to take in one sentence and now he's piping up.

'I'm right about what?' I ask. His book is open on his lap, but he clearly hasn't been taking a word in either. He looks as lost in thought as I feel, although maybe not quite so confused.

'What you were saying about our holiday,' Will remarks. 'This holiday with you has been easy. I was just thinking about when I went to Ibiza with Nathan and Jonesy. I suggested one afternoon that we go and check out the Roman ruins in the old part of the island and they laughed in my face. I get it, they were just there to let off steam and get smashed but one afternoon wouldn't have killed them. Oh, and there was this Irish pub by our hotel, and they wanted to eat there every day. The pub did fry ups until 4 p.m., can you believe it? 4 p.m.? That's how nocturnal everyone there was. We'd roll over there and have a big greasy fry-up every day.'

'Ewww. An Irish pub in Ibiza. Sounds like the least classy holiday ever!' I joke.

'Yeah, it did leave quite a lot to be desired,' Will says. 'I suggested to the guys that we try some other places, maybe the taverna down the road, but they weren't interested.'

'Poor Will,' I coo, giving his arm a squeeze with a mock sympathetic expression plastered over my face.

'Shut up, Nat!' Will pushes my hand away, trying hard not to smile.

I'm acutely aware of the feel of his fingers against mine. He's only lightly brushing my hand away and yet his touch makes me feel girlish and self-conscious all over again, adding lust back into the heady mix of feelings already whirling around my mind.

'I was just trying to say, that I haven't had any of those issues with you,' Will says, smiling.

'You mean, you're relieved I haven't wanted to sit on my arse in an Irish pub scoffing fry-ups and not do any sightseeing?'

'Yeah!' Will laughs. 'Basically.'

'Haha, well, you're welcome!' I grin, turning my attention back to my book. 'Can't promise I won't dare you to get a pajazzle later though,' I add, still unable to concentrate.

Will laughs. 'Gotta be done. Our honeymoon be without a pajazzle. Maybe we could get each other's names done?' Will suggests.

'Or just "Mr" and "Mrs"? Ultimate tackiness.'

'Perfect,' Will replies.

I look back down at my book, which at this rate is never going to get read. I focus hard on trying to read although now all I can think about is Will's private parts, albeit covered in diamanté. I need to stop thinking about that. Right. Focus on the book. I force myself to read another few lines but nothing's going in.

'Nat,' Will pipes up again.

'Yeah?' I reply, without looking up from my book. I'm determined I'm going to read at least a chapter while on this holiday and a sentence would be a good start!

'I mean it, you are a good travel companion,' Will says.

'Thanks, Will,' I reply blankly, still trying to read. 'You too.'

'I know I shouldn't say this, but there are times I've enjoyed this fake honeymoon more than my real one,' Will remarks.

My heart lurches. 'Ha! Well, I guess it helps that I'm not off riding horses!'

Suddenly Will's hand is on mine, properly on mine. He takes my hand gently from my book and laces his long, tapered fingers through mine. I watch as though in slow motion. He's not messing around like he was a minute ago, he's being genuinely affectionate. I look across the pool for Medhi and Amira in case this is some kind of show he's putting on for them, but they're nowhere to be seen. Mohammed is still engrossed in his game of solitaire. I look up at Will. His eyes have sharpened in intensity. They're sincere, affectionate, almost loving. What's going on?

Will slides his fingers further through mine, interlocking our hands, and although every part of me yields to his touch, another part of me wants to dive into the pool and swim away as fast as possible. What is he doing?

'You're a good companion,' Will says. He strokes one of his fingers over mine.

Instinctively, I yank my hand away. 'A good companion?' I utter, half-laughing, half-expecting him to have simply been messing around.

Will frowns, looking a little hurt. 'Yeah. Or maybe you don't think so.'

'Oh God,' I sigh.

Part of me wants nothing more than to kiss Will, to hold hands with him, say sweet nothings, and more, and yet at the same time, the idea of actually doing that is as terrifying as it is enticing. It's not just a physical thing with Will. It's not just a holiday romance or a silly fling. He gets to me. He gets under my skin. He broke my heart when I was 16 and it took me years to get over it and he still has power over me. I could just about bounce back when I was a teenager, with no responsibilities beyond schoolwork, but what about now? The feelings I have for him are still intense, and yet I can't take any more heartbreak. Not after Leroy. Not now I have Hera to worry about. A business to manage. A life to lead.

'I'm sorry, Will.' A lump hardens in my throat as I get up and hurry away.

Chapter 15

Lauren. Where is she when I need her?

I sit in the hotel restaurant where the WiFi is strongest and type messages to on my phone, but she's not online. The last message she sent was last night – one I chose to ignore.

Lauren: Sooo … Have you hoped aboard the cruise ship yet?! :p

Typical Lauren. If only it were that easy. If only I could just have a fling with Will and not be the overthinking mess that I am. I need to talk to her and try to wrap my head around all of the feelings swirling inside my head, but she must be busy. I know my mum would probably reply if I messaged. She sent me half a dozen pictures of Hera while Will and I were in the taxi back from the souk, but I know exactly what she'll say. She'll simply tell me to go for it with Will. Even though Lauren jokes around, at least she knows how I feel and understands my reservations about getting involved with Will. My mum, on the other hand, would simply tell me to go for it. She'll tell me I was an idiot for pulling away, making an awkward excuse and scurrying off inside the hotel, leaving Will sitting by the pool, scratching his head.

I try Lauren again.

Me: Lauren! Will just made a move. Freaking out.

Still nothing. I sigh, contemplating going back out to the pool, where as far as I know, Will is still sunbathing and probably feeling completely put out. I'm about to get up from the table I'm sitting at, when the man I saw sitting by the pool on the first day of our holiday comes over, extending his hand. He looks as familiar now as he did then, although I still can't place him.

'Hi, sorry to interrupt, but I thought I'd say hello. I'm Lars,' he says, smiling warmly.

He's quite attractive up close. He's tall and has dark hair streaked with grey, but it's thick and slightly wavy, swept back from his face. His eyes are a deep brown shade, warm and intelligent-looking. His accent sounds like that of someone who's lead an international life, it's simultaneously American and European.

'Hi, nice to meet you. I'm Natalie,' I reply, shaking his hand.

'Is everything okay? You looked like you were having trouble with your phone,' he comments.

'Oh.' I shrug. 'I was just trying to message a friend, but she must be busy.'

Lars nods. He's standing by my table, a little awkwardly. Perhaps I should invite him to join me? It would beat hurrying back to Will right now, and it would be good to figure out where I know him from.

'Ah, I see. Shall I leave you to it?' he asks, a slightly vulnerable expression passing over his face.

'No! It's fine. Take a seat if you like,' I suggest, feeling a little sorry for him. I may have my own problems to deal with, but what if the poor guy just wants a chat? He might be feeling lonely as well. I can always book my flight later. It's not like I'm going to make it back home tonight anyway.

Lars' face lights up. 'Thank you,' he says as he pulls the chair back.

I hope Will doesn't come looking for me. While I think Lars could probably do with a chat, it might look a bit weird if Will sees me, five minutes after running away from him, sitting chatting to a stranger.

Lars has the same off-duty businessman look of the guys in the first-class carriage of the plane on the way here, with brown chinos teamed with a Ralph Lauren polo shirt. Smart casual and very preppy. I get a whiff of a musky richly scented aftershave as he sits down.

I place my phone face-down on the table.

'Given up on contacting your friend?' Lars asks.

'Yeah, she must be working or something,' I say, even though I know that when Lauren's working, her phone is usually on the desk next to her. It's more likely that she's busy with her new man or having a nap or something.

A waiter comes over and I order a G&T. Screw non-alcoholic cocktails. I could do with a drink right now. Lars does the same.

'So are you on your honeymoon? I saw the hotel had scattered confetti over the entrance when you and your partner arrived,' Lars remarks.

'Umm …' I squirm, wondering whether to lie to his face. I really can't face lying right now. My head is already swimming with thoughts and feelings about Will, the last thing I feel like doing is pretending Will's my husband.

'Erm …' I utter.

Lars eyes me curiously, as though trying to figure me out.

'Let's start with you!' I suggest instead. 'What's brought you here?' I ask, keen to establish how close to Medhi and Amira Lars is before I admit the truth to him. I can barely admit that Will and I are just long-lost childhood friends if it turns out Lars is Medhi's brother or something.

'Okay!' Lars laughs as the waiter places our G&Ts down on the table.

I thank him and pick up the cool, misted glass, taking a sip as Lars tells me he's on a work trip, having flown in from Dubai where he lives. He explains that he works with a charity over here that helps women in rural communities in Morocco gain access to education. He tells me how he used to be an investment banker but retired at 40 and turned his attention to philanthropy instead and is now an investor. Suddenly, it hits me where I know him from.

'Wait, did you donate to The Skin Project' I ask, remembering a campaign I worked on years ago for a charity that provide cosmetic surgery to people who'd suffered traumatic injuries like disfiguring burns or lacerations. I got involved with the charity after taking an interest in what they do from the beauty industry angle, but I've followed their work ever since and continued to donate to their campaigns.

'Yes!' Lars's face lights up. 'How do you know that?'

I explain about the campaign. 'I was convinced I knew your face from somewhere, and that's where! I must have seen your picture on the charity's website or something,' I tell him.

Lars grins. 'Yes, my picture was on there! I think it still is actually. The Skin Project are doing some amazing work.'

'Totally!'

I take another sip of my G&T and chat away about The Skin Project with Lars. He's a fascinating guy and it's clear that supporting charities really means something to him. He's incredibly animated when talking about the organisations he supports, from The Skin Project to the literacy charity he's in Marrakech visiting.

'The team are doing amazing work. They're setting up schools in the most remote rural communities, making sure that all children have access to education, no matter what their background,' Lars says, his eyes sparkling with enthusiasm.

'That's amazing!' I comment, feeling humbled. Here I am, having been fretting over Will trying to hold my hand when there are kids in the Moroccan countryside who don't even have access to running water.

'Yes, they're an impressive team,' Lars says, taking a sip of his drink. 'So, enough about me, tell me about your honeymoon. Where's your other half?'

I squirm. 'He's by the pool, but he's not quite my other half

156

though,' I admit, feeling confident now that I can trust Lars.

'He's not?' Lars looks thoroughly confused.

'It's a long story,' I warn him.

Lars shrugs. 'I'm free all afternoon,' he says, picking up his drink. 'Go for it.'

'Okay!' I take a sip of my G&T, before explaining everything that's brought me to Marrakech, from being a single mum in need of a holiday to winning Mick's raffle. I describe the blunder that meant that Will and I ended up on holiday together, and how somewhere along the line, our holiday together was mistakenly upgraded to a honeymoon, and that we, sort of, never put anyone straight.

Lars snorts with laughter. 'So, the hotel think you're newly-weds?'

'Yes. We even faked wedding pictures,' I admit, feeling slightly ashamed.

'You faked wedding pictures?!'

'Yes,' I admit shiftily, glancing over my shoulder to make sure Medhi or Amira haven't suddenly appeared.

'Oh my goodness!' Lars chuckles. 'That's brilliant. How on earth did you manage that?'

I explain about the park, dressing up in my 'boho' wedding dress, telling the random couple we were Instagrammers and getting Lauren to photoshop the pictures. As I explain the whole thing, I realise how completely ridiculous it's been.

Lars laughs. 'That's commitment to the cause.'

'I guess I just really wanted the holiday and I was worried if the hotel found out Will and I weren't really on our honeymoon, they might send us packing.'

He nods. 'I see what you mean, but it sounds like you got away with it.'

'Yeah! We did.' I take another sip of my drink.

'So why the long face then?' Lars asks. 'I saw you from across the restaurant and you seemed kind of upset.'

157

'Oh, yeah.' I grimace. 'I think maybe we got away with it too much,' I explain.

'Huh?' Lars looks understandably confused.

'It's just Will sort of made a move on me and I freaked out!' I tell him. 'Sorry if that's too much information.'

'Don't be silly. So you don't feel like a holiday romance then?' Lars says.

'I don't know. Not really. Will and I have known each other a very long time. It wouldn't be the kind of fling I could easily forget once we're back on English soil,' I explain.

It feels good to get my feelings off my chest, even if I am probably oversharing with someone who's pretty much a stranger. Yet there's something friendly, trustworthy and familiar about Lars that puts me at ease and makes me feel like it's okay to talk – that, in fact, sharing with him is probably a good idea.

'Well, maybe it could be more than just a holiday romance?' Lars suggests hopefully.

'Maybe …' I gulp. 'I suppose I'm just not sure I'm ready for that. I'm a single mum. I have a lot on my plate.'

'So you like this guy a lot, but you don't want any kind of relationship with him?' Lars clarifies.

'Yes, I guess …' I murmur.

Lars's face drops. 'That's a shame. If you like him, you should go for it.'

'But what about my daughter?'

'What about her? You'll still love her even if you choose to be with this Will character. He sounds like a good person.'

'Yes, but …'

'What are you scared of?' Lars asks suddenly.

'Getting hurt,' I admit quietly.

Lars shrugs. 'Life hurts. But life can also be brilliant, thrilling, funny, surprising, and joyful. Sometimes you have to risk getting hurt to experience all the other good stuff,' he says.

I glance down at his ring finger and realise he's not wearing one.

Lars catches me looking. 'I used to be married. I'm a widow now though,' he explains, his eyes sombre. 'My wife died from breast cancer five years ago. That's when I left banking and decided to do something more meaningful with my life.'

'I'm so sorry,' I utter.

'Thank you,' Lars says, with a sad, yet brave smile. 'But I'm speaking from experience. Even though my wife's death hurt, unbearably, she also gave me the happiest memories I have. Life is too short to miss out on being with people you love.'

Love.

The word hangs between us. Lars is so sincere that I can't bring myself to flippantly deny that I love Will. In a way, I do. He was my first love and on some level, that love has always been there. Maybe Lars is right. Perhaps it is worth taking a risk and giving Will a chance.

'You should talk to him. You clearly care about him,' Lars points out, eyeing me meaningfully.

'You're right. Thank you! And I hope you don't mine my emotional outpouring.'

'It's fine, it's been good to have a chat.' Lars smiles.

He's one of those people who sets you at ease. An older man whose life experience has made them wise and kind.

I gesture for the waiter to come over, and then I pay for our drinks, even though Lars tries to protest.

'By the way, do you have a card?' I ask, hesitating before I put my wallet back into my bag. 'I'd love to make a donation to one of your charities.'

'Sure,' Lars replies. 'That's very kind of you.' He reaches into his trouser pocket, flips open his wallet and hands me a business card with the simple title 'Lars Mansur, Investor,' with a link to a personal website.

'Thanks Lars.' I slide the card into my wallet, making a mental note to take a look later. I definitely want to donate to the charity he works with in Morocco and maybe a few others, but as well as that, for some reason, I have a feeling that Lars is a good person to stay in touch with, as though our acquaintance isn't going to end here. I get up and pull my bag strap over my shoulder.

'No problem, thank you. And good luck with Will. Some of the best things in life are often the scariest,' Lars says with an encouraging smile.

'You're probably right!' I reply, before heading off to talk to him.

Chapter 16

I head back to the pool, my confidence somewhat restored by Lars's encouraging words. I care about Will, to deny it would be to lie to myself, but I also don't want to rush into anything. I need to let him know how I feel, especially since he's probably feeling quite rejected right now.

It's still sunny outside, although not quite as blazing as it was before. The pool is shimmering in the hazy light. Shielding my eyes from the sun as I walk towards mine and Will's sun loungers, I spot that he's no longer there. There's just his book and his drink. Perhaps he's gone to the loo. I'm about to sit down and wait for him to return when I hear some voices. I look in the direction they're coming from and spot Will sitting playing cards with Mohammed. They're immersed in a game and they're happily laughing and joking away. I watch Will, taking in his sweet smile and effortless charisma, the natural and kind way he's engaging with Mohammed and drawing him out of his shell. It really is just like looking at the old Will, the Will from school.

Will senses me looking and glances over. He waves a little awkwardly. I wave back and smile, opening my book so he doesn't feel he needs to end his game and hurry back. I attempt to read while Will and Mohammed continue their game, but I can't concentrate. My thoughts keep wandering to me and Will. I keep thinking about what Lars said about having to risk being hurt in order to experience all the wonderful sides of life.

Eventually, Will comes over.

'Sorry about that,' he says, sitting down. 'I felt sorry for him playing on his own.'

'I know you did. He looked like he appreciated the company.'

'I think so,' Will replies, with a small smile that makes my heart do that twinge thing again.

Will reclines on his lounger. He lowers his sunglasses down the bridge of his nose and looks at me over the top of the frames. 'Nat, I'm sorry if I freaked you out. I didn't mean to come on strong,' he says sincerely, his voice lowered, even though Mohammed has headed back inside the hotel and we're the only guests by the pool.

'You held my hand, it was hardly coming on strong!' I joke, even though it's obvious to both of us that it did freak me out. 'It's not even first base!' I add.

'You still ran away though!' Will points out, laughing a little awkwardly.

The sun is beginning to dip in the sky, taking on a warm golden hue. It looks beautiful between the palm trees – an exotic dreamy sight that's completely at odds with the confusing swirl of feelings going on inside me. I close my book and place it on the table beside me, turning closer to Will.

'I know, I'm sorry,' I tell him, reflecting his sincere gaze. 'It's just, things went so badly wrong with my ex, and ever since then, I've been so focused on taking care of myself and Hera. I've been trying to heal and be a good mum to her and I guess I've become so protective of our little bubble, that allowing anyone in, even just a little bit, completely freaks me out.'

Will nods sympathetically. 'I know, I shouldn't have done anything.' He sighs, clearly feeling guilty.

'Don't feel bad, Will. You didn't do anything wrong. It's not your fault I'm completely weird about this stuff!' I let him know.

'I'm probably over-thinking everything, and I can't think of a way to say this without sounding weird and bunny-boilerish, but I don't know how you feel. I mean, are you just looking for a holiday romance? A bit of fun? Or what ...?' I ask in as casual a tone as possible, even though I don't feel particularly casual at all.

'I'm not just looking for a bit of fun, Natalie!' Will scoffs at the idea.

I feel an instant sense of relief, which quickly morphs into panic. If he's not looking for a bit of fun, that means he's looking for something serious and even though that is the answer I wanted to hear, I hadn't bargained for it.

'I wasn't looking for some random fling, but I shouldn't have tried anything,' Will says. 'I care about you and yes, I do still have feelings, but I really didn't mean to make you uncomfortable or confuse you or anything. This is our holiday. We're here to relax and I don't want to mess that up for you.' Will smiles sweetly, looking genuinely contrite, even though he has nothing to feel guilty about. He knows what he wants more than I do and there's nothing wrong with that.

'Thanks, Will. You haven't messed anything up though,' I explain, not wanting him to feel bad. 'It's not your fault I'm like this. When you held my hand, a huge part of me wanted to hold yours back! I wanted to do more than just hold your hand, but then I started thinking about Hera and everything else. You're not just some random guy, you're *you*! If we got together and it's likely more than a holiday romance, then I need to give that serious thought. Hera's dad already abandoned her before she was even born, I'm scared of getting involved with someone else and then things not working out. It's not just me that would be affected. I mean, I don't even know how you feel about kids!'

Even as the words leave my mouth, I'm aware of how ridiculous they sound. All Will's done is try to hold my hand and I'm asking him how he feels about kids. It's so embarrassing, and if it were any other guy, he'd be running for the hills right now, but Will seems to be taking it all in his stride. He's taking all of my concerns on board and I can tell from the thoughtful, pensive expression on his face that he's giving my questions serious consideration, despite how weird they might sound to a regular guy.

'Honestly, I didn't used to think I wanted kids,' Will admits. 'When I was with Elsa, neither of us were particularly keen, but I think that was more because we both knew deep down that we might not last and the last thing we needed to do was add a kid to that.' A flicker of sadness passes over Will's face and I can tell that he's not just the carefree 16-year-old he used to be. In some ways, he reminds me exactly of his old self, but it's clear that his own relationship has caused him to develop a more reflective, sensitive side.

'Since Elsa and I broke up, I've thought about family a lot more. I've been back home, and for the first time in years, I've been looking at all the photo albums of my dad, of us back when I was a kid. I hadn't been able to look at them before, it was just too painful, but I finally did it. At first it was really tough, but then the sadness gave way to a sense of just cherishing what we had. My dad was a great dad and my childhood was amazing. You look at pictures of your dad playing football with you, or your mum pushing you on a swing or the pair of them holding you as a baby, beaming with happiness, and you just realise that family is the most meaningful, purest thing,' Will says.

'It really is,' I agree, having come to the exact same conclusion through having Hera. In our own completely different ways, Will and I have arrived at the same understanding.

The sun is growing even more orange, a fiery shade, as it dips lower in the sky. Will's words are certainly reassuring, it's good to know that he feels the same way about family as I do, and I'm glad he doesn't sound like he's going to just mess me around, but I still feel a little unnerved.

'I don't want you to feel pressured or anything. We're on this holiday together and I don't want to make it awkward. I just got swept up in the moment,' Will explains.

Swept up in the moment? His words snag a little.

'That's the problem though,' I sigh, feeling a flicker of doubt and uncertainty creeping back in. 'What if this whole honeymoon thing has ended up making us feel romantic? What if all the romantic vibes have got to you?'

Will laughs. 'Are you saying the fake honeymoon brainwashed me?' he jokes.

I laugh with him, even though I don't think it's entirely out of the question. 'I guess so! It's a possibility, isn't it?'

'Nat, I still have a picture you drew of me when we were 15. I went to Mick's fundraiser just on the off-chance of getting to chat to you. You were my first love. I haven't been brainwashed by a Congratulations cake and some rose petals in a fancy honeymoon suite!'

My heart lurches in my chest. Will seems completely sincere, but there's still a small part of me that's worried something might happen over here in Marrakech where everything is beautiful and magical, and then we'll get back to Chiddingfold, return to real life and the sparkle might wear off.

'Okay! But I just think we should take things slowly,' I suggest. 'Maybe we should just do something completely unromantic, just to make sure that all this honeymoon stuff hasn't got to us.'

'Something completely unromantic. What are you suggesting?' Will raises an eyebrow.

'I don't know!' I shrug. 'Just something normal. Something that isn't *honeymoonish*.'

'Like what?' Will asks.

'I don't know, trekking or something?' I suggest. 'Didn't you want to go trekking and see the "real Marrakech"? Let's do that!'

'Trekking? Are you sure? I thought you wanted to lounge by the pool and stuff?'

I shrug. 'I can do that when we get back. If we still have feelings after trekking together up the Atlas Mountains together, then maybe this thing is for real.'

'Okay,' Will laughs. 'I never thought I'd have to climb a mountain just to hold your hand!' he teases.

I hold out my hand, which still has a greenish mark where my fake wedding ring sits. 'It'll be worth it!' I insist wryly.

'We'll see!' Will jokes with a cheeky grin.

Chapter 17

Stripping down and being slathered in oil is probably the last thing Will and I should be doing right now, but apparently, a honeymoon package at a five-star hotel wouldn't be complete without a couple's massage.

Just as Will and I were ready to don our hiking boots and venture into the great outdoors, we realised we had a massage booked at the hotel's spa – a traditional Moroccan hamman – and felt it would seem a bit ungrateful to just cancel it. So here we are, awkwardly following a spa therapist down a gently lit corridor lined with tea lights towards a treatment room where we're about to experience a traditional full body scrub.

I honestly thought the hotel couldn't get any better, but the hammam is incredible. Tucked away at the back of the hotel behind a brushed brass door, it's an oasis of calm and tranquillity. The walls are a gentle gold shade, lit by candles nestled in alcoves. The light is low and soft. The air smells zesty, like oranges and the only sound is the trickling of water from a fountain. I feel like I've died and gone to heaven as one of the therapists guides me and Will down a corridor towards our treatment room.

'This is your treatment room,' she says, gesturing for us to go through a door at the end of the corridor.

She holds it open and we step inside. I'm expecting a serene, relaxing room like the one pictured on the voucher, but this couldn't be any more different. It looks like a dungeon. It's nearly pitch-black, the air is thick with steam, and the walls are lumpy and dark like coal. They glisten with wetness in the faint silvery light of a small overhead lamp.

'Please undress and place your underwear and gowns here.' The therapist gestures at an alcove in the lumpy wall. 'Then take a seat and relax, the steam will open your pores and then your scrub will begin. Enjoy,' she says, smiling sweetly before shutting the door.

'What the …' I look towards Will, who seems equally perplexed as he takes in the dungeon-like room.

'Are we meant to just … get naked?' I balk.

'I think so,' Will replies, eyes wide.

'We can't do that!' I reply.

'I know. What shall we do?'

'I can't believe we're meant to just sit here, naked!' I balk.

'It's not very English, is it?'

It's only then that I realise we're both whispering.

'It's not very English at all,' I reply, glumly.

'Well, we're not in England, are we? I guess this is how they do it in Morocco,' Will says.

'I thought this was a conservative country,' I grumble.

A smile plays on Will's lips. 'It is, but I don't think women wear their hijabs when they're in the spa,' he says.

'Damn it,' I mutter. 'What are we going to do?'

We stand there, facing each other in our dressing gowns. It's getting hot under my robe and I can feel my body growing slick with sweat.

'I guess as far as they're concerned, we're married, so why on earth would we be uncomfortable with getting naked in front of each other,' Will points out.

'Oh my God,' I groan. 'So what you're saying is we now have to get completely starkers to keep up the façade of being married?'

'I'm not saying we have to, but it would look a bit weird if we didn't! I don't know. We could just say we don't want to do the treatment ...'

I contemplate that for a moment, but how ungrateful and weirdly uptight would we look if we just suddenly turn around and tell the spa that we don't want the traditional full body scrub?

'How about we just get naked, but don't look at each other?' I suggest.

'Okay, I suppose,' Will replies.

'Which one of us is going to get naked first?' I ask, feeling a little anxious.

'Ladies first!'

'Let's both do it.'

'Okay fine,' Will replies.

We both turn and face the wall, our backs to each other. This is *so* awkward. Getting a fake wedding ring and faking a wedding snap was one thing, but whipping my clothes off makes that stuff look like child's play. I tentatively pull my robe from my shoulders. It already feels good to remove the fabric from my clammy skin. I glance over at Will, feeling unnerved about exposing my breasts. He's removed his robe and I immediately get an eyeful of butt cheek as he pulls his boxers down.

'Natalie! You're not meant to look!' Will cries, catching me glancing over.

'Sorry! I wasn't checking you out! I was just checking you were actually doing it,' I explain.

'Yes, I've actually done it!' Will cups his hands over his groin. 'Unlike some.'

He walks over to the bench at the side of the room and sits down. 'Stop staring at me, Nat. I can feel your eyes on my bum!'

'I wasn't!' I insist, even though I totally was. I wasn't meaning to perve on him, even though he does have a nice arse. My gaze just sort of followed him. 'Sorry, I won't look.'

'Good,' Will replies.

I steal one last glance at him to see him lying on the bench, still cupping his groin area.

I let the robe fall from my shoulders and place it on the shelf, before pulling my knickers off and wandering over to the opposite bench, while trying to cover my modesty with my hands. Will is lying on his back with his eyes closed. I sit down on the opposite bench and even though I do feel awkward, I can't deny that the sensation of the hot steam drifting all over my naked body does feel nice.

'You know, it's really hard to cover yourself as a woman. Two hands just aren't enough,' I comment, as I struggle to cover my vagina and breasts.

Will looks over.

'Oi! You're not meant to look!' I point out.

'Well, don't make conversation about your nakedness!'

I sigh, leaning back into the bench. 'This is ridiculous,' I comment, still attempting to conceal my breasts. 'Are we just going to cup our private parts when the therapist comes in? We'll look like the weirdest married couple ever.'

'I know ...' Will admits.

'Maybe we should just get it over and done with?' I suggest. 'Be naked together.'

'Yeah, maybe,' Will replies. He's still holding his hands over his penis. 'This does feel a bit silly. We should probably stop being such prudes.'

'Yeah, exactly. Even though this is a far cry from how I imagined getting naked with you would be,' I say, thinking aloud.

Will looks over, eyes wide. 'How did you imagine getting naked with me would be?'

Oh God. 'Erm.' I grimace, kicking myself. 'I guess I just imagined that if we did ever get naked together, it probably wouldn't be in a Moroccan spa,' I explain, trying to sound blasé, even though I'd always imagined that if Will and I got naked, it would be in

170

the throes of passion. I'd imagined we'd tear each other's clothes off. I didn't think we'd be as awkward as this.

'Okay, let's just relax. Stop being so prudish,' Will suggests, tentatively moving his hand away from his crotch.

'Yeah, let's do it.'

I slowly inch my arm away from breasts.

A silence passes between us.

'So ...' I utter, staring at the ceiling. 'We're naked.'

'Yep,' Will replies. 'Completely naked.'

'Great!'

'Great!' Will echoes.

I glance over at him and there it is. His penis. Right there. Just out there. In plain sight. And I can see instantly how he got the nickname 'the cruise ship'. As far as ships go, it's a big one.

'I can see your penis!' I note.

Will laughs, looking over. 'And I can see your breasts!' he says.

I'm dying of mortification, but I try not to let it show. I watch as Will's gaze drifts down my body and suck my stomach in. This is the first time anyone's seen me naked since I gave birth to Hera in hospital, and even then I wasn't properly naked since I had a weird, flimsy smock thing on.

'I hope you don't mind me saying this, but you have an amazing body, Natalie. If I were you, I'd be showing it off,' Will says.

'You'd be showing it off?' I echo, surprised.

'Yeah, you wear all these big baggy clothes. Those baggy jeans and massive T-shirts. I don't see why you hide yourself. You have a great body. And you know what they say, if you've got it, flaunt it,' Will comments.

I roll my eyes. 'Firstly Will, you make me sound like a total scruff when you say baggy jeans and massive T-shirts. Those are boyfriend jeans and oversized T-shirts. They're meant to be loose, that's the fashion. And also, maybe I deliberately don't flaunt my curves.'

'You don't need to flaunt them, but why would you deliberately *not* flaunt them?' Will asks, his eyes still closed.

I consider his question as I lie down on the bench. The dark stone may look uninviting, but it's surprisingly warm to the touch and as I spread my body over it, it feels nice against my skin. Now that I'm lying on my back, Will can't exactly see my lady parts, but I'm still holding my forearm over my breasts.

'Well, perhaps I just don't want men to be salivating over my boobs,' I reply.

'We're not all Neanderthals. We can admire your figure without salivating,' Will remarks.

'Well, fine, but I don't dress for men's admiration. I just wear what I want to wear.'

'Fair enough,' Will replies simply.

A silence passes between us. 'I'm just saying, you do have a great figure, one that's definitely worthy of admiration, not that I want to admire it. At least not in a sleazy way,' Will blurts out.

'Oh God, Will just stop talking.' I laugh, letting my arm fall from my breasts. I gaze up at the dark ceiling, before sensing Will's eyes on me. I turn to look at him and catch him gazing at my naked body. He quickly looks away.

'Will!' I tut.

'Sorry,' he says. 'But wow ...'

'Wow?' I echo as it dawns on me that Will is the first guy who's seen my naked post-baby body. 'Wow' isn't a bad reaction. And neither is the awestruck way he said it.

'You're beautiful,' Will says matter-of-factly.

I let my eyes roam over his body too, taking in his tall sturdy frame. For once, unlike the times I've seen him whip off a T-shirt in the hotel room over the past few days, I don't politely look away. I let myself drink him in and it's liberating. His body is board, strong and masculine, without being overly ripped or muscular. His chest is covered in a light dusting of hair that traces down his stomach towards his pubic area. I try not to look directly at his penis – that would just be too pervy – but it's hard to miss it. I don't know if it's just the steam in the room or what, but I start to feel hot and lightheaded. I look away, gazing back up towards the ceiling, as I feel the steam condensing on my skin and dripping down onto the bench. The room is so warm, dark and wet, that it feels almost like a cave.

'This dungeon's growing on me,' I comment.

Will laughs. 'Yeah, I quite like it too. It's like we're in a crater in the middle of the earth's crust or something.'

'Same,' I reply. 'It feels so surreal, so cut off from everything.'

'It does. It feels like a different world. Our own little cave, all the way in Africa, just you and me,' Will says, his voice dreamy and wistful.

'Just you and me,' I echo, feeling a million miles away, while simultaneously finding myself completely at home.

Chapter 18

I don't know if it was our heart-to-heart or our spa day or what, but Will are getting along better than ever. Perhaps the full body scrub and long luxurious massages relaxed us, or maybe it's the effect of being honest and open with each other, but I feel like I really am on holiday with a good friend. The blunder that threw us together on this crazy trip now feels like a blessing and we both have a spring in our step as we head out of the hotel and make our way down to Jemaa el-Fnaa, where a rickety old bus awaits us packed with tourists heading to the Atlas Mountains to hike, ride camels and camp overnight.

I raise an eyebrow as I take in the bus. It's painted with the slogan 'Atlas Adventures' in peeling paint, the bright sunny weather showing no mercy in illuminating its flaking rusty exterior. The bumper is hanging is hanging off and looks like it might just fall free any second.

'Erm, Will,' I nudge him, pointing at the bumper.

'Oh …' Will pulls a face. 'I wondered why it was so cheap.'

'Oh no!' I laugh, trying to push the worries about boarding this claptrap out of my mind as Will hands our tickets to the driver.

We hop on board and make our way to our seats. A red-haired woman tuts as though we've been holding the group up and looks at her watch, but otherwise, everyone seems to be in good spirits.

The sight of a dozen or so happy-looking tourists who seem to have put their faith in this dodgy-looking bus reassures me a bit. We sit down at two free seats near the back of the bus, behind a Scandinavian couple who say hello, looking up from flicking through photos on their camera.

The scenery as we leave Marrakech and head into the mountains is like nothing I've ever seen before. The urban buildings of the city rapidly give way to the most rugged beautiful landscape I've ever seen. The earth is a rich reddish terracotta shade spattered with greenish purple-tinged shrubbery. I'd seen pictures of the rural landscape in my guidebook before the trip, but the photos didn't do it justice. They don't capture just how vast and awe-inspiring the mountains are or how vast and endless the desert looks.

'It's breath-taking, isn't it?' I turn to Will, who's gazing out of the window, taking everything in just as I had been.

'It really is,' he agrees. 'It's amazing to see this side of Morocco.' A faraway look suddenly enters his eyes.

'What was it like back when you first visited?' I ask.

Will looks away from the mountains rolling past beyond the window. 'It was awful. There were a lot of casualties. The café where the bombing took place had been blown to bits. Everyone was really traumatised. It was tough,' he says, regretfully.

'God, that must have been so hard,' I remark, realising just how different mine and Will's worlds have been. While he was at bomb sites interviewing people who'd just been through unimaginable trauma, I was in my trendy Camden office, writing about the latest beauty treatment or celebrity fashion trend, entrepreneurs playing games of team-building ping-pong in the background. I feel a twinge of humility coupled with admiration for some of the things Will's done.

'It wasn't the best trip I've ever been on,' he says, with a sad smile.

'I can imagine,' I comment. I decide not to ask too much more about it. We're on holiday now and it's not exactly the most uplifting subject for Will to dwell on.

Once we get settled into the journey, we start chatting to the Scandinavian couple in front of us. It turns out they're from Sweden/ Alice is a nurse and her boyfriend, Lucas, works for a bank. They've been celebrating their one-year anniversary and have been visiting Morocco as part of a two-week trip that started in Spain. They flew into Barcelona, which is one of the few travel destinations I've visited in recent years, and we have a fun time talking about the Gaudi architecture and the Picasso museum. They then flew down to Seville, exploring the Andalusia region, before flying to Marrakech. They don't say it, but I get the impression Marrakech isn't quite what they imagined and that it's possibly a bit too intense for them. They seem to have found Jemaa el-Fnaa a bit overwhelming and they're clearly looking forward to exploring the mountains, which will be a lot more serene. I smile sympathetically, remembering how I felt when I first walked through the square and collided with a donkey cart while coming face-to-face with a snake.

Will starts telling them about his previous trips in Morocco and some of his other, wilder adventures, like the time he got drunk with the Russian mafia on an overnight train to Moscow while on a reporting trip, or the time he nearly got taken hostage by insurgents at the Syrian border. I resist the urge to roll my eyes. Will's life has been incredibly interesting, but he knows it. The couple seem a bit flummoxed by Will's off-the-beaten-track exploration, which is probably worlds away from their idea of a holiday. Fortunately, before Will can recount any more even crazier tales, the driver turns off into a terminal and parks the bus.

We all look out of the windows, taking stock of our new surroundings. The terminal appears to be on the edge of a small village surrounded by rugged terracotta mountains, stretching into the distance. There are a few other tourist buses parked in bays.

The driver turns the engine off and gets up to address us.

'This is a traditional Moroccan hillside village, known for its skilled local craftspeople and bustling souk. There are many cafés where you can get lunch. Let's take a break and meet back here in two hours.' He glances at his watch. 'So we'll meet back here at 1.30 p.m., okay? Then we will head to the mountains. Everyone happy?'

Everyone agrees that this is a good plan and we all unload from the bus.

As lovely as the Swedish couple are, I'd rather explore the village alone with Will. Fortunately, Alice and Lucas seem to want to explore alone too and wish us an enjoyable lunch. Returning the sentiment, we split off in a different direction.

We pass through a beautiful ornate brass gate from the carpark and enter the village. It's a lot calmer and more laid-back than Marrakech, but it's still bustling with a busy vibrant main square surrounded by souks. There are more craft-sellers than in Marrakech, with potters and jewellery makers, laying out their wares on the pebbles of the square. The vibe is a lot more chilled and Will and I wander happily through the square, admiring the craft-sellers' wares and picking up a few more gifts for people back home.

Eventually, we nip into a restaurant to have lunch and sit by the window, chatting away while eating 'Sesku' – a traditional Moroccan couscous dish with vegetables, meat and raisins. It's so delicious that Will and I lapse into silence as we eat. I take another bite, before placing my fork down and picking up my glass of orange juice.

'What time is it?' I ask Will, before taking a sip.

He looks at his watch. 'Five past one. Don't worry, we still have loads of time,' he says, before sipping his beer.

'Well, not exactly loads,' I comment.

'Relax, Natalie,' Will says, with an encouraging smile. 'We're on holiday.'

'I know,' I relent. He's right. We're on holiday and I should just relax but I'm so used to having work pressure and Hera and being on a schedule that it's hard not to feel just a bit uptight when you know your time is limited. Plus, as nice as this village is, I know how excited Will is about this excursion and I really don't want us to miss it.

'Look, even if we are a tiny bit late. It's not like they would leave without us,' he says, before taking another bite.

'They might …' I murmur.

'They won't!'

Will distracts me from fretting by asking how Hera's doing. I show him the latest photo my mum sent of her, which came through while we were on the bus and Will was deep into his story about getting pissed with the Russian mafia. It's a picture of Hera fast asleep in her cot clutching Mr Bear.

'She's so cute,' Will comments. 'You know you see some kids and beauty seems to be in the eye of the beholder? Their parents adore them, but they just look a bit …' Will pauses, searching for the right words.

'Like wrinkled balls of flesh?' I suggest.

'Yeah,' Will laughs. 'But Hera isn't like that. She's actually really adorable.'

I smile, feeling touched. 'Aww, thanks Will. She's a beauty,' I reply proudly.

Will smiles warmly. 'It so sweet how much you dote on her.'

'I really do. Honestly, I didn't realise I was capable of this much love.' I take a sip of my juice and glance down at the table. I don't know if it's the fact that I've been away from Hera for three nights now or what, but I suddenly feel a bit emotional.

'It's been a hard year,' I tell Will, reflecting on everything that's happened back home. 'Hera was just two weeks old when Leroy, my ex, bolted. She was crying constantly. I was still exhausted from the birth and I felt like my world was ending. I honestly didn't know how I was going to cope.'

I gaze blankly out of the window of the café, my mind full of memories of that difficult time.

'Bastard,' Will remarks, taking me by surprise. 'Leroy, not you,' he adds.

'Yeah! You're right,' I laugh.

'I have to admit, my mum did mention it to me. What he did was so bad that word spread, I guess,' Will says, a little sheepishly.

'I figured. I know what Chiddingfold's like!'

'It's truly unforgivable. Does he have any contact now?' Will asks.

'Nope. He just disappeared. He blocked me on all social media. I haven't received as much as a text. I guess it was a case of out of sight, out of mind,' I say, aware of how bitter I must sound.

Will looks completely disgusted. 'What a complete scumbag,' he sighs, shaking his head.

'He is. There's no question about that. He's a complete scumbag, through and through. But I'm not angry anymore, believe it or not,' I tell him, meaning it. 'I was angry. I was livid, but I've moved on from that now. Now I just pity him, and pity is a better place to be. Pity doesn't eat away at you.'

Will nods, taking my words in. 'You're right, pity is a much better place to be.'

I take a bite of my wrap and place it back on my plate.

I finish chewing and decide to keep talking. I don't usually open up much about Leroy. It's still such a painful period of my life, but I feel comfortable speaking about it to Will, maybe because he opened up about his marriage.

'I had a hard time at first, and things still aren't exactly perfect. After all, I didn't think I'd be back living at home with my mum at 32, but I'm a hell of a lot happier now than I was. It's really thanks to my mum and my friends and my workmates, they pulled me through. I'm so lucky to have such strong inspiring women around me,' I say, feeling a bit emotional. I distract myself by turning my attention back to my lunch.

'You're strong too, Natalie. You're incredibly strong,' Will says, taking me by surprise. He holds my gaze. 'You're an inspiration.'

'Thanks, Will!' I reply a little taken aback.

'You really are. You're clearly completely devoted to Hera,' Will remarks. 'And you're a successful businesswoman. I think it's amazing what you've achieved, running a thriving business while being such a brilliant mum. You should be incredibly proud of yourself.'

'That's so sweet of you to say,' I reply, feeling genuinely touched.

'It's a shame Leroy was so intimidated by you,' Will sighs, before taking another mouthful of couscous.

Huh?' What's he on about? 'Leroy cheated,' I explain.

Will shrugs. 'That doesn't mean he wasn't intimidated by you,' he says. 'I reckon that's why he cheated.'

I narrow my eyes at him, trying to suss out what he means.

'What did Leroy do for a living?' Will asks.

'He was a furniture upcycler,' I explain, a little sheepishly.

'A what?' Will replies.

I describe what Leroy's 'occupation' entailed.

'I see …' Will murmurs, pulling a face. 'Yep, he was intimidated by you. Let me guess, he went for someone who wasn't a successful businesswoman? Maybe someone younger? More inexperienced? Someone who might look up to him?'

'Errr …' I utter, not quite sure how to react.

'Look, I know it sounds weird, but Leroy sounds like a pathetic excuse for a man and he probably wanted a woman who wasn't as successful as you, so he could feel like the big man,' Will explains.

'Maybe …' I murmur, looking down at my plate. Could it be true? I'd always imagined Leroy went for Lydia because he was just a pathetic spineless asshole, but could it have been about something else? Could it really be that he was just looking for someone who'd look up to him a bit more than I did? After all, it probably wasn't doing wonders for his ego that I was the one paying for holidays. I was essentially the breadwinner in our relationship. I suppose it's possible that Leroy wanted to be with a younger, more impressionable woman, who might actually be naive and gullible enough to look up to him and not see him for the work-shy no-good fool that he was. The thought is strangely comforting.

Will looks at his watch as the waiter retreats. 'We need to get going soon. The bus leaves in ten minutes.'

'Ten minutes?!' I gawp.

'Yeah,' Will replies casually.

'We'd better go then! Oh my God!' I look over my shoulder and call the waiter back, asking for the bill.

'Relax, the bus stop is only a two-minute walk away!' Will says, taking another bite of his lunch.

'I know, but the driver said to be there at 1.30 p.m. He specifically told us not to be late!'

'Don't worry. We'll head off now. We won't be late.' Will smiles.

I shovel in the last few mouthfuls of my wrap and wash it down with the rest of my juice. The waiter brings the bill over. Will and I both reach for our wallets and go fifty-fifty, placing dirham notes on the silver dish on the table, before thanking the waiter in a flurry of compliments and 'shukrans' and dashing out.

The square is even busier now than when we first arrived as even more sellers have set up their stalls. There are more tourists as well, milling around. The smell of kebab meat drifts from a few street food vendors. I can't spot the exit, so I look through the crowd to try to spy the shoe stall, but there are so many people and so many similar-looking stalls that it's proving impossible. I look to Will.

'Which way is it?' I ask, panicked.

Will's eyes dart through the crowd and even he, with all his roving war reporter travel experience, is beginning to look a little stressed out.

'I think it's this way,' I comment, spotting what looks like the ornate brass gate from the carpark in the distance.

'Cool,' Will replies.

We hurry across the square, towards the brass gate.

'Oh yeah, this is it.' Will lets out a sigh of relief as we reach the brass gate with its distinctive design.

I glance at my watch. 'We're only a few minutes late!' I tell him as we hurry through the gate.

'It was this way.' I point across the depot and cut between a donkey cart loaded with crates of live clucking chickens and a parked truck. Will follows.

We cross a layby, where a man is unloading boxes from a van. I look towards the space where our tourist bus had been parked.

'Hang on a minute, where is it?' I ask, scanning the empty space where our tour bus was. I turn, taking in the nearby bays in case I've missed it, but there's no sign of it. The bus is gone and the only vehicles in nearby bays are vans with what looks like business names painted in Arabic on the side, as well as a few parked juice carts.

'Will!' I turn to him, desperate. He's glancing around, looking as confused and worried as I am.

'I really didn't think they'd leave without us,' he utters, wiping the sweat off his brow. 'We're only a few minutes late. That's ridiculous!'

'Oh my God, Will! I told you we were cutting it fine.' I groan, exasperated.

Will frowns. 'Why would they leave like that? I don't get why they couldn't have just waited five minutes.'

'I don't know. This is so annoying!' I sigh, scanning the entire carpark again, in case the bus has moved, but it's nowhere to be seen. There are just a few other juice carts and a couple of transit vans.

'Five minutes late and they leave, that's so unreasonable,' Will huffs.

I slump onto a nearby wall. 'They probably just thought we were going to have our own adventure or something. You did go

182

on and on to Alice and Lucas about how much you love venturing off the beaten track. Maybe they thought we had just decided to abandon the touristy day trip and do our own thing,' I suggest.

'Now I feel like you're blaming me.' Will looks downcast.

'I'm not, I just … It makes sense, doesn't it?' I explain. 'And then there was that moody redhead woman, I bet she wasn't keen to hang about,' I add, thinking back to the redhead who was checking her watch as Will and I boarded the bus this morning.

'I guess. I'd get it if we didn't come back after an hour or something though, but five minutes? Urghh. Maybe I shouldn't have booked with the cheapest tour company. They're clearly unprofessional.' Will sighs. 'I was just worried the higher end ones might know Medhi.'

'Damn!' I grumble as I slump down onto the carpark wall.

The sun is beating down on us and I'm beginning to feel sweaty. It feels hotter out here in the mountains than it did in Marrakech and even though I expected to be gripped with panic if the bus left, the bright, warm light of the sun has taken the edge off my worries and I find myself feeling strangely okay about it. Will is still glancing around the car park as though by some miracle, the bus might suddenly appear.

'So, Mr Renegade Traveller, what shall we do now?' I ask.

Will smiles weakly and sits down next to me on the wall. 'Well, this is a curve ball. This isn't even a proper tourist village. They don't really have hotels,' he groans.

I can't help laughing. 'Hotels?! I thought you were all about camping and mixing with the locals and shunning the tourist trail? And now you're worried about going without a nice big bed and fluffy pillows?' I snigger, pinching him. 'Do you want rose petals too?'

'Hmph. I was thinking about you actually,' Will insists.

'Sure you were, Will!' I smirk.

The chickens in the nearby crate start clucking loudly. Will and I both turn to see what the commotion is all about, when we spot a man pulling the crates from the cart and carrying them towards a nearby market.

'So, what's the plan then? Shall we try to find somewhere to stay? Or maybe there's a bus back to the city?' Will asks, distracting me.

'Hey! What are you doing here?' the man unloading the chickens shouts over to us.

Will hops off the wall. 'We came to get our bus, but it's left unfortunately,' Will explains.

The man looks at us like we're crazy. 'What do you mean? There are no tourist buses here,' he says gruffly, looking annoyed.

'Yeah, we know,' I sigh.

'No, you are in the wrong place. The tourist buses leave from the other side of the square. This area is for trade. This is for locals only.'

'What?' My mouth drops open.

'You're in the wrong place,' the man reiterates impatiently as he reaches for another crate of chickens.

'Right, okay. Sorry about that. Which way is it?' Will asks.

The man sighs loudly as he places his crate on the ground, before pointing us in the right direction.

'Thank you!' Will says to the man, before turning to me. 'Come on, let's go.'

I can feel the man's eyes on us as we scurry out of the trade depot. Tourists are clearly not welcome.

'I can't believe we went to the wrong place,' I mutter under my breath. 'I was sure it was the right one.'

Will gives my arm a sympathetic squeeze. 'It's okay, hopefully they're waiting for us,' he says, smiling optimistically as we dash back across the square, weaving through the crowds.

Finally, we get to the bus station which has the exact same gate and layout as the depot – a mirror image. Bursting through the gates, Will and I scan the depot for our bus, and while the depot is full of buses, with no chicken crates in sight, the space

184

where our bus was parked is empty.

'Seriously? They've gone?' I stand in the empty parking space, looking around. A group of elderly tourists who look a little hot and bothered pile onto a nearby bus. Definitely not our group.

'We are half an hour late now,' Will sighs. 'You're right. Maybe they did think we'd gone off and decided to do our own thing.'

'Oh Will!' I sigh, shaking my head. 'So, what shall we do?'

'There's probably a bus back to the hotel. Let's go find a time-table,' Will says, looking across the station.

'Oh! Exciting!' I reply sarcastically.

'What do you mean?' Will asks, glancing back towards me.

'"Let's go find a timetable". Hardly the words of a free-spirited explorer,' I tease.

Will laughs. 'Well, I doubt you want to go venturing into desert. But we could, if that's what you fancy doing. We could camp under the stars.'

'I'm up for it if you are,' I retort, not quite believing he's serious.

'You do realise that you won't be able to plug your hair straighteners in and there won't be free breakfast and coffee in the morning if we camp, don't you?' Will asks.

I smile begrudgingly. 'Yes, Will. I do realise that. Now are you game or not?' I ask, calling his bluff. I don't actually believe he wants to camp. He'll probably be wanting to check into a local guest house soon enough.

'Of course, I'm game!' Will scoffs, although his voice is a little high-pitched and his brow is beading with sweat.

'Great! Well, if you're game, I'm game!' I reply.

'Great, well I'm definitely game,' Will insists. His voice sounds more resolute as though he might actually be warming to the idea.

'Great! So we're both game!' I wonder what the hell I'm letting myself in for.

Chapter 19

We might have decided to camp in the desert, but it turns out that making that happen isn't as easy as it sounds. While the souks in Marrakech are great if you want to buy spices and kaftans and tagine dishes, they're not exactly well stocked when it comes to tents. And Will, for all the intrepid explorer tales he always spouts, is definitely more than just a little uneasy about the prospect of actually venturing into the wilderness.

'I know camping under the stars sounds like fun, but I don't think you're meant to do it literally under the stars,' Will comments as we wander past the seventh or eighth spice stall. 'What if it rains?'

'Will!' I tut. 'We're in Africa. It's thirty-five degrees!'

'That doesn't mean it won't rain,' Will huffs, before pausing at a stall to admire a silver lamp.

'Honestly! I thought you were bloody Bear Grylls. You're more Mary Berry,' I tease.

'Shut up, Natalie!' Will places the lamp down and pokes me in the side, causing me to flinch. 'Even Bear Grylls wouldn't just go camping without a tent! We don't even have a torch. Or a stove or anything. And somehow, I doubt they sell them here,' Will says as he looks around the souk.

'Okay fine, so what are you saying? You don't want to camp after all? You just want to find a guest house and have a nice cup of tea? Hey, maybe they do scones?' I tease.

Will rolls his eyes.

The vendor spots me eyeing a bangle that I think Lauren would like. He approaches, offering a price. I do a quick pound to dirham conversion in my head. It's around two pounds. I accept and hand him a few dirham notes, before Will and I wander deeper into the souk.

'I thought you wanted to go camping and since we've done a ton of coupley things, I just thought we should try to make that happen, but we can head back to the hotel. It's up to you,' I tell him.

'Why don't we see if we can find the group?' Will suggests. 'I think I can find the name of the campsite they're heading to.' Will digs a crumpled brochure from his pocket. 'Maybe we can hire a car and meet up with them later tonight or in the morning.'

'In theory, that's good idea, but I don't see any car rental places,' I reply.

'I'm sure we can hire a driver. We'll just ask around,' Will says, looking around for someone to ask.

'Okay.' I shrug.

'How about that guy?' he asks, spotting an older man standing by a stall selling rugs. His stall is packed with hundreds of rugs and he appears to be giving instructions to a co-worker. He definitely looks local.

'Yeah, go for it,' I tell him, even though I'm not feeling too positive about our prospects.

We approach the stall and Will asks the man how to get to the tourist campsite in the mountains where our group's heading. He laughs.

'It's twenty minutes away. No more than a few kilometres,' he says. 'You can walk.'

'Really?' Will balks.

'Yes, it's not far at all,' the man says.

I can't help laughing. All this time we've been fretting over missing the bus and we were only walking distance away from where we needed to be.

Will asks the man exactly how we get there, paying attention as he describes which exit to take from the main square, which path to take out of the village and the correct road to head down. I can tell Will's making a deliberate effort to double check each of the instructions so that we don't get lost again.

While Will's locked in conversation, a man with a monkey comes up to me and tries to get me to pose for a photo.

'No, it's okay!' I insist, but the man is insistent and dumps the monkey onto my back.

Suddenly images of it biting my ear off flood through my mind. I even heard that monkeys can carry rabies. I read an article about a girl who needed a face transplant after being mauled by a chimpanzee. I scream and Will spins around.

'Photo?' the man says, as though me screaming is a great photo opportunity.

'Oh my God, get it off me,' I cry. As much as I love animals, I don't trust monkeys. I sneak a glance at it, and it eyes me cheekily.

'Help!' I shriek as I reach up to the monkey and attempt to pull it off my shoulder. A few people, tourists and locals, have turned to watch, taking in my predicament with a combination of shock and amusement on their faces. One woman has even got out her phone and is filming the whole thing.

The monkey grabs my hand and yanks the wedding ring from my finger, sliding it off in one skilled move.

'Oh my God, he took my ring,' I gawp.

Will watches in shock as the monkey jumps back onto its owner and they hurry away through the crowd.

I'm so glad the monkey's off me that I let out a huge sigh of relief.

Will places his arm around me and rubs my back. 'It's okay,' he says comfortingly.

'Thief!' someone cries out.

I look over and see a local, pointing at the man. Another guy joins in, screaming 'thief' as well. Someone even insists that we call the police.

A woman rushes up to me. 'You poor thing! That monkey stole your wedding ring. That's so awful.'

I look back at her blankly. I couldn't care less about the cheap crappy ring, I just wanted to get that monkey off me.

'Umm … Yes, I'm devastated,' I reply.

I glance over at Will, who's looking at the commotion in the crowd, an inexplicably panic-stricken expression on his face.

'Sorry, I need to speak to my husband,' I say, turning away from the woman.

'What's up?' I nudge Will.

People are still pointing down the road in the direction that monkey man disappeared to. Will watches. Word seems to be getting around between tourists about how awful it is that my wedding ring has been stolen.

'I think someone's called the police.' Will turns to me. 'If the police come, they might want to question us. They might wonder why we're not actually married,' Will whispers.

Oh God, he's got a point. Will and I could go from victims of a crime to potential suspects. What if they contact Medhi and Amira? What if we get done for fraud or something?

'We should go, Will,' I whisper.

'Yeah, we definitely should,' Will replies.

'I think he went that way!' Will shouts, pointing down an alleyway.

Everyone turns to look, and Will and I seize the opportunity to hurry away. We nip down a tiny alleyway, which leads to another alleyway, and another, and before we know it, we've found our way to the outskirts of the village. A road stretches into the distance.

'I think this might just be the road the man I asked directions

189

from was talking about,' Will says.

I eye the non-descript road. 'How can you tell?'

'He said it had a boulder by it,' Will says, gesturing at a boulder.

'Right,' I reply, shrugging as we wander down the road. It's not like we have any other options. If the police start investigating the monkey thief in the village, they'll definitely want to speak to us and neither Will or I want to have that conversation.

We walk in silence for ten or twenty minutes, half-awed by the staggering rocky landscape all around us and half shell-shocked from the incident in the village.

Eventually, I look over my shoulder to see the village has retreated from view.

'So, where's this campsite then?' I ask, turning to look ahead. I can't see any signs of life, it's just red mountains and desert dunes.

'He said to just follow the road,' Will explains.

'But I can't see anything,' I point out, squinting into the distance.

'That's because there are mountains. It's probably obscured behind them. Once we're around this bend, I'm sure we'll see it,' Will insists, looking down the road, holding his hand up to shield his eyes from the sun.

'Okay!' I reply, as we continue down the road.

We walk for another ten or twenty minutes more, but the road remains desolate. Eventually, the rocky landscape gives way to desert. It's beautiful – a vast expanse of sandy dunes that glow golden in the bright light, and for a moment, I'm silent, awestruck by the landscape, which is the kind of thing I've only ever seen before in films. Then the wonder passes, and I'm left with the dawning realisation that there is no campsite in sight. Not one.

'Will …' I grumble.

'Yes?' he replies in a small voice, slowly tearing his eyes away from the scenery towards me.

'Where is the campsite?' I ask in a clear calm voice that belies the frustration building inside me.

'Erm ... I thought it would be here,' Will replies, looking puzzled.

'Where?' I ask.

'Around here,' Will says, gesticulating around him.

'I don't see a any signs of life, Will,' I utter, taking in the rolling dunes and the dusty baking ground stretching on as far as the eye can see. 'Let alone a campsite!'

'Hmm ... Well, that's odd,' Will replies, scratching his head. 'It should have been here.'

'What the hell?' I gawp. 'You sound like you've misplaced your sun cream or something! Will, this is serious! We've been walking for ages and there's no village in sight! We're in the middle of nowhere.'

'It's fine!' Will chirps. 'We'll just walk back.'

'To the village where we'll probably get arrested?' I balk.

'Erm ...' Will scratches his head, looking out to the desert as though for a solution.

'Oh my God,' I sigh, flopping down onto a nearby boulder. 'I thought you were listening to that guy when you asked for instructions.'

'I was listening,' Will insists. 'But I guess I got a bit distracted when you got mugged by a monkey.'

'What are we going to do?' I groan, fanning my increasingly sweaty face with my hand. 'We're in the middle of nowhere. With no water.'

'We're not exactly going to die out here, Natalie. We're a mile or two away from the village,' Will points out.

'Yeah, I guess they'll at least have water at the police station,' I sulk.

Will laughs weakly.

The sun has sunk lower in the sky and is no longer as blisteringly bright as before. Its light has tinged to a golden glow. It's beautiful and I can't help thinking how nice it would be to be riding a camel right now through the Atlas Mountains. Instead,

I'm sitting on a boulder, feeling hot and thirsty, in the middle of nowhere.

'What are we going to do?' I sigh.

'Let's just sit down for a minute and then decide,' Will replies.

'So much for our epic adventure!' I joke.

'Ha. Well, we did make it off the beaten track. Literally.'

I laugh, when suddenly the sound of hooves distracts me. I look up to see two Berber men riding down the path on camels. Their eyes widen when they see me and Will – two flustered tourists sweating on a boulder, far off the tourist track. We must look like quite a sight.

'As-salāmu 'alaykum,' they say as they approach.

'As-salāmu 'alaykum,' we echo, smiling awkwardly. What is the etiquette for running into two men riding camels in the middle of the desert?

'Are you lost?' The older-looking man asks in a heavily accented voice. I'm impressed that even in the most remote part of Morocco, people still speak English. He's probably around the same age as me and Will, although he's missing a few teeth.

Will looks a little embarrassed. It no doubt hurts his male pride that he was unable to navigate his way to the campsite.

'A bit,' Will admits, before explaining that we were heading to the tourist campsite but managed to somehow end up here. He leaves out the bit about running around in a panic because we thought we were going to get rumbled by the police after a monkey mugging.

'I see.' The man nods. 'The village you are looking for is a long way from here,' he says.

'Oh, right.' Will glances at me, looking embarrassed.

'It is that way,' he says, pointing far off across the horizon.

Will and I both squint into the distance but we can't see anything.

'You cannot go by foot. It's a long way,' the man tells us.

'How far?' Will asks.

'Too far to walk,' the man replies. 'Why were you going there?'

I explain about visiting the Atlas Mountains and camping, feeling a little embarrassed to be making such a novelty out of what is probably daily life for these Berber men.

As we're talking, I notice a familiar flash of colours peeping out from under one of the Berber's scarf.

'What's that?' I ask, pointing to the half-obscured logo on his chest.

He pulls his scarf back. 'This is the hotel where we work. We are chefs there,' he says. 'We're coming back to visit our family.'

I gawp at the logo: Marrakech Palace.

'Oh my God! That's where we're staying!' I tell the man.

'What?' His face lights up. Even his quiet companion's expression brightens. 'You are staying at Marrakech Palace?'

'Yes!' Will and I both reply enthusiastically.

I shield my eyes with my hand and squint at his face, spotting the mysterious jagged scar across his cheek. Suddenly, I recognise him from Amira's kitchen.

'I saw you the other day!' I tell him. 'Amira was making me some tea.'

He frowns for a second, before his face dawns across his face. 'Yes! I remember. You were looking at Amira's wedding picture,' he recalls.

'Yep, that was me,' I reply.

'And you are lost? Shall we call the hotel? Or you can come with us,' he suggests. 'Our village is not far. We can take you on a tour.'

I look at Will. He grins. He looks like he's unable to believe our luck.

'I think that sounds great, what do you think, Natalie?' he asks.

'Yeah!' I agree, taken aback by the whole coincidence. 'Why not?'

'You want to?' the man clarifies, looking between me and Will.

'Thanks. That's such a kind offer. We'd love to,' Will says.

Both of the men seem happy we've accepted and within

seconds, they're disembarking from their camels and offering them to us. We both object in our polite English way, but they insist. They even let us have a drink from the flasks of water they keep in pouches around their necks.

The men walk alongside us, steering the camels with a rope over the sandy dunes. The camels bob up and down with each step, their huge hairy feet leaving footprints in the sand. The older man, who seems to be the chatty one, tells us that his camel – the one I'm riding – is called Bob Marley, while the camel behind me – the one that Will's on – is named after Jimmy Hendrix. It turns out that the men are brothers and have lived in the mountains their entire lives but spend a couple of weeks per month working at Medhi's hotel to support their family. They tell us how they've never left the area and have no plans to.

'Why would we leave?' The older man, Hamza, says, gesturing across the desert, which glimmers in the golden sun. 'We live in paradise.'

I smile. He's right. It is beautiful. It's heavenly. Why on earth would they want to leave? As I gaze out over the stunning landscape, I'm struck yet again by the colours. The shimmering gold sand, the azure blue sky, the warm orange sun and the faint wisps of pale white cloud across the horizon. I turn and look over my shoulder at Will and smile. This may not have been the day trip we were meant to be on yet somehow, it's almost turning out better. We're riding on camel-back through the desert, and instead of being surrounded by other tourists, we're with local Berber guys! Now I know what Will means when he says he likes adventure travel. This may have seemed a disaster at first but now it feels like an adventure. It feels incredible. I can barely believe I – Natalie Jackson – am traveling on a camel across the Moroccan desert on a camel called Bob Marley. With Will Brimble of all people.

I look over at him, chatting amiably with the brothers, and smile

Chapter 20

When Hamza and his brother said they were heading to their village, what they actually meant by village turns out to be three caves where they and their extended family live. Not that I'm criticising. They seem to have everything they need. The caves aren't like regular caves. They're not dark or gloomy. They're proper homes, with bedrooms, kitchens and bathrooms, but they just happen to be set within mountains. They're really remarkable. They're embedded in a rockface overlooking the desert and the view is spectacular. Hamza, and his brother, whose name is Sajjad, presented us to their family as though we were long-lost cousins. The whole family were all incredibly excited by the arrival of two Westerners and even though they can't speak much English, they immediately started fussing over us. They gave us water and freshly-baked bread, and then Hamza took us out on a tour of the mountains on camel back. The scenery and the views were spectacular. He even took us to the most beautiful tumbling waterfall in a red-rock gorge. Will and I took so many pictures, unable to believe our luck to be shown such extraordinary sights.

Now we're back at the camp, where Hamza's mother, Salma, makes tea over an open fire, placing a metal teapot on a stove over the flames until it starts bubbling. The smell of burning wood drifts on the languid desert breeze. The sun is beginning to set and a chill sweeps across the sandy dunes. Hamza's father Abdul goes into the cave and retrieves a blanket that has a musty, burning wood smell as though it's frequently brought out for gatherings around the fire. He drapes it over mine and Will's shoulders.

Will and I thank him in our awkward, effusive way, making sure he doesn't need the blanket, but he simply smiles and gestures that it's no trouble. Unlike Hamza, who explains that he's picked up English from working at the hotel, neither of his parents speak much English so they communicate with us through gestures and the occasional word. But somehow, the language barrier doesn't matter. Their intentions are clear through the warm look in their sparkling eyes. Even though if Will had told me last night that we'd end up in the middle of nowhere around a fire with a family I barely knew, I'd probably have freaked out, I feel completely relaxed. I feel completely comfortable.

The teapot boils and Salma pours the steaming mint tea into a mug. She tips it into the cup from a great height, and the boiling water reminds me of the waterfall as it crashes into the cup. She hands the steaming mug to Hamza, who hands it to Sajjad, who hands it to another relative, who passes it along to Will. Will then hands it to me. There's no one left to pass the mug to, so I thank everyone, particularly Salma and bring the tea to my lips, taking a sip. It's minty and delicious. Salma smiles broadly. She's lost several of her teeth and her face is lined. I try to picture her on the streets of London, but the image simply makes no sense. She looks like someone from a completely different century, because, I suppose, she's living the lifestyle of another era. A century without dentists or high street shops or anti-ageing cream. And yet even though her haggard toothless face is somewhat strange to my Western eyes, she seems so kind and warm. So giving.

She passes mugs of tea around until we all have one, then Abdul emerges from the cave with a tin.

'Sugar,' he says, with a toothy grin, presenting the tin to us with a spoon, before sitting down and taking a steaming cup of tea from his wife. We pass the sugar around, spooning it into our cups and then we just sit there, around the fire, sipping the tea. Hamza makes conversation, asking us questions about England and our jobs, while relaying information back to his parents in Arabic, who nod and smile. The gulf in our worlds is huge and I don't even begin to go into detail about the kind of work I do. It feels a bit embarrassing to admit that I spend most of my time promoting superfluous treatments like vajazzles and semi-permanent eyebrows. I don't think these people even frequent the dentist, what on earth would they make of getting glitter tattoos on your lady parts? Definitely best to keep that to myself. Will avoids telling the family he's a journalist, and just describes himself as a writer. He doesn't mention that he writes about politics – it would probably ruin the mood – and instead says he writes about football, which he does write about from time to time. I think I saw an article about a Spurs player by him a few years ago. Hamza laps this information up and starts listing football teams.

'Manchester United!' he says proudly, scratching the scar on his cheek, which was apparently from a run-in with Bob Marley. 'They are very good.'

'Yes, yes they are,' Will laughs, even though I know he supports Arsenal.

'And Liverpool. Chelsea.'

'Yes, yes, very good teams,' Will agrees.

Abdul places his cup down and heads back into the cave. Will and Hamza continue trading football team names, before moving on to discussing the Morocco football scene. I tune out at this point, my attention waning, until Abdul brings out a tray loaded with bread and dishes. He asks Hamza to bring over a small table and then places the down. There's a bowl of something that looks like a tomato sauce or soup, glistening green olives, hummus and

197

tabbouleh. It looks delicious. Will and I tell him that he shouldn't have and tell him how grateful we are, but he doesn't seem to have a clue what we're on about and simply smiles and heads back to the cave to retrieve some plates.

We give up attempting to thank him and just enjoy the meal. The tomato sauce turns out to have a sharp, tangy flavour and tastes absolutely delicious mopped up by the fluffy bread. The olives are salty and succulent. I hadn't realised quite how hungry I was until I tuck in. Bread has never tasted so good and I tear a hunk off my roll and savour it, dipping it into the sauce while gazing out over the desert. I smile to myself. This is truly incredible. The food, as well as the scenery and the sense of connection. Hamza and his family have taken us in with such a spirit of warmth and kindness that it makes me glow with happiness. People can be so divided. Nations are so fractured and there's so much hostility in the world and yet here we are, strangers who lead completely different lives coming together in a moment of kindness, hospitality and humanity. I feel so grateful and content as I finish the food, accepting the second roll that Abdul encourages me to have, and I know that I'll cherish this memory. I'll remember it for a long time.

We have a second roll of bread and finish off the meal with another cup of the delicious minty tea and crumbly Moroccan biscuits, which Abdul brings us in another tin. The sun starts setting over the desert. It's taken on a darker, reddish tone and makes the sand dunes glow an almost orange shade. It's so profoundly beautiful watching the colours change as the sun dips below the skyline that conversation slips away. Hamza stops listing football teams and Salma and Abdul stop fussing over us. Instead we all sit by the fire which crackles and flickers, the wood singing and splintering in the flames and we watch the sunset together, silenced by the insane beauty of it.

I cosy up to Will under the blanket. He gives me a questioning look as though to check I'm okay with the intimacy. I nod and smile encouragingly, thinking of what Lars said: *Life hurts. But life can also be brilliant, thrilling, funny, surprising and joyful. Sometimes you have to risk getting hurt to experience all the other good stuff.* He was so right. Will wraps his arm around my shoulders as we gaze at the view. It's truly magical and it strikes me that tonight is the most romantic, inspiring and memorable night of our trip. It just goes to show that you don't need five-star hotels or money to be content. Sometimes, happiness and beauty can be found simply in nature, adventure and people. Will and I keep exchanging these sweet, affectionate looks and it's as though finally, now that we've dropped the act of faking being together, our hearts are free to actually feel something.

The light gradually darkens as the sun dips below the horizon. Soon after, the light rapidly changes from an amber glow, greying around the edges to a dark impenetrable black. The kind of blackness that neither Will or I are used to. Night-time at home is never truly dark, there are always streetlights and shop signs and houses or offices with the lights on. This plain, unbroken darkness is new to me. It's impenetrable – you blink, expecting your eyes to adjust but the darkness is thick and dense. The staggering landscape we were admiring just minutes earlier is now nothing but a vast dark void, the only light is that of the fire, which is beginning to fade. The pieces of wood have burnt up and shrunk from slabs to small chunks, almost embers, burning bright orange. Soon they'll burn out and there'll be no light at all.

My thoughts turn to bedtime and I can't help wondering where Will and I will be sleeping. Abdul insisted earlier that we stay but are Will and I going to sleep in the cave? Do they have space? Will it be awkward? What is the Berber bedroom etiquette? I start to feel a little nervous about it when Abdul comes over and gestures for us to follow him. He leads us into a tent by the cave.

It's lined with Moroccan rugs and throes in dark red shades with blankets and a paraffin heater glowing in the corner.

'You can sleep here,' he says, gesturing towards a mattress, made up with blankets and pillows.

'Really?' I ask, hoping we're not depriving him of his bed for the night.

'Yes, this okay for you?' he asks, a hopeful look on his face.

'Of course, this is more than okay. This is perfect!'

I turn to Will, who looks as surprised and delighted as I feel.

Hamza come in and shows us how to turn on the small paraffin heater in the corner of the tent. He hands us towels for the bathroom – a small shed-like outbuilding with a shower, toilet and sink. Then he brings us a bottle of water before bidding us goodnight. Will and I are both insanely grateful, but we don't try to protest or get awkward and English about it anymore. It's clear that the family are just really kind nice people, and feel tickled and excited to have guests, especially ones from the hotel where their sons work. I can't imagine it happens often. It'll probably be the kind of thing they'll talk about for years. The strange English couple they found sweating on a boulder in the middle of the desert.

Will and I thank them and settle in for the night, stripping down to just our underwear and T-shirts. We get under the blanket. Unlike the massive king-sized bed at the hotel, it's not possible to lie down without touching and bodies brush against each other's.

'I can't believe this,' I comment as I get in under the blanket. It smells a little musty but it's thick and warm.

'I know.' Will shakes his head, unable to believe his luck. 'This is quite something. That sunset.'

'That sunset, that tea, that bread, the olives, the mountains, the waterfall, the camels. It's just been … wonderful,' I enthuse.

'It really has. Beats the tourist day trip, eh?' Will says, adjusting his pillow.

'Oh yeah! They're probably at some boring touristy campsite right now having an early night. So inauthentic!' I scoff.

'Totally inauthentic. Not like this.'

'Nothing like this,' I reply. 'What a night.'

We spend a while going over how extraordinary our evening has been and trying to wrap our heads around the beauty of the landscape and the kindness of Hamza and his family. We speak in hushed whispers, although we're both speaking over each other, over-excited and invigorated by our adventure.

'And now here we are,' I comment.

'Yep. The middle of the Moroccan desert. Unbelievable,' Will replies.

'No, I was thinking, here we are. You and me. Back in a tent. Together. Sixteen years later. It's almost like we're picking up where we left off,' I comment, gazing into Will's eyes in the weak light. He looks back at me with an unsure expression in his eyes, as though not quite sure where he stands.

'I know I freaked out at the hotel, Will, but I do really care about you.' I lace my fingers through his.

His eyes widen in surprise.

'I still have feelings too and I'm willing to give us a shot. Sixteen years on, I think we should try again,' I say, my stomach full of butterflies – a combination of excitement and nerves.

Will traces his thumb against mine, his gaze intensifying. 'Are you sure?' he says.

'Yes,' I reply, feeling completely confident that I'm making the right decision. It may be scary for me to get close to a man again, but Will isn't just any man, he's *Will*: he's my first love He's still the gorgeous, interesting, adventurous, funny, charming man I fell for so many years ago. The man who deep down, I've always adored. And even though things didn't work out between us the first time around, it strikes me that perhaps they were never meant to. Perhaps, despite all our flaws and all the things we've been through, the timing is perfect right now. We've both matured and even though we both have a bit more baggage than we once did, we also have a lot more

201

sensitivity and wisdom. Maybe now, things might actually work out between us.

'I don't want you to feel pressure,' Will insists.

'Honestly, Will, I'm sure,' I tell him.

Will smiles. Our eyes lock in the darkness and my heart pounds in my chest, as we draw closer together and finally, we kiss.

Chapter 21

A year later

It's a beautiful sunny day and I'm sitting in the park.

Not a strange park with a beautiful hidden lake, like the park Will and I found this time last year in Marrakech, but my local park in Chiddingfold. Yep, I'm still in Chiddingfold, but thankfully, I'm no longer living in my childhood bedroom with its Take That poster and Beanie Babies. I've swapped my bedroom for a small terraced house, but my living situation isn't the only thing that's changed.

'Cake!' Hera cries, reaching for a cupcake.

Will laughs and hands her one from the delicious picnic spread we're having in the sunshine to celebrate our one-year anniversary.

I gaze at him, adoringly. It still takes me by surprise just how well everything's worked out. When Will and I got back from Marrakech, despite being totally smitten with each other a part of me was still worried the whole thing might lose its sparkle once real life set in, but things just got better. The more time Will and I spent together, the deeper our feelings became. My anxieties and worry over giving my heart to a man again disappeared as I fell deeper and deeper in love and saw what a kind-hearted person Will is, realising how vastly different he is to Leroy. Unlike Leroy, he's invested so much time and energy into not only our relationship, but Hera too. He dotes on her, like a father would. She's even started calling him, 'Daddy'. It still surprises me that one holiday could have changed everything and that one silly blunder in a raffle could have transformed our lives so much.

Our fake honeymoon didn't just change our lives romantically, but professionally too. I stayed in touch with Lars after I got back home and donated to a few of his charities like I'd promised. Then one evening, Will and I were watching the news together and he was complaining about the negative way social issues are covered, with stories offering nothing but an opportunity for people to moan or feel bad. I suddenly remembered about Lars and suggested that Will get in touch with him to write about some of his initiatives.

Will ended up writing a few articles covering some of the work Lars's charities are doing. He really dug into the stories, finding the human-interest angles, and then had a brainwave for a website featuring stories about current social issues told in a relatable way, with calls to action at the end, showing readers how they can get involved either by donating, signing petitions or simply sharing the story on social media. Will created a business plan and Lars loved the idea so much that he gave Will funding to launch the project as a proper enterprise. The site went live a few months ago and it's already proving a success, with each article attracting thousands of hits and a substantial amount of donations in return. Will's been loving it. He gets to chase stories like he's always done but while covering important issues, he's also making a difference. He's even started appearing on TV again, with one of his old contacts from Sky inviting him to discuss a few of the social issues covered by the site. It's been great to see Will get his lust for life back.

But he's not the only one who's succeeding in business. I

managed to secure some press coverage for Medhi and Amira just like I'd promised myself I would as a way of alleviating my guilty conscience over faking being newlyweds. They still think Will and I are married, but I don't feel so bad now that their honeymoon suite is booked out thanks to the national newspaper feature I managed to arrange for them. In the process of contacting travel editors, I started making a new contacts list and ever since, I've been dipping my toe in the travel PR market, collaborating with a few boutique hotels looking to raise their profile. It's added another string to my bow and it's proving lucrative, helping me save money for the deposit I'm putting together for a house with Hera, a permanent house. Even though we moved into our little terraced house around six months ago, it's rented and it's still my dream to have a proper home.

Did I mention that Will lives with us too? We moved in together fairly quickly, but I needed to get out of my mum's place and Will was living in a cramped studio flat so it just made sense to move in together. I was a bit worried about it at first, particularly as Hera would be with us. Although Will adores her, I was concerned that living with her might be another story – but things have been great. We've had a few challenges. Will's definitely not the tidiest of people and his habit of leaving his stuff strewn about everywhere does annoy me, but then he finds the way I take up half the bedroom with my clothes rails annoying too. On the whole, we get along amazingly well and it's been lovely having him around. There have been times when I can barely get my head around how my life ever felt normal without him. He really does feel like the missing piece, not just to me, but also to Hera. My mum is over the moon that we're together and has practically already adopted Will as her new son-in-law. Our relationship makes what Leroy and I had feel like child's play. I thought I was in love back then, but it wasn't love. It was just lust and loneliness. With Will, it's the real deal. I love everything about him, from his kind. sweet nature that I fell in love with back at school, to the adorable nurturing way he is with Hera and his passion for his work. He's just incredible and I feel so lucky that we found our way back to each other after so many years.

I open my backpack and pull out a canvas sack.

'What's that?' Will asks as I place it down amongst all the picnic food.

I take out the tagine dish inside.

Will raises an eyebrow. 'You made a tagine?' he asks.

I've been building up to this moment for weeks, but my stomach is swarming with butterflies. I look between Will and Hera's curious faces.

'Not quite. Open it,' I suggest.

'Okay!' Will raises an eyebrow and reaches for the lid.

I brace myself as he lifts the lid to reveal a cheap costume jewellery ring I picked up in town. It's nothing fancy, but it's only meant to be symbolic.

'What?' Will's eyes widen. Our eyes lock and it feels like it's just me, him and Hera in the entire world. The park shrinks away, the sounds drowned out. The kids playing, the dog walkers, the ducks quacking by the lake disappear and it's just us on this picnic blanket, with a ring between us.

'Will you … Will you marry me?' I ask, my words choked.

I can't believe I'm doing this and yet it feels completely right. Will's been quite gentle and tentative in his approach to our relationship, knowing how hurt I was by Leroy. I know he loves me and he's willing to take things slowly. I don't think he realises I'm ready now. I'm ready for a life-long commitment. I've never felt more ready to be with anyone in my life. I want to make things official and become a proper family.

'Aren't I supposed to ask this?' Will says, a grin spreading over his face.

'I'm a modern woman, Will!' I reply, grinning back.

'I can't believe it!' Will gazes in shock at the ring lying in the dish.

'I love you, Will. I never thought I'd be this happy, I really didn't. You're the one. I want to spend my life with you.' I pick up Hera and pull her onto my lap, blinking back tears. '*We* want to spend our life with you!'

Will picks up the ring. It's a symbolic ring really, since I don't think men wear engagement rings. Will holds it between his fingers and for a terrifying moment, I fear he's going to say, 'No', but then he looks up at me, his eyes as damp and full of emotion as my own.

'Of course, I'll marry you, Nat,' he says. 'I love you.' He looks at Hera. 'I love you both.'

'We love you!' I gush as I reach over and slide the ring onto his finger, my heart bursting with joy.

Hera claps her hands together and we all laugh. Will holds out his hand, taking in the ring.

'We're engaged!' he enthuses, his eyes sparkling, before leaning forward and sealing the deal with a kiss.

Acknowledgements

A huge thanks to my fantastic editor Charlotte Mursell for her invaluable editorial insights. I'm so fortunate to work with such a talented editor.

If you loved *As Luck Would Have It* then turn the page for an exclusive extract from *When Polly Met Olly* ...

Chapter 1

Surely, I'm not qualified to be a matchmaker?!

You'd think getting a job at a dating agency might actually require you to have found love, or at least be good at dating, but apparently not. I've been single for three years and I haven't had a date for six months, yet I'm pretty sure I'm nailing this interview.

'So, what kind of message would you send Erica?' Derek asks, handing me a print-out showing a dating profile of a pretty, tanned brunette. Derek is the boss of To the Moon & Back dating agency, although with his nicotine-stained teeth, lurid purple shirt stretching over his giant pot belly and cramped city office, he's not exactly what I imagine when I think of Cupid.

What kind of message *would* I sent Erica? When Derek says 'you', he doesn't mean me, as in Polly Wood. He means me pretending to be 34-year-old bachelor Andy Graham, because that's what my job as a matchmaker would involve. While Andy, and the rest of the busy singletons on the agency's books, are out earning the big bucks, too busy to trawl internet dating sites looking for love, I'll be sitting here with Derek, firing off messages on their behalf in the hope of clinching dates. It's a little morally questionable I suppose, since the women will be chatting to me beforehand, and will no doubt become enamoured with my witty repartee and effortless charm, but to be honest, I haven't really given the moral side of it much thought. According to Derek, it's what all dating agencies do, and anyway, ethics somehow stop being so important when you really need cash.

I try to put myself in the mindset of Andy, while thinking up a message for Erica. I only know about him from reading a form he's supposedly filled in, which Derek gave me to study five minutes earlier. According to the form, Andy is an ex-army officer turned property surveyor. He grew up in a small town in Ohio where his family still reside. His younger brother, aged 31, has already settled down with a wife and three kids, and reading in between the lines, I get the impression that Andy feels he's beginning to lag behind. He works long hours, reads Second World War history books in his spare time, enjoys visiting aviation museums and likes to play tennis at the weekends. Oh, and he has a penchant for Thai food.

I take a look at Erica's profile. She's 32, lives in the Upper East Side and works as a fashion buyer. Her interests are listed as: 'yoga, fine dining, dinner parties (hosting and attending!), dancing, cocktails with the girls, travelling, tennis, and festivals'. Erica sounds cool. She sounds fun. She seems like a girl about town. And to be perfectly honest, she strikes me as a bit too cool for Andy. I can't imagine her wanting to visit aviation museums or discuss Second World War history. But for all I know, Andy could have stunningly handsome looks that somehow make up for his yawn-inducing interests. But from what I do know so far, he and Erica hardly seem like a great match. I glance up at Derek, scanning his face for any sign that this might be a trick question, but he simply looks back, keen with anticipation. He doesn't seem like he's testing me; he clearly thinks Erica is in Andy's league, although as far as I can see, the only thing they have in common is tennis.

'So, what do you think?' Derek presses me.

'Erm, I'd keep the opener light. From Erica's profile, you can tell she's a breezy, happy kind of person. I'd try to mirror that tone,' I tell him, biding time while I attempt to think of a witty opener.

'Good tactic,' Derek agrees with an encouraging nod.

'Thanks,' I reply as I desperately try to come up with an attention-grabbing message. Something that will capture Erica's attention among the deluge of 'hey, how r u? x' type openers she probably receives all the time. But what can I write? What could Andy possibly say that would grab Erica's attention when their only mutual interest is tennis?! Then suddenly, it hits me. I smile to myself.

'I'd probably go with something along the lines of "I'm glad to see you're a tennis player, because I'm going to court you",' I tell Derek.

He snorts with laughter. 'Good one! Cheeky! I think Erica would like that.'

I grin, feeling a flush of pride. 'Thank you.'

'Great line! Very good!' Derek laughs.

'Thanks. I mean, why play singles when you can play doubles?' I add, cringing internally. I think I might be taking the tennis puns too far now. Fortunately, Derek laughs again, clearly not adverse to a good sports-themed chat-up line.

'Indeed!' he says.

A couple of cars honk loudly outside and for a second, I'm taken out of this surreal alternative reality of pretending to be Andy messaging Erica and it hits me that the real me has probably got this job. In fact, I know I have. I'm 99.99 per cent sure. I can tell by the way Derek is regarding me like a proud father. I can tell in the easy, relaxed way we've been chatting the entire interview. We seem to have really hit it off, which is a little disconcerting seeing as I'm, you know, a respectable (okay, at least semi-respectable) person and he's a middle-aged owner of a slightly shady dating agency. Maybe it's because I'm British, having grown up in Cornwall before moving to the States when I was 18. Derek said he used to date a Brit, recounting how they went on holiday to Cornwall one summer. He even described it as 'heavenly'. Or, perhaps we click because we went to the same university. Derek's barely looked at my CV but he glanced at it for a second as I came in and when he saw that I went to Wittingon Liberal Arts College, that was it. He was gone. Even though our degrees were thirty years apart, he was treating me like an old chum, reminiscing about his times at the college bar, where he insisted with a chortle and a wink that he'd had 'many a wild night'.

He went a bit misty-eyed talking about those days, which isn't that surprising really. I only left three years ago and sometimes even I get misty-eyed thinking about it. Probably because everything has gone a bit awry since. I moved to the States for university convinced I'd make it big here, but now I'm beginning to think there's a reason my dad, who grew up in New York, left to marry an English woman and live in Cornwall. Because while my student days were idyllic, it turns out real life in Manhattan is nothing like the dream world of a liberal arts university. The chaotic streets of New York bear no resemblance to the tree-lined pathways of the campus; people in the city don't spend hours having picnics and reading poetry; and a degree in photography, although widely revered among my college peers and considered of utmost importance by my professor, seems to hold little to no currency in the real world. I've found that out the hard way, which is why I'm here, trying to clinch this job, which despite being a bit shady, is surprisingly well paid. Well, by my standards anyway. It pays twice as much as my last job as a barmaid and I'm pretty sure I won't have to wash pint glasses or deal with annoying drunks. Although you never know.

Derek studied an equally impractical course – media studies and communication skills – and from a quick Google search this morning, it doesn't seem like he's managed to put it to much real-world use either, unless he was a very communicative boss in his former career as an adult entertainment company director. Or in his stint as a used car salesman. Yep, it's fair to say that neither of us would quite make the list of our college's star alumni. Despite Derek's questionable background, his latest venture, To the Moon & Back, seems to be doing surprisingly well. The company won Dating Agency of the Year at the prestigious US Dating Awards a few years ago. And it's received a ton of rave reviews online with former clients claiming that thanks to the agency, they finally met the love of their life after years of struggling to find a partner. It was even profiled by *The New Yorker*, which described it as an, 'innovative and ambitious dating service with a friendly personal approach'.

The website of To the Moon & Back is incredibly slick too, which is why I was a little surprised when I rocked up to find that in person it consists of nothing more than a client lounge and a cramped back office. With a central address on Wall Street, I thought it was going to be as swanky as its zip code, but it's tiny. Located at the top floor of a financial advisory firm, it's nothing like the salubrious offices below. The client lounge, which Derek showed me through earlier, is like a kooky cocktail bar, with a huge sofa laden with sparkly cushions and throws, two comfy armchairs, an ornate coffee table, low-hanging gold lamps and sumptuous curtains. Leading on from the lounge is this pokey office, which features Derek's worn-looking old desk, a dated Mac computer, a filing cabinet, a shrivelled pot plant in the corner and an incongruous and oddly distracting waving Chinese cat ornament which sits proudly next to Derek's monitor. Derek told me he's been running the whole operation himself since he launched the business two years ago, but apparently, he now needs extra help looking after his client list of 'successful single bachelors' and fighting off competition from rival agency, Elite Love Match, which Derek claims are 'scum, a bunch of charlatans, the worst dating agency in New York'.

Derek's stomach growls and he reaches into his desk drawer, pulling out a pack of Oreos.

'Fancy a biscuit?' He thrusts the pack towards me.

'Sure!' I reach for one, smiling gratefully.

Derek sips his coffee and takes a bite.

'So …' he ventures through a mouthful of crumbs. 'Where would you suggest taking Erica for a first date?'

'Oh!' I feel my face light up. Now *this* is my forte. I may not be a natural when it comes to love, but I do know New York's fine dining scene inside out.

Not because I frequent such establishments, just because I know them. I read about them. I follow every major food critic in the city on Twitter and I have an encyclopaedic knowledge of Manhattan's high-end dining scene. I suppose it's to me what Second World War history is to Andy Graham. These places represent the glittery side of New York. The side of the people who've made it. The holy grail, if you will. And yes, I'm more likely to order in from Domino's than actually go to such places, but I like knowing that they're there. Just in case.

'How about Zuma?' I suggest. Zuma is a new Japanese fusion restaurant in Midtown. It was opened a couple of months ago by a Michelin star chef and it's been getting rave reviews.

'Interesting, why Zuma?' Derek asks.

'Well, the food's meant to be great, but it's also classy and cool. It's not just your run of the mill bar or café, it's the kind of place you take someone to impress them and I think Erica would feel complimented by the choice. It sets a good standard for a first date. Oh, and it's not far from the Upper East Side so it's convenient for Erica too.'

'Very convenient! Especially if she and Andy hit it off,' Derek adds, raising an eyebrow suggestively.

'Yes,' I laugh awkwardly.

'Zuma is a great choice,' Derek says. 'Have you been?'

'No.' I admit. 'I've just heard about it.'

I'm about to ask Derek if there'll be any opportunities to go to such places within the job role. The online ad mentioned 'networking with clients' and you never know, such networking might take place in fancy bars and restaurants, particularly if the clients are as successful as Derek makes out. But as I open my mouth to speak, a buzzer sounds, a shrill bleep chiming through the office.

'Sorry Polly, I'd better answer that.' Derek gets up and crosses the room.

'Hello?' he answers, pressing the button on the intercom. 'Brandon! Sure, come on up!'

I glance over my shoulder to see Derek buzzing his visitor up.

'Brandon's one of my clients. Great guy,' Derek tells me, with a warm smile. 'He's a super successful lawyer, a real high-flyer but not so successful in the love department.'

'Oh …' I utter regretfully.

'Yeah, well, I'm working on it.' Derek sighs.

'Right.' He claps his hands together. 'I'm going to have to wrap things up I'm afraid,' he says, pulling a face, as if calling time on the interview is going to come as a major blow to me. 'But it's been excellent meeting you, Polly.'

'It's been excellent meeting you too!' I enthuse, a little too brightly.

Derek smiles at me with that broad paternal smile and I smile politely back. I put on my jacket and we head out of the office.

'"I'm going to court you!"' Derek chuckles as he leads me back through the client lounge. 'I think you'd be a natural at this job, you know.'

'Really?' I ask with slight trepidation as we pause at the exit.

'Yes, really.'

Derek reaches over to shake my hand. 'Thanks for coming in. I'll be in touch very soon,' he says, with a conspiratorial wink. A wink that tells me, without a shadow of a doubt, that the job is mine. Any sliver of doubt I had has now been wiped out. It's in the bag and for the first time in my life, I feel both relief and dread at the same time. My dream has always been to be a photographer, not a matchmaker, but money is money.

I pump his hand, thanking him, before heading out the door.

As I walk down the narrow office corridor with its ugly hexagon-printed carpet, I try to imagine pacing down it daily. Every morning and every evening. On my way to and from that tiny office with Derek and his waving Chinese cat. Could this be my domain? My new life? My new routine? Could I look at this ugly hexagon pattern every day? This building and this job are hardly where I imagined I'd end up.

'Excuse me.' A male voice interrupts my thoughts and I look up to see a man, an incredibly handsome man, who must be in his early thirties. He's tall, with dark hair and striking blueish green eyes.

'Sorry!' I move out of the way to let him pass. He's wearing a smart grey suit and carrying a briefcase; he looks every inch the corporate city worker. He must be here to visit the financial advisory firm downstairs. 'Umm, that's To the Moon & Back,' I inform him, gesturing down the hallway. 'You know, the dating agency.'

'Yes.' The man smiles. 'I know …' He eyes me with a bemused look. Then suddenly, it dawns on me.

'Oh! Are you Brandon?' I ask, fully expecting him to say no. He is definitely not how I imagined Brandon. Or any other of To the Moon & Back's clients, for that matter. In fact, when I pictured them, I envisioned different incarnations of Derek: balding, overweight and middle aged.

'Yes … and you are?'

Yes? I try not to gawp. Brandon?! How is this guy Brandon? How is he single?

'I'm Polly. Polly Wood. I just had a job interview with Derek,' I tell him, with an awkward laugh.

'Right. Nice to meet you, Polly,' he says, with that bemused, sparkly-eyed look.

'Nice to meet you too!' I reply.

He smiles, causing the skin around his eyes to crinkle and

dimples to appear in his cheeks. He has the most perfect smile. In fact, everything about him is perfect. He's around six-foot tall but not too towering. He's slim and lean-looking, and even though he's wearing a suit, I can tell he's muscular without having the ripped build of a gym addict. He looks clean-cut with his corporate suit and short brown hair, but he doesn't look boring. His eyes tell you that there's more going on and a light dusting of stubble along his jawline makes him look sexy rather than slick.

'Well, good luck! I hope you get it,' he says, and for a second, our eyes lock and a charge of intensity passes between us.

He hopes I get the job? So he can see me again? I can't quite figure out whether he's just being polite and glib or if he actually wants me to get the job so that our paths might cross. Because I, for one, would definitely like that.

'Brandon!' Derek bursts through the door, arms outstretched as though greeting an old friend.

'Derek!' Brandon turns towards him with equal enthusiasm.

'See you around, Polly,' he says, smiling over his shoulder before heading down the corridor.

'See you,' I echo as I walk away.

Chapter 2

The first thing I see when I arrive home is my flatmate with what appears to be a giant spider stuck to his cheek. He plucks at one of the legs before letting out a shrill scream.

'Ouch!'

'Gabe! What are you doing?' I close the front door and cross the flat to where he's standing peering at his reflection in the mantlepiece mirror. A garland of fairly lights is strung around it, illuminating his face, and as I get closer, I realise that what I thought was a spider is in fact a humungous false eyelash that Gabriel appears to have glued to his cheek.

'Oh my God,' he groans. 'I got these cheap lashes, ninety-nine cents a pair. Total bargain! But now I see why. These things come with industrial glue. My finger slipped at I tried to apply the damn thing. It fell on my cheek and now it won't come off!' Gabe yanks at the lash, causing his skin to pull. 'Ouch!' He winces in pain.

'Stop pulling it!'

'But it won't come off!' he whines. 'I can't go to work like this. I'm freaking out!'

'Honestly!' I tut, hanging my jacket by the door, before walking over.

Gabe looks me up and down. 'Why are you dressed like a secretary?'

I glance down at my outfit. I donned a black shift dress and a suit jacket that have been gathering dust at the back of my wardrobe for my interview at To the Moon & Back. It's not exactly my usual attire.

'I had a job interview,' I tell him. Derek only invited me for an interview a few days ago and mine and Gabriel's paths haven't crossed since. He works for a HR firm in the city and often stays over at his boyfriend's place, which is closer to his office.

'A job interview?' Gabe raises an eyebrow and scans my outfit once more. 'For a proper job?'

'Umm ... kind of.'

'Kind of?' Gabe tugs at the eyelash stuck to his cheek and winces.

'Yeah.' I reach across and gently pull the eyelash, but it won't budge. It's well and truly stuck. 'Wait, I've got an idea.'

I head to my bedroom to retrieve some nail varnish remover that's hopefully strong enough to cut through the glue. Gabe doesn't normally wear false lashes, but on Friday night's it's part of his work uniform. While he spends most of the week in his office job, he unleashes on Friday nights, going from Gabriel, HR consultant, to Gabriella, drag queen. Gabe performs at The Eagle, a gay bar downtown. I think it's how he lets off steam – he shakes off his corporate shackles by swapping fusty suits for over-the-top dresses, trading boring meetings for belting out pop songs. Gabe always says he's going to quit, but I can't see him doing so any time soon. He loves The Eagle, even if he doesn't want to admit it. No one really wants to admit they love The Eagle. It's most definitely not the place to be seen with its sticky floors, fluorescent lights, and over-the-top camp entertainment. And yet even though people don't exactly brag about going there, it's always packed and everyone seems to have a good time.

It's actually where Gabe and I first met. I used to work behind

221

the bar. As far as bar jobs go, it was a good one to have since most of the guys were fun as opposed to sleazy. Gabe used to perform there nearly every night, back when he was trying to make it as a singer. We instantly clicked over our mutual love of Blondie, Madonna, Amaretto sours and purple eyeshadow, as well as having both moved from small towns to the city in pursuit of our dreams. Gabe wanted to be the new Prince, while I wanted to be the next Mario Testino, even though we were just working in a crummy gay bar. We decided to abandon the crappy house shares we'd been living in and get a flat together. That was a couple of years ago now. After a while, Gabe quit singing there every night and got a job in HR, while I stuck to bar work, trying to get photography jobs on the side. I had a stroke of luck a few months ago when I managed to clinch a freelance job with a marketing agency which involved taking staff photos for the company website. It paid so well that I decided to chuck in my bar job and try to make it as a full-time photographer. Except I think I had beginner's luck, because ever since, work's dried up. I've emailed my portfolio to hundreds of companies, but no one's been interested, and I've been struggling to find work that pays a living wage. My money's running out, which is why I ended up trawling through job adverts online, looking for a regular job. My mum keeps telling me I should come back home to Cornwall. She works as a receptionist at the local GP and apparently, there's a job opening at a nearby surgery, but I can't face moving back home, with my tail between my legs, to take a job my mum's sorted out for me, even if it is sweet of her to suggest it. It's too much like failing.

Unlike me, Gabe's been doing well for himself. In fact, with his HR job, he could probably afford a slightly better flat than the grotty two bed we share in Brooklyn, but he sticks around. We get on well and I think he prefers to spend his extra money on nice clothes and good nights out rather than rent. I find my nail varnish remover on top of my chest of drawers, grab a bag of cotton wool pads and head back to Gabe, who is still peering into the mirror while tugging at the eyelash.

'You're making it worse!' I tell him, observing the red patch that's appeared on his skin. He pulls a glum face as I wet the cotton wool and begin dabbing at his cheek.

'Be gentle!' he insists, eyeing the bottle of nail varnish remover with caution. 'Christ, do you think that's going to work? I don't think that stuff's meant to go near your eyes.' He squirms.

'Then stay still!'

'Fine!' He sighs, squeezing his eyes closed as I dab the cotton wool against the giant eyelash in an attempt to dissolve the glue.

'So, tell me about this job then,' Gabe says.

I fill him in on the job interview, describing Derek and the strange set-up at To the Moon & Back while I remove the eyelash. As I recount the interview, I realise I've hardly been thinking about it at all. The interview itself has been totally eclipsed in my mind by meeting Brandon in the hallway. I can still feel the excitement of how he made me feel – the frisson of attraction I felt when looking into his gorgeous aquamarine eyes. I still can't get my head around how someone like him would need a dating agency. He intrigues me more than the job, but I don't bother mentioning him to Gabe. At least not for now. I fill him in on my conversation with Derek instead.

'Ha, got it!' I declare eventually, pulling the eyelash free.

'You did it!' Gabe grins, reaching up to touch his cheek. 'Thanks babe!'

'No worries!'

Gabe grabs a wet wipe from the pack on the coffee table and dabs at the red patch on his cheek as I settle down on the sofa. 'So, you ... A matchmaker?'

'Yep!' I reply brightly. Gabe, of all people, knows how woefully unqualified I am for this job.

'But don't you have to have, like, good dating skills?' Gabe asks, raising an eyebrow.

'I have good dating skills!' I huff. I may not have been on a date for a while, but that's not because I'm bad at dating. I can date. I may not be in a relationship, but I can date just fine! I simply took a break from dating to concentrate on my photography work – clearly that hasn't worked out so well.

'You haven't been on a date for *ages*,' Gabe reminds me.

'I'm aware of that, thanks! I've had other stuff to do. Anyway, my job isn't to get myself dates, it's to arrange dates for other people. They might be infinitely cooler than me, it could be easy!'

'Oh yeah.' Gabe nods. 'Good point.'

I poke him, laughing. I think back to Andy Graham. Okay, maybe he isn't infinitely cooler than me, but I can't imagine it would be much of a challenge to get someone like Brandon a date. I think back to his gorgeous smile; no, it definitely wouldn't be difficult.

Gabe peers into a handheld mirror and dabs a concealer stick over the red patch on his skin. I reach for a glass of Coke with ice that he's left on the coffee table and take a sip. It's laced with vodka.

'So, you'll just be messaging poor unsuspecting single people all day, trying to charm them on behalf of the agency's clients?' Gabe asks.

'Exactly.' I nod.

'So basically, you just have to be really good at making conversation?'

'Yeah, I guess!'

'Hmm …' Gabe muses. 'Remember that guy you fancied – you know, that hot Greek guy, Darius or something, that we met in Soho. The one with all the necklaces …'

'Demetrius,' I correct him, thinking back to the man in question – an extremely sexy, tall, dark guy I met while sipping a mojito at a street party last summer. He was wearing a ton of hippy necklaces and had that cool, boho, traveller look.

'Yeah, him. Didn't you send him a peach and aubergine emoji with a question mark and a winky face when you were drunk?'

'Shut up!' I hiss, feeling a fresh flush of shame even though it was months ago. Demetrius and I struck up a great conversation in person, but then I ruined it a few days later with my appalling texts. Naturally, I never heard from him again.

'Trust you to remember that,' I grumble, taking another sip of the drink before placing the glass back down.

'As if I'd forget. That was classic.' Gabe laughs as he powders over the concealer on his cheek.

'Hmmph.'

'What about that guy you called Mike for four dates then it turned out his name was Matt,' Gabe sniggers.

'That was his fault! He should have corrected me!' I insist, recalling the man in question: an overly polite British guy who sheepishly admitted on our fourth or fifth date that his name was, in fact, Matt. I'd even cried out 'Mike' in bed by that point. I shudder at the memory.

'That was brilliant.' Gabe sighs. 'Oh, and remember that guy you saw in the hall who asked if you needed someone to "service your pipes" and you thought it was an innuendo.' Gabe chuckles.

I roll my eyes, recalling the cringe-worthy incident in question. It may have been years ago, but I'm still mortified by the memory. A few days after Gabe and I first moved into our flat, this really attractive guy started talking to me in the hallway. When he asked if I needed anyone to 'service my pipes', I thought he was just being really flirty and forward. I didn't realise that he was literally a plumber. It was only when we were in the flat and I was offering him a glass of wine, and he pulled out a toolbox from his bag that I realised that he really did want to service my pipes. I tried to style it out and ended up with a $150 bill for pipe servicing. Literal pipe servicing, that is. The incident was so embarrassing that two years later, I still scan the hallway every day before I leave the flat just to check he's not there.

Gabe giggles at the memory as he begins applying winged eyeliner.

'Okay, I think we've established that dating chat isn't quite my forte,' I admit. 'But for your information, I'm pretty sure I got the job, so there!'

'Seriously?' Gabe scoffs.

'Yeah!' I tell him about the way Derek responded to me in the interview while Gabe perfects his eyeliner flicks. 'Honestly, I think the job's in the bag!'

I expect Gabe to be happy for me, but he seems a bit off. He screws his eyeliner closed and places it back in his make-up bag. 'Don't you think the job's a bit ...' He pauses, searching for the right word. 'Wrong?'

'Wrong?' I echo.

'Yeah.' Gabe shrugs as he rummages in his make-up bag again, before pulling out a lipstick. 'Don't you think it's a bit messed up? To message women pretending to be someone else? What if they start to like your banter? What if they like cheeky emojis or being called Delia instead of Diana?!' Gabe jokes.

'Ha! I don't think it's a big deal. It's just messaging, right? Everyone seems different over messages to how they are in real life. They probably won't even notice.'

'I don't know,' Gabe muses as he pulls off the lid of his chosen lipstick – a bright pink shade he used to wear all the time called Back to the Fuchsia. 'I think I might feel a bit cheated if I'd been talking to someone for a while and it turned out they'd just hired someone to write their messages.'

'Well, it's not like I'm going to message them about their deepest darkest secrets, I'm just setting up a date,' I insist.

'I suppose,' Gabe reasons as he applies the lipstick, but I can tell he's not on board.

'Look, I need the money,' I remind him. Gabe knows better than anyone how much I've been struggling lately. I've been living off horrible ready meals and barely going out thanks to the crummy pay of my intermittent freelance photography jobs. I even had to borrow a hundred dollars from him to cover last month's rent.

'I guess,' Gabe says. 'But can't you get a different job? Like a normal office job. Admin or something?'

'Admin?'

'Yeah.'

'You need qualifications for those jobs. Or experience,' I point out. 'I've seen ads for admin jobs online and even the dullest-sounding positions still require a degree, a secretarial qualification or relevant experience.

'Hmm ... you have qualifications though,' Gabe says, a little hesitantly.

'I have a photography degree, Gabe. They don't want arts degrees. Trust me, I applied to a few and heard nothing,' I tell him. After all, it's not like getting a job as a matchmaker for To the Moon & Back was my first choice of role.

'Well, it just seems a bit morally dubious, that's all.' Gabe perfects his pout, before popping the lipstick back into his make-up bag.

'Well, no job is perfect, is it?'

'I suppose.' Gabe sighs. 'So are you going to take the job then?'

'I don't know.' I shrug. 'I haven't officially been offered it yet. But I probably would take it. It's not like I have any other options right now.'

'Hmm ...' Gabe murmurs. 'Well, why don't you come out tonight? Have a night out, let your hair down, and then sleep on it. You might feel totally differently in the morning.'

It's clear that Gabe really doesn't want me to take the job. He isn't a fan of online dating. He met his boyfriend Adam in the coffee shop near his office. He's all about real life over online. Perhaps it's because one of his friends got catfished once; he sent the guy nudes and then found them on some creepy website.

'I shouldn't ... I don't have any money,' I say.

'Come on.' Gabe shoots me a look. 'You know you're going to get free drinks at The Eagle.'

'I guess,' I murmur. That's another great thing about The Eagle.

Since I used to work there, I always get free drinks from my old work mates whenever I go. I should probably just have a quiet night, stay home and consider my options. I even agreed to take on an unpaid freelance job tomorrow for an Instagrammer who's releasing a cookbook and I'm meant to be at her flat bright and early in the morning to photograph the recipes. But a night out at The Eagle is kind of tempting. It would be fun to just dance and let my hair down, especially after all the job-hunting I've been doing over the past few weeks.

'Come on! We'll have fun!' Gabe insists brightly.

'Okay, fine!' I relent, reaching for the vodka and Coke.

Chapter 3

When I set out to be a photographer, I didn't think I'd end up photographing turnips, yet here I am, in a swanky kitchen in Chelsea taking what feels like the one-hundred-and-seventy-fifth shot of a turnip resting on a bed of wilted spinach, pomero and chopped dates.

'Darling!' Alicia Carter, famous health food Instagrammer, bursts through the doorway carrying another bowl of salad. She places it down on the table. 'This is one of my favourites. Absolutely delicious!'

'Great!' I insist weakly, eyeing the latest salad bowl. I could really do with some toast and a cup of coffee. After a late night at The Eagle, that's precisely what the doctor ordered – not another bowl of salad to photograph.

'Can you make sure it's in sharp focus? Try to capture the colours,' Alicia advises me.

'Yep, definitely!' I insist. 'Just need five more minutes on this one.' I glance towards the turnip.

'No problem! Take your time!' Alicia says, clapping her hands together before turning on her heel.

She's preparing the salads in the kitchen next door with all her cool, health-conscious friends. All morning, I've been overhearing them discussing the importance of balancing macro and micro nutrients and debating the merits of hot yoga versus hatha. They're all tanned, athletic and glowing and not one of them has even acknowledged me. I'm clearly not worthy of attention, like the cleaner who's minding her own business as she dusts and tidies the house. I know it probably shouldn't bother me, but it does. Manners go a long way, particularly when you're not even being paid. I agreed to take on this job photographing recipes for Alicia's new cookbook, because I thought it might open doors. After all, Alicia does have nearly a million followers on Instagram and her cookbook, based solely on raw vegan recipes that aim to help readers 'rediscover the fruits of the earth and enjoy an invigorating plant-based diet', is probably going to be huge. But then, as Gabe reminded me this morning, while I lugged my camera, tripod, lights and screens out of the flat, that's what I said about my last job when I got paid peanuts for taking wedding photos for an actress who promised me she'd put me in touch with all her friends. She didn't. It was a similar story with the job before that. I keep hoping that one of these jobs is going to kickstart my career, but it doesn't seem to be working out like that. I've just been lumbering from one rubbish job to the next. I peer down my lens at the salad, adjusting the focus until it's in perfect definition.

Having taken a dozen or so pictures, I scroll through the images on the back of my camera. They're okay, but there's still too much shadow on the left-hand side of this goddamn turnip. I adjust the bowl and take five or six more pictures until I get one I like. I examine the picture. The turnip glistens, its purple to beige skin capturing the light, almost glowing. If a turnip could be described as beautiful, then this is one beautiful turnip. I smile, feeling a twinge of professional pride. And then a second later, I kick myself. A swell of pride over taking a good picture of a frigging turnip?! Oh, come on. The day I start revelling in taking pictures of vegetables for pretentious cookbooks is the day I declare my true photography dreams officially over. I always imagined I'd be some cool portrait photographer, taking pictures of singers, artists, filmmakers and intellectuals, the movers and shakers of my generation, not vegetables! I like to get an intimate rapport with my subjects, getting to know them, so that they don't just look beautiful and striking in shots, but unmasked too. Like when Mario Testino shot Kate Moss or when Sam Shaw shot Marylin Monroe. They don't just look stunning in the photographs, they look vulnerable, off-guard and real. But here I am, taking intimate off-guard shots of a turnip instead.

'Polly!' Alicia bursts back into the room, looking flustered. 'I'm so sorry, but I completely forgot about the pumpkin seeds.' She reaches into a bag of seeds she's holding and scatters some over the salad.

'Can you take a few more pics? With seeds.'

'Okay?'

'Yeah, it's just this one, the last and about half a dozen more. I'll bring them back out from the kitchen,' she says.

'Half a dozen more?' I gawp. I don't think she has any idea how long it took to capture each salad at just the right angle with just the right focus and light. I have almost two hundred pictures on my camera for those half a dozen salads, and now I need to take them all again, with bloody pumpkin seeds?!

'Is that okay?' Alicia asks brightly as she scatters a few more seeds over the turnip.

'Yes, of course!' I insist, trying hard to conceal my frustration.

'Fab! I'll go and get them'

I let out a sigh once she's left the room. All of my efforts for the past hour have been reduced to nothing because of the stupid pumpkin seeds. I want to go home, but now I'm going to be stuck here, taking more photos of salads. *Think of the credit*, I tell myself. Having my name in Alicia's book is going to be great. Surely, I'll get more jobs. Better jobs. Paid jobs. I pick up my camera and start snapping away.

Alicia starts bringing in the salads, placing them on a table nearby. I take a few more shots of the turnip salad, before swapping it for the bowl of chopped fennel, cucumber, radishes and lettuce that Alicia's placed on the table.

'Try to get a shot of that one quickly, the lettuce is going to go limp any second. I can tell.' Alicia eyes it warily.

'Will do.' I position it in front of the lights. Alicia scatters some pumpkin seeds over it and I snap away.

Alicia brings in a few more salads as I try to get the perfect shot.

'Polly, hun ...' Alicia says.

'Yep?'

'We're just heading to Diabolos,' she says. Diabolo's?! Diabolo's is the coolest restaurant in New York and I can't believe Alicia's going there. She's cool and everything but this is Diabolo's! It's the place to be seen. It's A-list central.

'Oh, nice!' I look up from behind my camera, to see her placing two more bowls of salad on the nearby table.

Alicia flaps her hand anxiously towards the salad. 'Get a good shot. That lettuce is going to turn. Bad batch! Trust me.'

'Of course, will do.' I look back down the lens and snap away.

'So ... are you coming?' Alicia asks.

The salad is in perfect focus and I take a few more pictures, not wanting to ruin the shot. But my ears have pricked up. Am I coming?! Just when I thought I was having a terrible day, it's about to get a hundred times better! Even though this job has been frustrating and unpaid, Alicia's making it up to me by taking me out for dinner at Diabolo's! No wonder her friends haven't acknowledged me all day. They've just been busy preparing the salads, and they probably knew they'd have a chance to get to know me over dinner. Am I coming? Of course I'm coming!

'I'd love to!' I pull away from my camera, confident I've got the shot I need, a massive grin on my face, only to see Alicia and one of her friends looking back at me, confused.

'Oh ...' Alicia grimaces. 'Sorry Polly, I was just talking to Seb.'

Seb, a skinny guy with a mound of dreadlocks piled on top of his head, smiles awkwardly.

'Of course! Haha, sorry!' I feel my cheeks burn crimson. How embarrassing. How completely embarrassing.

'We would invite you, but we booked a table months ago. It's so hard to get bookings there!' Alicia rolls her eyes. 'And you're coming, aren't you, Seb?'

'Well, I was going to, but it's cool, Polly can go in my place,' Seb suggests.

Alicia frowns and casts him a sideways look but he just smiles encouragingly. I think he means well, but as if I'm going to be a tag-along like that!

'No, it's okay! Sorry, I just overheard you and err, you know ...'

'Don't worry about it!' Alicia insists. 'Look, we have to run, but you'll be okay here, won't you?'

I glance over the salads. There are still five left to photograph. 'You're leaving now?'

'Yes! Our table's booked for lunch and we have to get across town. Don't want to be late.'

Seb winces, smiling apologetically.

'Of course not!'

'So, shall I just let myself out when I'm done?' I ask.

'Yes! Martina will clear everything up.' Alicia glances towards the cleaner, who is busy rearranging some books on the coffee table. She smiles over politely. 'She'll let you out. Oh, and feel free to tuck into the salads after you're done, if you want?' Alicia suggests.

I look down at the lettuce, which is beginning to wilt, going brown at the edges, as predicted.

'Great, thanks!' I enthuse.

'Thanks so much, Polly.' Alicia comes over and envelops me in a hug. 'Can't wait to see the pics!' she adds, before bouncing out of the room. Seb follows, giving me a limp wave.

I wave back and let out a sigh the second they're out of earshot. 'Idiot, absolute idiot,' I curse myself.

'Don't worry about it,' Martina says, giving me a sympathetic

233

smile. 'One of my clients went to that restaurant last week. Apparently, it's completely overrated.'

'Really?'

'Yeah. You're not missing out on much.' She gives me a mischievous wink and I smile back.

My phone buzzes. It's an email from Derek.

From: *derek@tothemoonandback.com*

To: *Polly.wood@gmail.com*

Dear Polly,

Thank you for coming in yesterday. It was great to meet you.
I was very impressed by your interview and would like to offer you the position as matchmaker at To the Moon & Back.
I hope to hear from you soon.
Kind regards,
Derek

I write a reply. Part of me has been resisting taking the job at To the Moon & Back, but who am I trying to kid? I keep hoping that doors will open in the photography world, but the only door that's opening is Derek's.

From: *Polly.wood@gmail.com*

To: *derek@tothemoonandback.com*
Dear Derek,
Thanks for your email. It was great meeting you too and I'm delighted to be offered the job as matchmaker.
When would you like me to start?
Best wishes,
Polly